MURDER
at
MIDWINTER
FARM

BOOKS BY HELENA DIXON

THE SECRET DETECTIVE AGENCY SERIES

The Secret Detective Agency

The Seaside Murders

HELENA DIXON

MURDER
at
MIDWINTER
FARM

bookouture

Published by Bookouture in 2025

An imprint of Storyfire Ltd.
Carmelite House
50 Victoria Embankment
London EC4Y 0DZ

www.bookouture.com

The authorised representative in the EEA is Hachette Ireland
8 Castlecourt Centre
Dublin 15 D15 XTP3
Ireland
(email: info@hbgi.ie)

ISBN: 978-1-83525-781-4
eBook ISBN: 978-1-83525-780-7

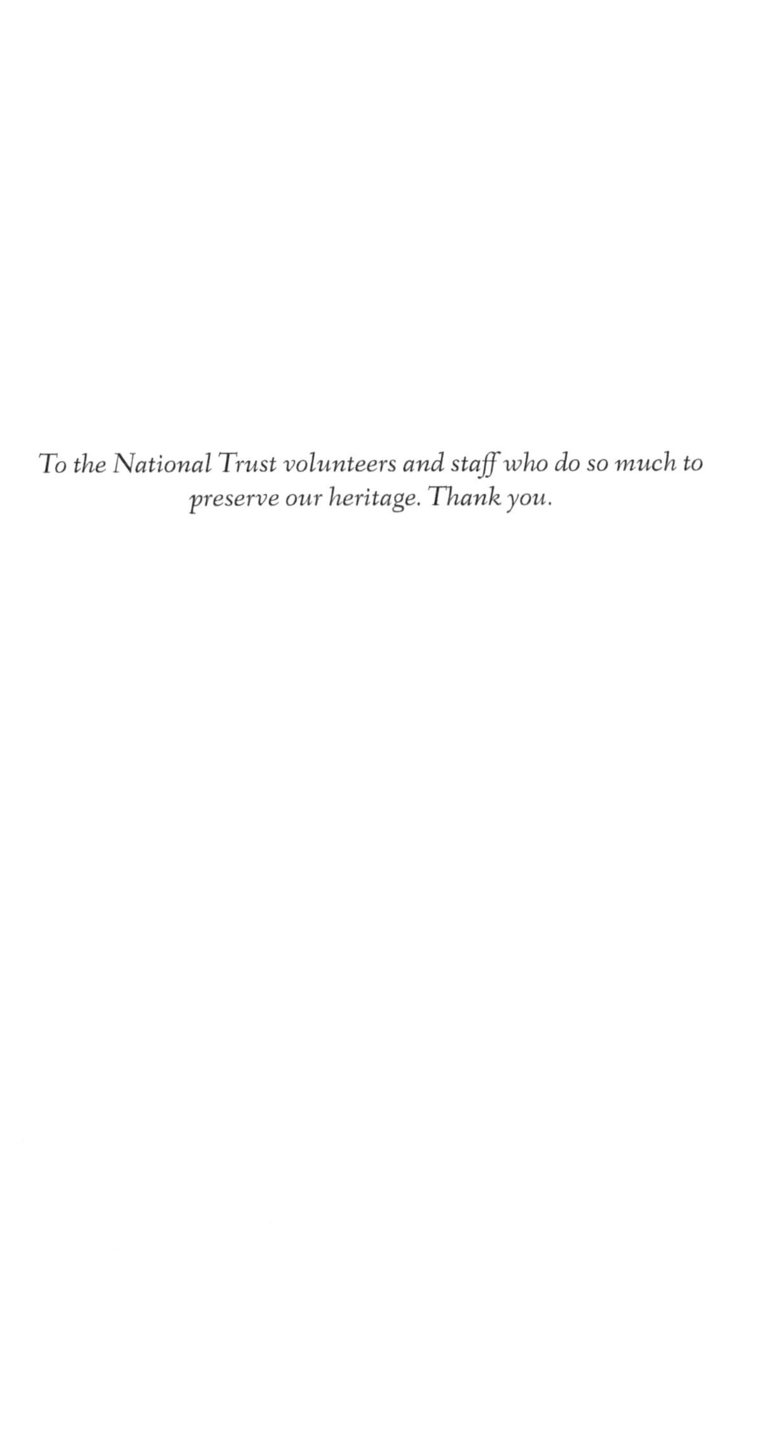

To the National Trust volunteers and staff who do so much to preserve our heritage. Thank you.

PROLOGUE

Torbay Herald November 1926

A robbery took place yesterday evening at Seacliffe House, Hillhead, home of Lord and Lady Massey. During the night, thieves forced their way into the house, breaking into the safe and stealing a large quantity of silver and valuable jewels. The stolen jewellery includes the famous Massey tiara which contains the Kimberley yellow Empress, a remarkable yellow diamond stone of particular colour, size and clarity. Lord and Lady Massey were fortunately not at home during the robbery and are offering a substantial reward for the return of their property and conviction of the thieves. Anyone with information is asked to contact Sergeant Greville at Torquay Police Station.

January 1927

Mystery continues to surround the disappearance of local man, Thomas Crabtree, of Midwinter Farm, Hillhead, near Kingswear. Mr Crabtree, who lived alone at the isolated small-

holding, disappeared without trace shortly before Christmas. The farm was found deserted by the landlord's agent during a routine inspection. Supper was uneaten on the table, the dogs were in the yard and the animals still grazing. Mr Crabtree's property and personal possessions were still in place inside the farm. The missing farmer was last seen on the 10th of December in Dartmouth and was found to be missing on the morning of the 13th. Anyone with any information is asked to contact Sergeant Greville at Torquay Police Station.

AUGUST 1935

Sale of valuable freehold farm and lands.

To be sold at auction by Richard Kemble and Sons.

At Paignton Auction House on 6th August 1935 at 6.00 in the evening precisely if not previously disposed of, and subject to the Law Society's General Sale Conditions of 1934, and in the following or such other lots as may be determined upon at the time of sale.

Lot One

Midwinter Farm. A valuable smallholding of some twenty acres and farmhouse situated at Hillhead near Kingswear. The farmhouse is offered with vacant possession and is in need of some remedial work.

Lot Two

Several stone-built barns and outbuildings suitable for a variety of needs with hardstanding for vehicles.

Further information, maps and guidance can be found by contacting Messrs Lowton and Burridge Solicitors, Totnes 362.

CHAPTER ONE

DECEMBER 1937

Kitty leaned back in her seat and toasted her toes in front of the roaring fire. Outside the diamond-leaded panes of the bay window of her grandmother's apartment in the Dolphin Hotel, Dartmouth, the wind howled along the embankment. A sudden squall of sleet hit the glass sounding like a shower of stones. Kitty wasn't looking forward to leaving and crossing the river on the ferry to return to her home at Churston.

'The weather today is really not very nice,' she observed as her grandmother placidly sipped her tea.

'Well, it is less than two weeks now until Christmas,' Grams said with a smile. 'Your great-aunt says they already have some snow.'

Grams's sister lived in Scotland near the Highlands and Kitty had spent the morning assisting her grandmother to pack ready for a stay there. 'You'll need all of those warm woollens we've put in your trunk. I don't want you to catch pneumonia again,' Kitty remarked.

'Indeed no, once was enough. At least the house is always warm, and it sounds as if she has a host of activities planned for Christmas and Hogmanay. You will be all right, Kitty, dear, keeping an eye on things here at the hotel? I know that Mr Lutterworth and Dolly will have everything in hand, but we are fully booked for Christmas this year.'

'Of course, Grams. Mr Lutterworth is an excellent manager, and Dolly is the most wonderful asset to the hotel,' Kitty reassured her.

They had appointed Cyril Lutterworth to the manager's position just before Kitty's wedding a few years ago. He had previously been manager of the Porteboys Gentlemen's Club in London. Dolly Miller, his assistant, was the younger sister of Kitty's best friend, Alice. She had joined the hotel after leaving school and had quickly proved herself to be excellent at her job.

'I know I am probably worrying about nothing, but I feel happier knowing you and Matthew will still be overseeing things,' her grandmother said. 'It's just that, well, Mr Lutterworth's nephew, Henry, has been released from prison again.'

'Ah.' Henry, Cyril's nephew, was the son of his late sister. Although the boy was no good, Mr Lutterworth still tried to assist the man where he could to keep him on the straight and narrow.

'I suppose I should think about getting home. I'm going with Alice tomorrow to her new house to help her hang the curtains she's made.' Kitty reluctantly drew herself up in her seat.

'I take it that Robert has finished painting the inside of the house now then?' her grandmother said.

'Yes, I believe so. The man from the telegraph company will also be at the farm tomorrow to install a telephone. The house is a little remote and Robert wants to run his business from there after their wedding,' Kitty explained.

Alice was engaged to Robert Potter, the son of her grandmother's favourite taxi driver. Robert had his own business running bus tours locally to Exeter and Plymouth and onto the moors in summer.

He had bought a run-down farm not too far from Kitty and

Matt's house. The farm was at Hillhead just up from Kingswear on the opposite side of the river to Dartmouth. The stone barns and large area of gravel hardstanding were perfect for him to store the tour buses. He had been working hard all summer to renovate the farmhouse ready for his and Alice's wedding which was planned for Valentine's Day.

'I'm so pleased Alice liked the house when she finally saw it.' Grams set her cup and saucer down on the side table next to a pile of Christmas cards that she had been preparing for the post.

'Yes, I think Robert was afraid at first to show it to her because it was in a dreadful state. You know how much trouble that caused between them when she found out what he'd done. Then, of course, Midwinter Farm has a bit of an odd history.' Kitty frowned. 'Alice is dreadfully superstitious too.'

Grams raised her eyebrows. 'Yes, it has been an unfortunate house in the past. That man who went missing from there a few years ago and then a succession of bad tenants, I believe. No wonder Lady Massey decided to sell. She and her late husband never felt the same about coming to their own home, Seacliffe House, after that dreadful robbery in 1926. There were a few robberies locally around that time, I think. I believe there was also an attempt at Lupton House.'

'I don't think I know about that.' Kitty's frown deepened.

'Their house was burgled and the thieves got away with all the silver and the contents of the safe. The Massey tiara was very famous for its yellow diamond centrepiece. There was a big reward offered but they never got it back. Such a shame. Their daughter, Victoria, was supposed to wear it for her wedding,' Grams said.

'Well, I'm sure Midwinter Farm will be a wonderful home for Robert and Alice. It's an ideal place for him to run his business from and, of course, Alice can easily get into Paignton to her shop,' Kitty said.

Alice had set up her own business some eighteen months or so ago. She was an expert seamstress and had a shop selling haberdashery, where she carried out repairs and alterations. She also made and sold various clothing items.

'Perhaps you and Robert can convince her to learn to drive,' Grams said.

Considering Grams had been quite opposed for a long time to Kitty learning to drive and owning a car, this was quite an about turn. Kitty decided to say nothing on that, however, and merely murmured her agreement.

After a few more minutes listening to her grandmother's reminders about various small tasks, Kitty picked up the pile of Christmas cards to post on her way home. She kissed her grandmother goodbye and snuggled into her thick winter coat.

It was already growing dark, and her grandmother switched on a lamp flooding the room with soft yellow light as Kitty tugged on her hat.

'Have a wonderful holiday and a lovely Christmas,' Kitty said.

'You too, my dear. I shall telephone once I have arrived safely in Scotland,' Grams said as Kitty let herself out of the apartment.

The lobby downstairs in the hotel was busy with guests. The large Christmas tree in the corner glittered with silver tinsel strands and red and silver baubles, filling the air with the scent of pine. She popped her head into the office to say goodbye to Mr Lutterworth and Dolly before stepping out into the cold.

The bitter wind stung her cheeks as she hurried to the bright red post box near the boat float and posted her grandmother's Christmas cards. Her task completed, she was glad to get into her small, red car ready to drive onto the ferry which crossed the River Dart and connected the town to Kingswear on the opposite bank.

The waters were choppy today from the wind and she was glad when the boat bumped up against the ramp on the opposite side and she could drive off onto dry land. Once through the village she had to pass the turn that led towards Coleton Fishacre. This was where Alice's new home was situated. Her route then took her along the main road towards the small village where she and Matt had their home.

It was pleasant to think her friend would be closer to her when she was married. At present Alice lived in a tiny flat above her shop in Paignton. The wedding was set for Valentine's Day and seemed to be drawing very close now.

Matt's motorcycle was on the drive when she pulled in. He had been out earlier visiting Chief Inspector Greville at Torquay Police Station. They ran Torbay Private Investigative Services together and Matt had been to see Chief Inspector Greville to ask if there was any progress on a case they had been following since January.

Bertie, her roan cocker spaniel, let out a welcoming woof when he heard her key in the door and she scurried inside, glad to close the door against the sleet which was coming down quite heavily now. She was relieved that Matt was home since she didn't like him riding his motorcycle when the weather was bad.

'Hello, darling, is your grandmother all set for tomorrow?' Matt looked up from his newspaper when she entered the sitting room, having left her hat and coat on the stand in the hall.

'Yes, she's all packed and fussing about the hotel as usual. The weather is really nasty now out there.' She shivered as she stood in front of the coal fire, enjoying the welcome heat on her chilly legs.

Matt had already drawn the curtains and turned on the silk-shaded lamps. The Christmas tree was set up in the corner of the room, cards they had received were on the mantelpiece and all looked snug and comfortable. Rascal, her cat, was asleep on the armchair opposite Matt. Bertie sniffed around her hopefully in case she might have some treats about her person.

'I assume the sleet is heavier? I thought I heard it beating on the glass a moment ago. It had just started when I got home,' Matt said.

'It's much worse now and the wind has picked up too.' Kitty dislodged Rascal from her chair and sat down. 'How did you get on with Chief Inspector Greville?'

Matt set aside his paper. 'There is still no news on Redvers Palmerston. The chief inspector believes he has either fled abroad, is dead, or may be in prison under a different name. There has been neither hide nor hair of the blackguard since that fire in Plymouth in the summer.'

Redvers Palmerston had been a brother officer of Matt's when they had served in the Great War. Whilst they had been convalescing together back in England, unbeknown then to Matt, Redvers had faked his own death to avoid being sent back to the front. In January Matt had at first thought he had seen a ghost when he had sighted Redvers on the docks at Plymouth when Kitty and Matt had returned from America.

Since then, they had uncovered a whole list of crimes which Redvers had apparently committed. These included several bigamous marriages where he had defrauded the women of their money and jewellery. In June there had been a terrible fire at a boarding house in Plymouth. A man had died wearing Redvers's signet ring with his family crest.

The identity of the man remained a mystery, and no one knew how he had come by the ring. The origin of the fire was felt to be suspicious. One thing was certain though. The body had not been that of Redvers Palmerston. The police had been trying desperately since then to trace him, but it seemed he had completely vanished.

'It seems we are at a standstill then once more, for now at least. I fear though he is the proverbial bad penny and may well turn up again at some point.' Kitty fussed the top of Bertie's head as the dog rested his nose on her knee. 'What else did the chief inspector have to say?'

Matt grinned at her. 'I do have some more interesting news. Guess who is returning to Torquay Police Station?'

'Oh no, not Inspector Lewis? He has been at Exeter for so long I thought he had gone for good,' Kitty responded with a groan.

Inspector Lewis was not fond of private investigators and especially female private investigators. He and Kitty had crossed swords now on several cases. He had been working temporarily at Exeter Police Station hoping to secure a promotion to Chief Inspector. It sounded as if this wish had not come off.

'From the way Chief Inspector Greville was talking it sounded as if Inspector Lewis had requested to return,' Matt said.

Kitty stared at him. 'But I thought he wanted to remain at Exeter so he could be more in the notice of the Chief Constable.'

The dimple in Matt's cheek flashed as his smile widened. 'Apparently, there is a young lady in the matter.'

Kitty's eyes widened. 'Inspector Lewis is courting? Good heavens, do we know who she is?' She bounced in her seat with excitement at this tantalising titbit of gossip. 'I mean, the man has always been completely focused on his career.'

Matt laughed. 'That's as much as I know, I'm afraid. Even the chief inspector thought he was speculating but from things that Inspector Lewis has let drop, that's what seems to be the case.'

'I have to say I am astonished.' Kitty returned her husband's smile. 'I wonder who the lucky lady might be?'

Matt shook his head in mock despair. 'I daresay all will be revealed in due course.'

CHAPTER TWO

It was cold and damp with steel-grey skies and a brisk wind when Kitty went to collect Alice the following morning. She pulled up outside her friend's shop on Winner Street in Paignton and tooted the car horn. Alice emerged a few minutes later carrying a large bundle of cloth wrapped in brown paper which she placed carefully on the rear seat of Kitty's car.

'I've one more lot to fetch and I need to make sure our Betty and young Rose are all right managing the shop,' Alice explained breathlessly before darting back inside her business.

Kitty smiled and waited, admiring the clever festive display in the shop window. Tiny baby garments and embroidered ladies' handkerchiefs and other gifts were all artfully displayed with red ribbons and hanging clusters of red and silver baubles trimmed with holly.

Alice emerged with another large brown-paper bundle over her arm which she placed on top of the first parcel before jumping into the front passenger seat of the car.

'Is that everything?' Kitty asked as she started the ignition.

'I hope so. The hooks are already up at the house and

Robert has fixed up the rails and wires,' Alice said, glancing at her shop window as Kitty turned the car around.

'I take it your cousin Betty is working out all right as your new shop assistant?' Kitty changed gear and headed out of Paignton back towards Churston and Hillhead.

Betty, her friend's cousin, was an only child, unlike Alice who was the eldest of eight children. When Alice had started to become swamped with requests for alterations to evening gowns and party dresses for Christmas, she had taken Betty on to help out in the shop. Betty usually worked as a maid but never stayed at one house or job for too long, always looking for a better situation or a new boyfriend.

'Yes, thank goodness. You know our Betty, she has the gift of the gab and can sweet talk customers like nobody's business. It's freed up my time to do more alterations.' Alice was gazing out of the car window at the sodden fields and bare trees as they headed up towards the small villages on the outskirts of Paignton.

'It was fortunate she was looking for a post when you needed help,' Kitty observed as she overtook a man on a bicycle.

'She says she wants to get out of service. She reckons shop work suits her better. It certainly gives me time to get the sewing done while she manages the shop. Young Rose is a good help as well.' Alice turned her head to smile at Kitty. 'I reckon as the hours suits our Betty better too. You know she likes to go dancing and to the pictures.'

Kitty smiled. Betty was an attractive young woman and enjoyed a busy social life. She knew that the long and unsociable hours of working as a maid in a large house certainly impacted Betty's fun.

'Talking of a social life, wait till you hear what Matt told me yesterday.' Kitty told her friend about Inspector Lewis and his reason for returning to Torquay.

Alice's neatly arched brows rose. 'Well, that's a turn up for the books and no mistake. I suppose he's not that old really. Late thirties or so?' She looked at Kitty. 'He's got a good job and can drive, so I suppose he'd be a catch for someone. He's not ugly.'

'You're not selling him well.' Kitty gurgled with laughter as she passed the lodge and kennels belonging to Lupton House. A gust of wind shook water down from the leaves of the trees overhanging the road onto the roof of her car. Her friend had a point. Apart from being rather foxy-looking with his sharp eyes and reddish-brown hair, the inspector was quite passable.

'I don't expect as he'll invite you to his wedding,' Alice said.

Kitty took the turn to the small hamlet of Coleton Fishacre. 'No, I suppose not.' There was little love lost between Kitty and Inspector Lewis.

'I hope Robert has lit the fires in the house ready for us. He was going there first thing.' Alice looked out across the bare red fields for a glimpse of smoke.

'I think he has.' Kitty spotted smoke curling up in pale wisps against the dark sky as they turned into the narrow lane leading to Alice's house.

The farm stood on its own just off a small track. The farmhouse was built of the local grey stone with a thatched roof. A small patch of ground was at the front, currently somewhat forlorn and neglected but Kitty thought it would make a pretty garden with some care in the summer. The white wooden gate stood open and Kitty drove through.

To the side of the farmhouse was a large gravel hardstanding and a big stone barn where Robert could house the vehicles he used for his business. There was also the remains of what she suspected must once have been a small piggery, the low walls of which were now tumbling down and overgrown with weeds. Robert had promised Alice he would clear them all away. He intended to build an office there at some point.

At the rear of the house was an apple orchard and a place to keep hens. The rest of the fields, Robert had rented to a local farmer so that they would have a small income and none of the worries of the upkeep of the ground.

Smoke was indeed curling up from the chimney stack. Kitty hoped that meant the chill would be gone from the house as she pulled to a halt near the barn. Alice jumped out and went to unlock the freshly painted green front door. There was no sign of Robert and Kitty assumed he must have gone to work since his trips to the Christmas markets were popular and lucrative at this time of year.

She climbed out of the car and went to get the curtains from the rear seat. Matt had promised he would ride up to help them hang them once he had walked Bertie and attended his meeting at the bank.

'It's not too cold inside,' Alice said as she came to help her retrieve the bundles of material.

'That's good. It's quite horrid out here. What time is the man coming about the telephone?' Kitty asked.

'In about half an hour. It's a good thing they built that new house down the road a few years back or we would have been a bit stuck. Since they had to put all the poles and things in for them it meant as we could hook onto them as well.' Alice led the way inside the house.

Kitty knew the house Alice meant. It was a rather lovely holiday home for a wealthy London family and the cables and poles needed to service that house had been a boon for the other houses nearby.

The farmhouse had a small square hall with a red quarry-tiled floor. To the back of the hall was the kitchen and scullery. On one side of the house was the sitting room and on the other side was a small dining parlour. Outside at the rear of the house was a toilet and woodstore. Upstairs there were two good-sized bedrooms and a box room. Robert had turned the small fourth one into a bathroom.

Alice was very proud of this, and Robert had worked hard

calling in all kinds of favours from friends and neighbours to have it installed. Kitty followed her friend into the kitchen and draped the curtains over the back of one of the pine chairs that stood around a matching table.

'Now then, shall we have a cup of tea before we get going?' Alice suggested. 'I'll get the kettle on, and we can set the steps up ready in here and do this window first.'

'That sounds like a plan,' Kitty agreed. The kitchen window was long and low, overlooking the orchard at the rear of the farm. She could see that Robert had put up a wire ready for the pretty pale-lemon and green patterned curtains that Alice had made for the kitchen.

They set to work, and they had put up the kitchen curtains and were just finishing their tea when there was a knock at the front door. Alice hurried to open it.

'Miss Miller? I've come about the telephone.' An older man in navy overalls stood on the step carrying a large work bag of tools. His van was parked on the gravel next to Kitty's car.

'Oh yes, my fiancé said to expect you.' Alice stood aside to allow the man into the hall as Kitty watched from the kitchen doorway. 'Can we offer you some tea?' Alice asked as the man studied the walls of the hallway and the frame around the door.

'Thank you kindly, miss. I assume as you will want the telephone in the hall?' he asked.

Kitty went to put the kettle back on the hob while Alice answered the engineer's questions.

She heard the front door close again as she poured the tea.

'He's gone to his van to get his ladders. He thinks it might be a stretch to get the wire from the lane to the house, but he says he will try his best.' Alice looked worried as she took the blue and white striped mug from Kitty. 'I hope he can do it. Robert needs the telephone for his business, and I must admit I should be worried being here by myself with no way to contact anyone if something were to happen.'

'I'm sure he'll find a way. You know what men are like, they always have to find a problem first before they can do what's been asked,' Kitty reassured her.

Alice brightened and smiled. 'Yes, you're probably right. I'll take him his tea and perhaps it'll help him work out how to get the wires into the house.'

Kitty smiled to herself as Alice slipped away to sweeten the engineer's disposition with a mug of tea. She carried a bundle of fabric labelled sitting room through and draped it on an old sofa that Alice had been given by one of her relatives. She had just opened it up and was trying to sort out the contents when her friend returned.

'Are these all curtains, Alice?' Kitty asked as she studied the soft, green-coloured material.

'No, silly. I made slipcovers for the sofa and the chairs to match the curtains. It'll smarten them up a bit.' Alice smiled as she took the fabric from Kitty. 'See, this one is for a chair.'

'Oh yes, I see now.' Kitty helped her friend to fit the cover over the ancient armchair that had been placed near the fire which was burning merrily in the stone fireplace.

'That's better,' Alice declared, surveying their handiwork. They moved on to the other fireside chair before tackling the sofa.

'Right, I'll fetch the steps, and we'll do this window next,' Kitty said.

There was another knock at the door when she went into the hall.

'Matt, you got here quick!' Kitty greeted her husband with a smile as she opened the door.

'I met the engineer in the lane. He asked me to return this with his thanks.' Matt grinned and handed her the cup that Alice had taken out earlier.

'Come in, you're letting the heat out,' Kitty instructed as Alice came out of the sitting room to greet him.

Matt obeyed and Kitty closed the door, the draught already chilling her ankles.

'Your engineer chappie wants to sink another pole to support the cables. He believes it'll stop the wires from sagging. He can't do that today, but he needs to assess where it has to go. It looks like it will be in that old piggery that Robert wants to demolish. Did you want to go and take a look with him, or do you want me to do it?' Matt asked, looking at Alice.

'Would you mind going? Only we've the curtains to see to and I don't know much about engineering and cables. Robert plans to build an office there eventually so it sounds like that would be a good place,' Alice said.

'Of course. I already have my coat on so it shouldn't take long.' Matt smiled at her and disappeared back outside.

* * *

Matt crossed the yard, his boots crunching against the gravel. The engineer stood in the midst of the remains of the old piggery holding a shovel. His theodolite was set up nearby to gauge the best site for the additional pole.

'Mr Potter intends to demolish this anyway,' Matt informed the man when he reached him. 'So you can site the new pole wherever you wish.'

'I was just looking around. Some of this has been cemented so it might be a bit hard for the lads to break through to set it up.' The engineer banged his shovel against the cracked and discoloured floor to illustrate his point.

'How about over there?' Matt suggested. 'Would that work?' He pointed to a space near the edge of the tumbledown wall. The rotting remains of a wooden feeding trough lay on top of what appeared to be bare earth.

'We can take a look,' the engineer conceded.

Matt helped him to clear away the broken wood and the engineer scraped at the surface underneath with his spade.

'This seems more promising. Best check as there's no more of that concrete further down.' He stuck the shovel in and dug out a few spadefuls of the red earth before stopping suddenly, his complexion turning pale as he stared at the disturbed earth.

'What is it? More concrete?' Matt asked, before peering into the freshly excavated hole.

To his dismay he saw a piece of dirty and discoloured check fabric, what seemed to be bone and the unmistakable glint of a ring.

'I think as we had better get the police.' The engineer continued to look at what he'd uncovered as if unable to believe what he was seeing. 'That there looks like a body to me.'

Matt nodded. 'I agree. Head down to the big house just along the road. They have a telephone there, I'm sure, and the housekeeper will probably be in. I'll go and tell Miss Miller what's happening.'

The engineer nodded and hurried away to his van leaving his theodolite still in the piggery. The man was clearly shaken and anxious to get away from his discovery. Matt swallowed hard and braced himself to deliver the bad news to Alice. It seemed the long-lost former tenant of Midwinter Farm had finally been found.

CHAPTER THREE

Alice was perched on the edge of her freshly covered armchair. She anxiously twisted her cotton handkerchief in her hands as Matt gently explained what they had discovered in the derelict piggery. Kitty was torn between wanting to comfort her friend and longing to take a look at where the body had been concealed.

'It doesn't bear thinking about. That poor man, murdered and buried all this time in his own piggery. No wonder Robert managed to get this place at such a good price at the auction. I reckon as people knew as there was something wrong here.' Alice shivered and dabbed at her nose with her handkerchief.

'Well, we don't know for certain…' Kitty broke off from what she was going to say. It was true they didn't know for sure that he was the farmer who had vanished all those years earlier or that he had been murdered.

It was unlikely though to be anyone else, and someone had been at great pains to conceal the body.

'I don't know what to do now.' Alice jumped up and paced about in front of the fireplace. 'Robert has taken a coachload of shoppers into Totnes today for the Christmas market. Whatever will he say when he knows about this?'

'I'm sure Robert will take a sensible view of the matter when he finds out,' Matt said reassuringly.

'Yes, please don't upset yourself, Alice,' Kitty added.

'That sounds like the engineer returning.' Matt peered out of the window at the sound of a van rumbling into the yard.

Kitty went to open the door to let the man inside.

'I've telephoned the police, and they are on their way from Torquay. A Chief Inspector Greville it was,' the engineer said. The man still seemed to be shocked by what had happened and shuffled his feet awkwardly in the doorway to the sitting room.

Kitty was a little surprised by this since Matt had said that Inspector Lewis had returned to the Torquay station.

'I shall go and get the kettle back on then. Alice, do you have any biscuits here at all?' Kitty asked.

'Yes, and there is a fruitcake in a tin in the pantry. We left them here while we were doing the work decorating and measuring up.' Alice had sat back down on the armchair after inviting the engineer to take a seat near the fire.

Kitty exchanged a worried glance with Matt and went to put the kettle on the hob in the kitchen. She was concerned about how her friend was taking the news of the shocking discovery. She busied herself with preparing a tea tray ready for the arrival of the police.

Matt stayed in the sitting room, and she could hear the low murmur of his voice as he spoke to Alice. She couldn't imagine how her poor friend must be feeling. It was hardly the ideal start to her new life, unearthing a body on the premises.

The police arrived some ten minutes or so after she had finished preparing the tray. Matt opened the door to the chief inspector and promptly led him and the constable who had accompanied him to the piggery. The engineer remained in the sitting room with Alice. He too still seemed very shaken by the discovery.

Kitty went to sit on the end of the sofa closest to her friend. 'Don't worry, Alice, the chief inspector will soon sort everything out.' Kitty tried to sound confident.

'Oh, Kitty, Robert has put so much work into this place and all our money and now no one would want to live here, would they? Not with a murder having taken place here. We won't be able to sell it and how can we move in after the wedding now, knowing that man was just in our garden?' Alice burst into tears.

The telephone engineer shifted a little uncomfortably on his chair.

'Lots of things happen in houses and streets and gardens. Whatever befell that poor man is in the past. You and Robert are making a wonderful, comfortable home here.' Kitty patted her friend's arm. 'It'll be all right, you'll see.'

The sound of gravel spinning out from a car making a rapid entrance into the yard had Kitty jumping up to peep out through the window.

'Doctor Carter is here.' She recognised the dark-green sports car immediately even before the chubby, cheerful doctor had climbed out. Doctor Carter always reminded her of a smiley cherub. No matter how dreadful the task he had to deal with as the police doctor he was always unperturbed. He also had a fondness for fast cars.

The doctor crossed over to the group gathered in the piggery. The constable appeared to be using the telephone engineer's spade. No doubt to uncover the rest of the victim. She decided to go and add another cup to the tea tray and make sure the kettle was hot. The wind was icy outside, and a few snow flurries had started to flutter down.

She had just set the kettle onto the hob once more when she

heard the front door open and the sound of male voices in the hall.

'Mrs Bryant, always a pleasure to see you, although not necessarily in these circumstances,' Chief Inspector Greville said as she emerged from the kitchen bearing the laden tea tray.

'Do allow me to assist you, Kitty, my dear.' Doctor Carter took the tray from her and bore it into the sitting room, where he placed it carefully on the broad wooden windowsill since Alice did not yet have a coffee table.

Matt introduced the telephone engineer to the chief inspector, while Kitty and Alice poured tea and passed around the biscuits. The chief inspector took the engineer's statement whilst demolishing most of the plate of biscuits, much to Kitty's private amusement.

Chief Inspector Greville was very fond of his food, despite his wife's attempts to moderate what he ate.

'Thank you, that is most helpful. Now I have all your details you are free to go. I would ask that you don't tell anyone about this matter, at least for now,' said the chief inspector, brushing crumbs from his moustache.

The man seemed glad to leave, apparently reassured that the chief inspector would inform the company of what had happened.

'What happens next?' Alice asked, looking at the chief inspector once the telephone man had gone.

'Well, we get our chappie out of the piggery and that's it at this end, eh, Greville,' Doctor Carter remarked matter-of-factly.

'I suppose it was the man who went missing ages ago?' Kitty asked.

'Yes, Doctor Carter here will confirm his identity but the remnants of clothing, his ring and everything else fits the description we had at the time of Thomas Crabtree,' the chief inspector said.

'And was it murder, do you think?' Alice asked.

'I'm afraid so, Miss Miller. Fellow has a hole in the back of his skull. At a guess he was struck from behind.' Doctor Carter beat the chief inspector to the last biscuit on the plate.

'Are you familiar with the case, Chief Inspector?' Matt asked as he sipped his tea.

'Unfortunately, yes. I was a sergeant back then. It was just before I was promoted. We were very busy and short-staffed as it was this time of year he went missing funnily enough. A few weeks before, there had been some high-profile jewel robberies in this area. We suspected that Crabtree and his friends might have some knowledge of that, but we couldn't prove anything. Then Crabtree went missing. The farm agent called, and the supper was on the table, dogs in the yard, doors unlocked. No sign of the man. All his clothes still in the cupboards but he'd vanished into thin air.' The chief inspector's brow furrowed as he recalled the case.

'I presume the farm was searched at the time?' Kitty asked.

'Oh yes, as best as we could and there was no trace. At the time we suspected there had been a falling out amongst thieves and that perhaps Crabtree had scarpered with the loot.' The chief inspector looked regretfully at the empty biscuit plate. 'I wanted to bring in some dogs. Lupton House Kennels suggested they might assist but the chief constable at the time felt it wouldn't be of any use.'

Alice shuddered. 'It's so awful. Did you suspect anyone at the time who might have wished to harm this man, Mr Crabtree?' she asked.

'He had a number of undesirable associates and he'd quarrelled with his family. His son and daughter-in-law still live locally, I think. Thomas, the father, had borrowed a great deal of money from his son, William, and had refused to repay it. At first it didn't matter, but then William became seriously ill, and he and his wife had a young daughter. With William not able to work they desperately needed that money. At the time

Thomas went missing, his son hadn't spoken to him for over a fortnight. I'll have to break the news to them that he's been found, once Doctor Carter here has officially confirmed his identity.' Chief Inspector Greville set his cup and saucer down on the tray.

'I suppose they will at least have some closure on the matter,' Alice said.

'Hmm, I'd like to keep the discovery of his remains quiet for a bit while I revisit some of his old friends.' Chief Inspector Greville looked thoughtful.

'You may need to see the housekeeper then at the D'Oyly Carte house. That's where the engineer telephoned from and you know how word spreads fast around these parts,' Alice advised.

'Thank you, Miss Miller. A good thought,' Chief Inspector Greville agreed.

'Will you be taking charge of this case, sir, or will Inspector Lewis be handling it?' Kitty asked.

'I shall certainly handle all of the preliminary enquiries. I'll have the records fetched from storage. It may be useful to have Inspector Lewis go over everything. A fresh pair of eyes may spot something that Inspector Park, who was my superior at the time, may have missed,' the chief inspector said.

'Well, thank you for the tea, Miss Miller. Lovely to see you again, Kitty, Matt. I think Mrs Carter is planning a pre-Christmas supper party so do look out for an invitation. I had better go out and supervise the removal of our friend in the piggery. I think my men have arrived.' Doctor Carter excused himself and ventured back out into the cold.

'I had better go and visit the D'Oyly Carte house before tongues begin to wag.' Chief Inspector Greville rose and brushed biscuit crumbs from his tie. 'I'll be in touch, Miss Miller, and with Mr Potter when we know more. Thank you for the refreshments.' He followed after Doctor Carter.

'Are you all right, Alice?' Kitty asked as she added her own empty cup to the tray.

Her friend seemed to be frozen in shock. A tear escaped and slid slowly down Alice's pale cheek. 'No, not really. I thought I were going to have a lovely day, putting up curtains and getting a telephone sorted. Now I have a dead body in the piggery and the person who done it is probably still just down the hill in Kingswear or Dartmouth.'

'Chief Inspector Greville clearly seemed to remember a lot about the case when this Thomas Crabtree went missing. I'm sure he'll have the person responsible under lock and key in no time,' Matt said.

'What if he doesn't though? Suppose as this all stirs something up? 'Tis a lonely place up here if Robert is working and I'm on my own. What if that man was caught up with those robberies? I don't know as I can do it. I don't know if I can live here now.' Alice bit her lip.

'Oh, Alice.' Kitty placed her arm around her friend's shoulders in a supportive hug.

'This is a fine house and perfect for Robert's business. There's no need to be worried. I know that what's just happened is ghastly and unsettling, but it was all a long time ago. Ten years or so. There's no reason to suppose anything bad will happen now. People have lived here since then and it's all been all right,' Matt added in a reassuring tone.

'It's still horrid. I just don't think I can go ahead with the wedding unless whoever killed that man is caught. It feels like a bad omen.' Alice fumbled for her handkerchief again and dabbed at her eyes.

Kitty stood and picked up the tea tray. 'Let's get these things washed up and put away. Matt can give us a hand with the rest of the curtains, then, if you like, we'll go down into Kingswear and have some lunch.'

'Good idea. A spell away from the house will help you feel

better. I'll get up the steps if you want to hand me the curtains,' Matt offered, taking his cue from Kitty.

Alice looked at first as if she was going to refuse but then seemed to think better of it. 'Very well,' she agreed. 'We might as well finish what we come to do.'

Kitty breathed a small sigh of relief and went to wash up the cups and tidy them away, while Matt assisted Alice. Her husband was usually a calming influence so hopefully Alice would feel better once they had finished their task.

The curtains were up in the sitting room and the dining room by the time Kitty went back to see how they were getting on. She was pleased to see that Alice had more colour in her cheeks and seemed less distraught.

'Is that all the curtains for today?' Kitty asked.

Alice nodded. 'I've a bit of hemming to do on the upstairs ones so I thought as I'd do those next week.'

'It'll be nice to have them up before Christmas. They make the house feel so homely. Once the new year arrives it won't be many weeks until the wedding,' Kitty said.

Alice didn't reply but busied herself folding up the brown paper which had contained the seat covers and curtains. She placed the paper in the log basket beside the fire in the sitting room ready to be used when the fire was next lit.

'Have all the police gone yet?' she asked.

Matt looked through the window. 'I think so and Doctor Carter's car has gone too.'

Alice's shoulders relaxed. 'Then I'd like to go, please. I don't want to be here any longer today.'

They fetched their coats and hats from the hall stand and Alice checked that the back door was secure before they left the house. Alice locked the front door while Matt went over to his motorcycle.

'I'll meet you at the Waterside Tea Rooms. I'll go ahead and secure us a table.' He hopped onto his Sunbeam and kicked it into life.

Alice slid into the passenger seat of Kitty's car, her face woebegone under the brim of her dark-green felt hat.

'You'll feel better after we've had lunch,' Kitty said as she started the car engine ready to follow Matt. She certainly hoped something to eat would lift Alice's spirits.

'I hope so. The way I feel now I could just give Robert back my keys and never lay eyes on the house again,' Alice said.

Kitty glanced back at the farm through her car mirror as she set off into the lane.

She hoped the chief inspector would solve the case quickly or it sounded as if Alice and Robert's wedding could be in some jeopardy.

CHAPTER FOUR

Matt arrived at the tea room a few minutes before Kitty and Alice. He parked the Sunbeam at the side of the road and went inside to find a table. Kingswear was a pretty village built into the sides of the steep hill on the opposite bank to Dartmouth. It had a station, a few shops, a church and village hall, two public houses and a number of properties ranging from humble cottages to a large hotel.

The Waterside Tea Rooms was sited in a street above the river looking down on the water and offered a good view of Dartmouth on the opposite bank. Luckily, a table was free in the window, so he removed his heavy leather motorcycle coat and took a seat.

A moment or two later the brass bell above the door jangled and Kitty and Alice entered. They wiped their feet on the coconut matting in the doorway and hung their coats beside his on the dark oak stand before coming to join him.

'Brr, it's so cold out there. It's much nicer in here,' Kitty said, looking around her in approval.

The interior of the Waterside Tea Rooms was decorated for

Christmas with paper chains hanging from the black beams that spanned the ceiling and a large Christmas tree beside the fireplace. A fire crackled merrily behind the polished brass guard and a few Christmas cards from customers had been strung above the window where they were sitting.

The inclement weather seemed to have put off visitors to the tea room as it was relatively quiet. It was also after the usual lunchtime rush. A couple of ladies were taking tea, and an older man was eating a sandwich in the corner. The proprietor bustled over to them, notepad in hand as they studied the blue leatherette-bound menu.

'Now then, what can I get for you?' she asked.

'I think the vegetable soup, please, with a roll and butter,' Kitty said. The others all agreed they too would like the soup.

'I think I've just enough left. It's been popular today as it's so cold out there,' the woman said as she made a note in her book. 'Is it still sleeting?'

'Just spitting a little but the wind cuts right through you, especially up at Hillhead,' Kitty said with feeling.

'Oh yes, 'tis high up there. Lovely in summer though,' the woman agreed. 'Summat going on round there today, so I heard. Police business.'

Alice exchanged a glance with Kitty.

'Oh?' Kitty asked innocently as the woman tucked her notebook back in the pocket of her white frilly apron.

'Yes, somebody said as it were to do with that farmer who went missing years ago up there near Coleton. Bad business that was and so strange.' The woman shook her head sadly.

'Did you know him at all, the man who went missing? Erm, Crabtree was it? Thomas Crabtree,' Matt asked, as if suddenly recalling the name of the missing farmer.

'I knew of him, and I know his daughter-in-law, Lavinia. She still lives in the village here. Treated her and his son terrible, did old Thomas. Not a respectable man. I wouldn't be surprised if it turned out that he had a bad end.' The woman pursed her lips and walked off back to the kitchen to prepare their lunch.

'Everyone seems to know of this Thomas Crabtree, and so much for the chief inspector keeping things quiet,' Alice said in a gloomy voice.

'It certainly looks as if word may have already got out,' Matt said.

He knew all too well that in a small place like Kingswear gossip was rampant if there was even a hint of something interesting. Discovering the body of a man who had been missing for ten years would certainly give the locals a field day.

'If it has then Robert and I will be subjected to all kinds of gossip. There'll be people trying to get up to the farm to take pictures. It'll be in the papers.' Alice looked horrified.

'I'm sure the chief inspector will do something to try and prevent that. Besides the farm is your private property. Robert can put a chain through the gate to stop the nosy parkers,' Kitty said.

'Mother will be mortified if it goes in the papers,' Alice said.

The woman arrived back at their table with their soups and bread, so conversation paused for a moment. Once she had returned to her counter, Alice resumed in a low voice so as not to be overheard.

'It will be a scandal,' Alice said as Matt offered her the glass dish containing fresh curls of creamy-yellow butter.

'It's old news, Alice. Even if the papers did report it, everything will die down in a day or so,' Kitty assured her as she stirred in the cream on top of the thick pale-green soup.

'What if it doesn't?' Alice persisted as she picked up one of the white fluffy bread rolls that accompanied their meal. 'Then what? I don't want to have folks whispering every time I come to Dartmouth. People saying as that's the woman who lives in the farm where there were a murder.'

'I really wouldn't worry too much about other people. Any negative talk will soon fade away. Robert is a successful businessman now and you have a flourishing shop of your own. People are much more likely to say that's the place where Robert's business is based,' Kitty reassured her kindly.

'Kitty's right, Alice. Once the chief inspector has caught the person responsible any gossip will quickly die away,' Matt agreed. He suspected there was a grain of truth in what Alice had said.

Alice's mouth was set in a stubborn line, but she didn't argue. Matt, however, could see that his wife's friend was not convinced.

They finished their lunch and settled the bill. Matt took his motorcycle to drive home to Churston. He intended, however, to drop in at the golf club near their home first. Quite often he would find members who had called in for social reasons since the weather was too bad for a game. Many of those members had long memories and a good knowledge of local gossip.

Kitty and Alice headed back to Paignton so that Alice could ensure all was well in her shop. Matt guessed that Alice might have more to say to Kitty on the subject of the farm on her way back to Winner Street. He couldn't help feeling sorry for Robert since he had worked so hard on the house and the land, ready to make a home for himself and Alice after their wedding. Now it looked as if it might all be for nothing.

The bar at the golf club was quiet, as he had expected. He hung his heavy leather coat in the cloakroom and tidied himself up before entering the members' area. The lounge was a pleasant room which usually offered an open aspect to view the greens nearest to the clubhouse.

While they had been having lunch, however, the fog had

moved in from the sea shrouding everything in thick white mist. The eerie sounds of the ships' fog horns sounded from the harbour below in the bay and echoed mournfully even inside the building.

The bar steward was leaning on the polished wooden bar top idly chatting with a man Matt knew in passing.

'Captain Bryant, sir, a surprise to see you in today. Terrible weather out there. What can I get for you?' The man straightened up to greet him and the older man seated on one of the wine leather-topped wooden bar stools nodded his head in acknowledgement.

'Just a half of cider, please,' Matt said.

The steward reached for a glass and served him his drink. The other man requested another pint of bitter.

'I suppose the wind has dropped seeing as the fog has come in,' the man said to Matt as he accepted his drink from the steward.

'Yes, I was just up near Hillhead and it's quite dense now up there.' Matt raised his glass and took a sip of his drink.

'That'll be bad driving home to Kingswear, especially if it's coming off the river. I thought I'd get out of the house for a bit while the missus got on with her cleaning. Preparing for the family to come for Christmas she is. That means turning all the rooms out, annoying our maid and finding me a million jobs to do,' his companion said gloomily.

Matt and the steward made suitably sympathetic noises while the man looked mournfully at the small Christmas tree in the corner of the lounge.

'Ah well, it doesn't last long, does it? Christmas is for the kiddies. Then it'll be New Year and celebrations for the grown-ups,' the steward remarked as he took a cloth to polish the top of the bar.

'It wasn't so bad at Kingswear while I was having lunch,'

Matt said. He hadn't realised his companion lived so close to the river.

'That's lucky then,' the man said.

'We were hearing that the police had been in the village. The rumour was that it might be something to do with a farmer who went missing years ago up near Coleton.' Matt was careful about what he said. Since there were already rumours abroad he didn't wish to add to them, but he also wanted to find out what people thought of the matter.

'You mean old what's his name, Thomas Crabtree up at Midwinter Farm? That was a rum go. I'd be surprised if it was anything to do with that though. It must be what ten years or so ago by now.' The man looked surprised.

Matt shrugged. 'Who knows. Did you know him at all, this Crabtree?'

The man chuckled. 'No, I didn't know him, but I did know of him. His son, William, was upset with his father, and I don't think anyone could blame him. He owed William money, and the lad needed it at the time. He was unwell, and they had a little girl. Flu it was, he couldn't work for ages. They were almost made homeless. Then Thomas just ups and disappears. There's not many in Kingswear would give Thomas Crabtree a good name.'

'Oh, who else had he upset?' Matt asked.

'Arthur Maldon, he was the landlord at the time of the Steam Packet. He barred him from the place. Something to do with Maldon's daughter, Tilly, I heard. Only a young lass she was at the time. Then, of course, that meant that Fred Smith, Tilly's young man, he fell out with Crabtree as well.' The man paused and took another swig of beer. 'Still, I think they were all a bit foxed at him disappearing the way he did. You heard about that, I suppose?'

'Wasn't there something about his supper being half eaten on the table and all his belongings still in the cupboards and the dogs in the yard?' The steward stopped his polishing to join in the conversation.

'That's right. The papers said it was like that ship, the *Mary Celeste*, when those folks disappeared. Regular nine days' wonder it was.' The man rubbed his chin thoughtfully.

'Did no one have any idea where he might have gone?' Matt asked.

The man snorted. 'He had a bad reputation in the village. Some said as he'd been involved in that robbery at Seacliffe House. Nothing was ever proved, mind you. I think everyone assumed he'd just gone off with the jewels and the silver. Perhaps he thought the police were onto him. Or there had been a falling out and he thought he'd better scarper.'

'I'd forgotten about that robbery. There was a necklace or a tiara taken. It was in all the papers with a big reward. I don't think they ever got it back. I expect it was all broken down and sold in London or somewhere,' the steward said.

'Funny how that's come up now though. The farm was sold again not so long ago. A young chap from Dartmouth owns it. Been doing the place up and going to run his touring company from there I heard,' the man said.

'So I believe,' Matt agreed and finished his cider.

* * *

Kitty drove Alice back to Paignton. The wind had dropped but the fog had rolled in from the sea and the river. By the time she reached Winner Street and Alice's shop she had slowed her car to a crawl.

Alice had barely spoken on the way back. Kitty had been glad since it had taken all of her concentration to follow the barely visible road through the fog. Now they were stopped in front of her friend's shop, and the bright lights of the shop window cast a soft yellow light onto the street.

Alice had her hand on the car door as if ready to jump out when she turned towards Kitty. 'I suppose you think I'm being foolish? Making so much fuss over not feeling easy in my mind about living in that house?'

'Goodness me, finding a body in one's garden is enough to make anyone upset,' Kitty said. 'I would feel just the same way. But it's a lovely house and perfect for Robert's business. You are so lucky in some ways not to have to rent rooms or live with Robert's parents. I can see why you're upset but I do truly think everything will settle down. Everything will soon be resolved and you'll feel so much better about everything.'

Alice nodded. 'I know we're lucky. The house was cheap at the auction, or we couldn't have got it. It's just, well, it doesn't feel like the best of starts to married life. I was so excited to be fixing up my things and making it look nice. Now I don't know what Robert will say when he finds out. He's coming over tonight after he finishes work to take me out to supper.'

'I'm sure once Chief Inspector Greville finds who's done this everything will feel much better. Talk to Robert, he's a very sensible person,' Kitty urged. She hoped her friend wouldn't take against her new home before she was even living there. It was a lovely house now Robert had done so much to it. She knew how superstitious her friend could be though. Finding a murdered man in the derelict piggery was enough to make anyone feel superstitious.

She said goodbye to Alice and turned her car around to drive home. It took her a while to return to the square white villa she shared with Matt. To her surprise his motorbike was not on the drive, and she wondered where he could have gone.

She disliked him being out on the Sunbeam in bad weather and hoped he wasn't too far from home. Bertie greeted her enthusiastically when she entered the hall and took off her outdoor things. Their housekeeper, Mrs Smith, had put the day's post on the hall table and she could see there was quite a pile of what looked like Christmas cards. She fussed Bertie and gathered up the cards to take them into the sitting room.

It was getting dark out now, so she switched on the lamps and drew the curtains against the cold. Rascal, her cat, was curled up asleep on one of the armchairs beside the fire as Kitty sat down to open their post.

Mrs Smith must have banked up the fire before leaving so the room was warm and cosy as Kitty tucked her feet up beneath her on the chair and slit open the envelopes. There were several cards from acquaintances and a couple from hotels they had done business with during the summer.

The last envelope bore a Yorkshire postmark and Kitty guessed it was probably from her cousin Lucy and would almost certainly include a letter. The card had a picture of a fat robin on a holly bough and sure enough a letter was enclosed.

Darling Kitty and Matt,

I hope this finds you both well? And Bertie and Rascal too. We are so looking forward to baby's first Christmas here. Mother and Father have said they are bringing parcels from you both for us. I must admit I am ridiculously happy they are coming until New Year. Cousin Hattie is also joining the party and, this is why I'm writing: she has a new gentleman friend! We can't wait to meet him and find out more. Dear Hattie deserves some happiness. I shall, of course, let you know what we think when we see him.

All my love,

Lucy, Rupert and William xxxx

Kitty's eyebrows rose as she read the letter. Hattie had been the older, unmarried distant relative with no money or fixed home for years. Then she had inherited a small cottage and a little sum of money which meant she at last had a home of her own and some independence.

Kitty just hoped this new friend would be kind to her and make her happy. She was fond of Hattie and knew Lucy would like nothing better than for her to have a companion.

CHAPTER FIVE

Matt arrived home just as she was adding the newly arrived Christmas cards to the others on the mantelpiece.

'I wondered where you were. The fog is so bad and it's getting dark outside now,' she exclaimed when he strolled in and kissed her cheek.

'I called in at the golf club on the way home,' he explained. 'I wanted to do a spot of fishing to find out more about that Thomas Crabtree. I thought perhaps there might be someone who would know something which could help put Alice's mind at rest.'

Kitty immediately perked up. 'Oh, was there anyone in the club today?'

'Yes, just one fellow who lives in Kingswear. He didn't know Thomas Crabtree, but he did know some of the other people that Chief Inspector Greville may have been thinking of when we saw him earlier.' He told her what he'd learned.

'Hmm, interesting. This Thomas Crabtree definitely didn't sound a very pleasant man. Any time his name has been mentioned people seem to have the same reaction.' Kitty gave a little shiver as she took a seat on the black leather sofa to avoid disturbing her cat who was still snoozing on one of the fireside chairs.

'No, I agree. I wonder if the chief inspector might allow us to read some of the old notes on the case,' Matt mused. He guessed if they could get permission they would have to wait until after Inspector Lewis had examined them.

'Chief Inspector Greville might permit it, but Inspector Lewis is a different kettle of fish. You know he is a stickler for policies and procedures. Allowing us access to police files would be unlikely to meet with his approval. If he did give permission, we would no doubt have to complete a huge stack of paperwork first.' Kitty grimaced and wrinkled her nose.

Matt smiled. 'That's very true but the chief inspector usually manages to find a way.'

'I take it we are going to officially investigate this then. I mean, it's for Alice and Robert's future happiness. She really is dreadfully upset about it and who can blame her.' Kitty stroked the top of Bertie's head as he rested his nose on her knee. 'It was such a shock finding Mr Crabtree after all this time.'

'Yes, I think we need to try and get to the bottom of what happened if only to give Alice peace of mind,' Matt agreed. He knew his wife. Even if it hadn't been Alice and Robert's house she would probably still have wanted to investigate.

'Oh, talking of marital happiness.' Kitty handed him a folded sheet of writing paper. 'This came in Lucy's Christmas card. It's about Hattie.'

Matt took the letter and read it, smiling as he did so. 'That does sound good news. Hattie deserves some joy in her life. She's spent years shuffling from one relative to another running all kinds of errands and putting up with so many slights in return for her keep.'

'I know. She once told me that her stays at Enderley with my aunt and uncle were some of her happiest moments. My aunt and uncle have always treated her well and she's always been close to Lucy.' Kitty took the letter back and tucked it behind the clock on the mantelpiece, gently dislodging Bertie as she rose.

'Let us hope this gentleman proves worthy of her,' Matt said as Kitty resumed her seat.

'Yes, she deserves the best,' Kitty agreed as she soothed Bertie's ruffled feelings with lots of pats. Rascal merely opened an eye to see what the fuss was about, then went back to sleep.

* * *

Later that evening after supper they were seated in front of the fire listening to a Christmas story on the radio when a knock sounded at the front door. Bertie gave a woof of disapproval at the unwarranted disturbance to his pre-bedtime nap.

'Whoever that is, it's dashed late.' Matt set aside his glass of whisky and went to see who was there.

'Robert, my dear fellow, come in, come in. This weather is beastly, isn't it?'

Kitty turned off the radio when she heard her husband greet her friend's fiancé.

A moment later, once Robert had removed his outdoor things, he entered the room accompanied by Matt. Robert's pleasant face looked anxious and concerned as he accepted a seat on the sofa.

'I'm sorry to call so late but I've just left Alice,' Robert explained as Kitty called Bertie away from his investigation of Robert's trouser legs.

'How was Alice when you left her?' Kitty asked. 'Was she still upset? She told you what happened today, of course?'

'About the body of that man who went missing turning up in the old piggery. Yes, she did. I telephoned the chief inspector and spoke to him, and he confirmed the man was murdered. It was definitely Thomas Crabtree. They think as he was lured outside, and someone was waiting and bashed him over the head. It's a bad business right enough.'

Kitty thought Robert looked tired. No surprise really since he had been up very early to light the fires at the house and had then driven a busload of Christmas shoppers around Totnes, before returning to Paignton to have supper with Alice. To then be told a body had been found on their property must have been a terrible shock.

'Did he say anything else?' Kitty asked, while Matt poured Robert a whisky in a small crystal tumbler and handed it to him.

'Just as they were looking over the old files and would be reopening the case.' Robert accepted the glass. The amber liquid glinted in the light from the fire and the lamps as he stared gloomily at it.

'That's to be expected, I suppose,' Kitty said as Matt retook his own seat.

'It is since it's now a murder investigation. I only hope as the chief inspector can get to the bottom of who killed this Mr Crabtree before our wedding or Alice might not even walk down the aisle,' Robert said.

Kitty exchanged a glance with Matt. She had been afraid that Alice might refuse to marry until something was done.

'Please don't worry. Alice is just shocked and upset at the moment. Matt and I are going to see what we can unearth too. Everything will work out, I'm sure of it,' she said.

'That's right kind of you, Kitty. All my money is sunk in that farm. 'Tis mine and Alice's future. It's perfect for business and the house is nice now I've fixed it up. I swear though it's as if a jinx is on it.' Robert took a sip of his drink.

'It's a lovely house. I know that you and Alice didn't initially see eye to eye over the purchase.' Kitty tried to phrase things delicately. Alice had been furious when she had discovered Robert had bought the farm behind her back and had just expected her to fall in with his plans. It had almost parted them for good.

'It was a good buy at auction. The land isn't really enough to be profitable these days as a farm, so it made sense to lease the ground to the neighbour. The house itself were in a complete state. Mould in all the upstairs where the gutters had leaked and no electric. But all that is fixed now with a new indoor bathroom and all done up nice,' Robert said.

'It looks lovely. The curtains Alice put up today make it very snug,' Kitty agreed.

'But what if there's no one caught for this man's murder? Alice will be counting magpies and all sorts every day between now and our wedding looking for signs why we should or shouldn't marry and live there. You know how she fell out with me over buying it in the first instance.' Robert raised his gaze and looked at Kitty.

'Then we must do our best to find out who was responsible and find some good omens to satisfy Alice. I'm sure she'll come around,' Kitty assured him.

'We shall do everything we can to solve the case,' Matt agreed. 'After all, I am your best man.'

This brought a smile to Robert's naturally rosy cheeks, and he downed his drink before rising from his seat. 'Thank you, both of you. Alice and I appreciate everything you do for us. I had best be off. It's been a long day and I've yet to tell Father and Mother what's happened before they have chance to find out from elsewhere.'

He said his goodnights and Matt went with him into the hall to see him out.

'I think that means we are officially hired,' Kitty said with a mischievous smile when Matt returned. 'Just in case Inspector Lewis objects to our interest in the murder.'

• • •

The following morning dawned wet and cold. Kitty hoped her grandmother's long journey to Scotland would go smoothly. One of the maids from the hotel was travelling with her as far as Carlisle since she was visiting family there for Christmas, so at least she would have company for much of the journey.

Kitty shivered as she got washed and dressed in a warm, dark-red woollen frock and went downstairs to let Bertie into the garden. The cold air seeped in through the back door chilling her ankles as she waited for the spaniel to complete his investigation of the shrubbery before returning to the house.

Mrs Smith, her housekeeper, arrived shortly afterwards and together they went through the list for the grocer while Mrs Smith prepared breakfast. With just over a week till Christmas Day Kitty was keen to ensure she had everything in hand. It would be nice to have Christmas at home, just her and Matt in their own house.

The year before they had unexpectedly been summoned to America by a false claim that her wayward father was dangerously ill. That had led to an unexpected murder case in New York. At least this year the murder they were trying to solve was closer to home.

Matt came downstairs just as Kitty carried their boiled eggs and toast into the dining room.

'Brr, it looks like another cold day today.' He took his seat at the table opposite her.

'At least the fog has lifted.' Kitty poured them both a cup of tea from the china pot. 'Now, where shall we start with this case?'

Matt grinned as he helped himself to toast from the chrome-plated rack. 'I see you don't intend to let the grass grow under your feet.'

'Alice and Robert are depending on us.' Kitty set the teapot down on a mat.

'Yes, I would hate anything to upset the apple cart for them again with the wedding so close,' Matt agreed.

'I was thinking, while I was waiting for Bertie to come back in this morning, about the people that man mentioned to you at the club. The landlord and his daughter and the girl's boyfriend. I wonder if she married him? The boyfriend. It was ten years ago, and the father may not be the landlord anymore,' Kitty said thoughtfully, ignoring her dog's begging eyes as she ate her toast.

'We need to discover if they are all still in Kingswear,' Matt said, stirring his tea. 'Arthur and Tilly Maldon and a Fred Smith.'

Their housekeeper entered the room with fresh toast as he spoke.

'Fred Smith? I've a distant relative called Fred Smith. Black sheep of the family he is. Works on the ferries at Kingswear.'

'Is he married? To a girl called Tilly?' Kitty asked.

Mrs Smith looked surprised. 'He was seeing a girl called Tilly years ago when he were younger. Publican's daughter. Nothing come of it though in the end and he's still single.'

'We think he knew a man called Thomas Crabtree who vanished ten years ago from a farm near Coleton Fishacre,' Matt said.

'That's right. He was took in for questioning about it. My aunt was mortified. Still, he swore black and blue he knew nothing of it, and they never did find that man.' Mrs Smith refilled the toast rack.

'Is he still working the ferry?' Matt asked.

Mrs Smith gave him an assessing look. 'Lower ferry, so I heard. Not long out of prison again. He's not in fresh bother, is he?'

'Not so far as we know. We may want to ask him some questions at some point, that's all,' Kitty said as she took the top off her boiled egg with a teaspoon.

'Hmm, well it wouldn't surprise me if he were in trouble again. He only come out a few months ago. Got caught with some property that weren't his.' Mrs Smith pursed her lips disapprovingly and swept out of the dining room to return to the kitchen.

'Gosh, well we know where one of our suspects is at least. I wonder what became of the girl, Tilly, and her father? Do you think they are still at the pub?' Kitty asked as she plunged a toast soldier into her egg, causing the thick yellow yolk to rise up and ooze stickily down the side of the pale-blue china egg cup.

'We can see if his name is above the door,' Matt suggested.

'I should be able to spot this Fred Smith if I cross on the ferry. I use it so often I know most of the men,' Kitty suggested.

'Then I suggest we head down to Kingswear after breakfast,' Matt said.

CHAPTER SIX

Plans agreed, they finished eating and wrapped up against the cold to drive down to the ferry crossing at Kingswear. Bertie accompanied them, secured on the rear seat of Kitty's car with a tartan travel rug to lie on for warmth.

There were two ferries that crossed the river regularly. The upper ferry and the lower one. Mrs Smith had suggested that Fred was to be found on the lower ferry. This was the one Kitty usually used as it left from the centre of the village and was closer to home.

Since it was still early in the day and the weather so cold, there were not many people about as they drove into the village. Kitty noticed that the villagers had placed a large fir tree in a pot outside the railway station ready for Christmas.

She had slowed down as they passed the public house, and Matt had checked the landlord's name on the painted sign above the door. The pub had clearly changed hands after Thomas Crabtree had disappeared, and Arthur Maldon was no longer listed as the licensee.

'Hmm, well it seems we shall have to look elsewhere to discover where the old landlord and his daughter are now,' Matt said as Kitty carried on past the station entrance and the small post office to wait at the start of the slope for the ferry to return across the river from Dartmouth.

Kitty nodded. 'Let us hope that Fred Smith is amongst the crew on board this morning.'

There were two more vehicles queuing behind her car by the time the ferry had clanked its way back across the Dart. A small van and a cart disembarked before the ferryman gave her the signal to drive up the ramp onto the ferry. Kitty drove on and pulled up to the chain at the far end of the short deck. The other cars followed with one pulling beside her and one behind.

'Do you see him?' Matt asked.

Kitty knew the man who had guided her on board since he was usually working the ferry. She wound down her window as he approached her car for her fare.

'Good morning. Do you have a Fred Smith working on board today?' she asked as she stretched out a gloved hand to drop the coins in his palm.

The man eyed her with some surprise. 'Aye. Is there summat up?'

'No, just a few things we wanted to ask him. It's on behalf of a friend of ours, to do with a property she owns,' Kitty said as she accepted the ticket.

'I'll send him down from the wheelhouse. So long as he isn't in bother?' the man asked.

'No bother, just a couple of questions,' Kitty assured him.

The crossing was short so there wouldn't be time for an in-depth conversation. A few seconds later another man appeared at her window. This man was younger, in his early forties with a pale complexion and a dark bushy beard.

'You were asking after me?' the man asked as he gave her and Matt a swift, assessing glance.

Bertie gave a small grumble of disapproval from the back seat and the man moved back uneasily.

'Yes. Our friends have recently purchased Midwinter Farm, and we understand you knew the man who disappeared from there some years ago? A Thomas Crabtree?' Kitty said.

A wary expression entered the man's eyes. 'That were a long time ago, missus. What of it?'

'A relative of yours is our housekeeper. Mrs Margaret Smith. She said you knew him,' Matt added.

The ferry had passed the midpoint of the river and Dartmouth was drawing closer.

'He weren't a friend. Just someone as I knew. I don't know anything about what happened to him. One day he was there and then he weren't.' The man shrugged his shoulders and went as if to move away.

'You were walking out with a young lady at the time. Tilly Maldon, the daughter of the landlord of the Steam Packet public house in Kingswear. Do you know where she is now? Or her father?' Kitty asked.

'No idea, miss, I'm afraid.' The ferryman's expression hardened, and he moved off ready for the boat to dock and unload.

'He's lying,' Kitty muttered.

'Definitely,' Matt agreed.

Much to her annoyance there was no chance to ask anything else as the chain at the front of the boat was unhitched as the gate dropped onto the ramp. Kitty was forced to drive off into the town with a hundred more questions still on the tip of her tongue.

'What now?' she asked as she drove through the narrow streets.

'You know who probably will know something?' Matt looked at her.

Kitty's heart sank and she groaned as she took the turn leading out of the town towards the naval college. 'Mrs Craven.'

Her grandmother's very annoying friend was the former mayoress of Dartmouth. She knew everything about everybody and was on the committees for virtually every charity going. If anyone knew where Mr Maldon and his daughter might be, then Mrs Craven was probably the person to ask.

Unfortunately, she and Kitty were not exactly the best of friends. She always tried to recruit Kitty into running errands or serving on some committee or other whenever their paths crossed. Mrs Craven had very strong opinions on what was suitable behaviour for a young married woman in Kitty's position. These opinions were usually the opposite of Kitty's. She also fancied herself as a detective.

Kitty sighed and pointed the nose of her car towards the elegant street of smart houses where Mrs Craven resided.

'Remember we are not supposed to be letting on that we found a body at Alice's house,' she reminded Matt as she stopped the car.

'I know,' Matt said with a grin.

He hopped out and got Bertie from the back seat. Kitty followed at a slower pace. Mrs Craven's house was as smart as ever. The bay window gleaming and immaculate with a few Christmas cards just visible through the glass. A holly wreath tied with a large bow of red satin ribbon hung from the shiny brass lion's head door knocker.

Matt pressed the bell and waited for Dora, Mrs Craven's maid, to answer the door. The case they had solved in the summer had involved finding Dora's missing sister Agnes. The case had ended tragically but Dora had borne her sister's loss stoically.

The maid opened the door and smiled when she saw them on the step.

'Captain Bryant, Mrs Bryant, oh and Bertie. Mrs Craven is in the drawing room decorating the tree. Shall I see if she is free to see you?' Dora asked.

'If she could spare us a few minutes we would be very grateful,' Matt said.

Dora bobbed away to let her employer know that she had visitors. She returned quickly.

'Come right through and I'll take your coats.' She took their things, and they went into the drawing room. Kitty kept Bertie on his lead. If Mrs Craven was decorating her tree she didn't want her naughty dog stealing any of the glass baubles.

A seven-foot-tall pine Christmas tree stood in the far corner of the room almost reaching the ceiling. A small wooden step stool stood nearby next to several large cardboard boxes filled with tissue paper. Mrs Craven, resplendent in a lavender knitted twinset and a heather coloured tartan skirt, was admiring her handiwork.

'Good morning, Matthew, Kitty. Do you think I have sufficient tinsel?' she asked, her head on one side as she surveyed the tree.

Kitty blinked. The green of the tree was scarcely visible beneath the layers of fancy baubles, small ornaments and strands of silver and red metal tinsel strips.

'It looks very festive,' Matt said.

The usually tasteful room looked as if Christmas had exploded all over it. There were strings of cards everywhere. Red-berried holly arrangements in crystal glass vases and even a mistletoe ball hanging in an opportune spot near the door leading to the dining room.

'Wonderful. Matthew, you are nice and tall. Perhaps you could assist me and place the angel on the top of the tree? The ladies' Bible study group are coming for afternoon tea later and I am keen that all should be perfect for the occasion.' Mrs Craven handed him a golden-haired doll in a cream gauze dress.

Matt dutifully stood on the step stool and popped the angel on top of the tree where she gazed down at them with a suitably superior expression.

'How's that?' Matt asked.

'Perfect, thank you.' Mrs Craven beamed at him as he got down from the stool.

Dora immediately began to collect up the empty boxes. 'I'll get these away,' she said, looking at her employer.

'Thank you, Dora. Then I think a cup of tea?' She looked at Kitty and Matt.

'That's very kind, thank you. We're sorry to have arrived unannounced,' Matt said as their hostess led them across to the large comfortably upholstered sofa.

Bertie trotted obediently at Kitty's heels and sat nicely at her feet when she was seated next to Matt.

'Now then.' Mrs Craven took her place in one of the tapestry-covered fireside chairs. 'I assume you have come for my assistance with one of your cases?' She looked expectantly at them. The diamond brooch on her lapel glittered in the light from the fire.

Kitty's heart sank. This was what she had been afraid of. Mrs Craven loved to offer her advice on a case. She was always completely convinced that she would make a wonderful investigator.

'It's more just some background information to help Alice and Robert,' Kitty said.

'Oh, about the wedding?' Mrs Craven looked slightly surprised. 'Well, of course. I do have a great deal of expertise on social occasions.'

'Robert purchased Midwinter Farm at Hillhead, not far from Coleton Fishacre, a while ago at auction. He's been making quite a few improvements to the place since. You may remember the farm from when a farmer, Thomas Crabtree, vanished from there some ten years ago? It was a big story in the newspapers at the time?' Matt said.

Mrs Craven frowned. 'Hmm, let me think.'

Dora pushed a small gilt tea trolley into the room as Matt

spoke. Bertie lifted his head to sniff the air hopefully as the trolley approached in case it contained biscuits.

'Dora, do you recall someone going missing from Midwinter Farm across the river a few years ago?' Mrs Craven asked.

'Yes, miss. It were just after those robberies when them jewels were stolen from Lord and Lady Massey. You had more bolts fit to the back door and some catches changed on the windows to be on the safe side,' Dora said.

'I do believe you're right. I was very concerned as I obviously have some very valuable items and being a person of some standing, I would have been a target,' Mrs Craven said as she accepted a cup of tea from her maid.

'Do you remember anything about the missing farmer?' Kitty asked, ignoring Bertie's begging eyes as she took a slice of shortbread from the plate. Before Mrs Craven could speak, Dora answered.

'I know he weren't well thought of in Kingswear. Thomas Crabtree was said to have owed money to a few people at the time, and he'd been barred from the local public house for brawling.' Dora gave a disapproving sniff as she placed the teapot back down on the trolley.

'The landlord, Arthur Maldon, and his daughter, Tilly, have moved from Kingswear since then. Do you know if they stayed locally?' Matt asked, looking at the maid.

'They were at the Dolphin public house near the market in town, but I don't know if they'm still there. Tis a low place, not like your hotel for all it shares a name,' Dora said. 'The girl, Tilly, she was a brazen sort and caused a bit of bother herself.'

It seemed that Dora was a better source of information on this occasion than Mrs Craven. Their hostess was looking decidedly nettled by her maid's usefulness.

'Thank you, Dora,' Matt said.

'You'm welcome.' Dora whisked away.

'It seems my maid has quite an extensive knowledge of some

of the low-life of the town,' Mrs Craven remarked. 'Why is any of this of any interest to Alice Miller and her fiancé?'

Kitty glanced at Matt. 'Alice is quite superstitious, and she simply wanted to be assured there was no ill luck attached to their new house before the wedding.'

'Oh, what poppycock. She should be counting her blessings to have a home of her own at such a young age. I expect that farmer simply did a moonlight flit to avoid his debtors. It's hardly uncommon,' Mrs Craven said.

It seemed that news of the discovery of Thomas Crabtree's body had not yet reached their hostesses's ears. Kitty had a feeling, however, that Chief Inspector Greville wouldn't be able to keep the news quiet for much longer.

'We were just hoping to ease Alice's jitters,' Matt said as he took a mince pie from the holly-patterned china plate.

'Bridal nerves, I expect. I vaguely remember the farmer going missing now Dora has jogged my memory. He was quite a bad lot, I believe. The newspapers ran quite a few stories. Mainly I suspect because the animals had been left behind and the farm, of course, was part of Lord Massey's estate. With the last robbery being at Lord and Lady Massey's house I suppose it must have ignited the journalists' interest.' Mrs Craven sipped her tea with a contemplative air. 'Poor Hermione Massey was devastated over the loss of her tiara. It had been her great-grandmother's. Her daughter was to be married the following spring and obviously she would have worn the family jewels.'

Kitty could see Matt hiding a smile behind his cup. It was typical of Mrs Craven that she would know Lady Massey rather than a farmer or a publican and his daughter. Matt finished his tea and set his crockery down on the trolley.

'Thank you so much for the tea. I'm afraid we should really get going. It was good of you to see us. We must be hindering your preparations for this afternoon,' he said.

Kitty had finished her tea already and given Bertie half of a shortbread biscuit. 'Yes, you must have a lot to do. Thank you for the information. We'll be sure to pass everything on to Alice and Robert.'

'I'm always happy to help you, Kitty, dear. Now, before you run away, I could use a little bit of assistance myself. It won't take much of your time, but we are short of helpers to serve tea after the service at St Saviour's Church on Sunday morning at the hall. Can I count on you?' Mrs Craven fixed her gaze on Kitty who was half out of her seat.

'Well, I...' She started to try and think of an excuse but gave in with a sigh. 'I suppose I could help out just this once.'

'Splendid. I'll let the vicar and Mrs Hartlebury know to expect you. Don't worry, you don't need to bake anything. Dora is providing the mince pies and slices of fruit cake. I know how you struggle with baking.' Mrs Craven gave her a patronising smile and Kitty bit the end of her tongue to keep from retorting.

Once they had put on their coats and were back in the car, Kitty exploded. 'Grr, that wretched woman is so rude.'

Matt chortled as he fastened Bertie back on the rear seat of the car. 'In fairness, darling, cooking is not one of your skills.'

Kitty glared at him as he went to take his place in the passenger seat. 'I suggest you refrain from commenting further unless you wish to walk home to Churston.'

CHAPTER SEVEN

Since it was now almost lunchtime, they decided to drive home. Matt could see that Kitty was not in a happy frame of mind. He felt discretion was the better part of valour and dropped any discussion of the information they had discovered at Mrs Craven's house. He knew Kitty well enough to know she would soon recover her usual good humour.

There had also been no sign of Fred Smith on the ferry back across the Dart. Either he had gone off for a break, or more likely, was avoiding them. This had clearly added to Kitty's annoyance since he knew she had more questions she had wanted to put to the elusive Fred.

The ferry had been busy on the return and neither he nor Kitty had been able to ask the crew where Fred Smith had gone. Matt wondered how Chief Inspector Greville's enquiries were going. He suspected that no matter how discreet, tongues would start to wag.

Kitty was quiet as they arrived back at the house. He retrieved Bertie from his perch on the back seat, and they headed inside. A fresh stack of post had been placed on the hall table, and it looked as if more Christmas cards were amongst them.

Bertie trotted through to the kitchen to claim his lunch from their housekeeper while Kitty sifted through the mail.

'An invitation to dine with the Carters this Saturday,' she said, waving a card in the air and four more Christmas cards. 'Oh, and an early wedding anniversary card from Grams. She must have posted it before she left for Scotland.'

'Hopefully, she'll have a smooth journey to your great-aunt's house. I heard the weather on the radio last night and it seems the snow is not yet too deep in the Highlands,' Matt said.

'Unlike when we were last there.' Kitty gave a wry smile and disappeared into the kitchen to organise their lunch.

Matt took the cards into the sitting room to add them to the others. It looked as if he would have to add another string to hang them on as they now had so many. Still, it made the room look festive and cheery in contrast to the dreary winter weather outside.

Kitty had gone from the kitchen to the dining room, so he went to join her as she set their lunch on the table. Their house-keeper had prepared baked potatoes with cheese and bacon. Kitty shook out one of the white linen napkins onto her lap before adding a large knob of creamy-yellow butter to the top of her potato. He smiled as she sniffed appreciatively as the spread melted in golden streams down the crispy skin of her potato.

'I think I shall pop into Paignton later to see Alice at her shop. I want to make sure she is all right after yesterday,' Kitty said as she picked up her cutlery ready to eat.

'Then I think I may go back across the river and call at the Dolphin public house. I can at least see if Arthur Maldon or his daughter are still in Dartmouth,' Matt said as he added a sprinkle of salt to his lunch.

From what Dora had told them the pub had not sounded as if it had a very salubrious reputation so it wasn't somewhere that

Kitty could call without causing something of a stir. She was well known in Dartmouth and held in high regard.

'Yes, it would be good to try and discover where they might be. I expect the chief inspector will also be trying to find them,' Kitty said. 'I hope we get to read the notes from the case at some point. It would be really useful.'

Matt hoped that would be possible. It would be very helpful to see what they had discovered at the time Crabtree had vanished. He wouldn't mind reading the notes from the investigation into the robberies either. It seemed to him that there must be some connection between the cases.

From what the chief inspector had said, the police had also thought that might be true. Certainly, none of Thomas Crabtree's associates seemed to be pillars of society. Had Crabtree been involved with the robberies? If so, what had happened to the jewels? Nothing seemed to have come onto the market in the last ten years that could be attached to the thefts. At least Chief Inspector Greville hadn't mentioned anything.

After lunch was finished, Kitty set off to call on Alice while Matt donned his long leather motorcycle coat and headed back across the Dart. There was still no sign of Fred Smith on the ferry and when he bought his ticket he asked if he was still on board.

'He got called in by the police. An Inspector Lewis come to the dockside with Constable Biggs. Took him off to Torquay. I told him not to bother coming back. I only had him on as a favour to one of his relatives,' the ferryman said as he took the coins from Matt's hand and dispensed the pass. 'I reckon as he'll be more trouble than he's worth.'

Matt privately thought the ferryman was right. Still, it was interesting to discover that the police were already moving to talk to Fred Smith. Once the ferry had docked, he drove his Sunbeam off the boat and through the narrow streets of the town, past the Dolphin Hotel and towards the back streets near the market to the pub which shared its name.

Unlike the venerable black and white timbered ancient hotel, the Dolphin public house was a much smaller affair. Built of red brick with etched windows and shiny, glazed ceramic tiles decorating its exterior it overlooked the busy street. Its usual clientele were the local fishermen, and it had once served workers from the china clay works at Warfleet.

The name above the door was not that of Arthur Maldon so it seemed he was not the current landlord. The pub was due to shut so Matt knew he didn't have much time to try and get some information before it closed for the afternoon.

He parked his motorcycle outside and stepped into the pub. Inside it was quiet with just a couple of older men sitting at the bar talking to the landlord. The interior of the place was dingy, the formerly once white walls now a dark-yellowish brown stained by nicotine. The air smelt of stale beer which had been spilled over the years and had soaked into the broad wooden planks of the bar-room floor.

The conversation at the bar stopped as Matt approached and drew off his leather gauntlets.

'Afternoon.' He nodded to the barman and the two men. 'Pint of bitter, please.'

The landlord nodded an acknowledgement and took down a dimpled pint glass from the shelf behind the bar, placing it under the tap.

'Cold one out there today,' Matt remarked affably as the landlord pulled on the large ceramic beer pull to fill the glass.

'So they say.' The landlord placed the full glass on the top of the scarred and battered wooden bar.

Matt dug in his pocket for his wallet and paid for his drink. The landlord accepted the coins and handed back the change.

'It was busy over in Kingswear when I crossed the river.

Lots of police around asking questions,' Matt said, before taking a careful sip from his glass.

He had sensed that he would get no answers from any of the men in the pub if he asked direct questions so decided to try getting them to ask him questions instead. Then he might be able to obtain the information he was seeking.

'Oh, what was they about then?' one of the men asked. He was nursing the dregs of his pint. His nose was flushed red and his jacket and cap were worn and dirty.

'I don't know. Something about a farmer who went missing years ago. Somebody called Crabtree.' Matt kept his tone casual.

He noticed all three men stiffen and they exchanged glances between themselves.

'That must have been ten or twelve years back now,' the landlord observed as he leaned on the counter.

'What they hoping to discover now, after all this time?' the other man asked. He looked slightly younger than the other two, with a thin tanned face even in winter which spoke of a life spent outside.

'I don't know but I heard the police had taken one of the ferrymen in for questioning.' Matt felt rather than saw the unease increase in his audience.

'That might be young Fred.' The landlord looked at his customers as if for confirmation.

'I suppose he must have known Thomas Crabtree,' Matt remarked and took another sip from his drink.

'Probably,' the landlord agreed.

'If he did, then I suppose the police will be talking to anyone who knew the missing man from back then,' Matt continued.

'Did you hear what they was asking about? Has summat turned up, you reckon?' The man in the cap looked at Matt.

'I only caught bits of the conversation. I think they might be looking for somebody called Arthur Maldon. He used to have a pub apparently,' Matt said.

'I knows Arthur. He used to have a pub across the river, and he were landlord here for a short while.' The landlord straightened up and reached for his cloth to clean the bar ready to shut for the afternoon.

'Is he still in Dartmouth? Only he might want to know the police are asking after him, oh, and his daughter?' Matt frowned.

'Tilly?' The other customer glanced at his drinking companion.

'Yes, that was the name.' Matt had almost finished his drink now.

'Arthur went to Paignton, didn't he?' The man in the cap looked at the landlord.

'I think so. Tilly went off with a chap from Totnes. I don't know if hers still there, mind. Never one to settle for long was Tilly.' The landlord gave a wheezy laugh.

'Not unless they had a bit of brass in their pockets.' The younger man joined in with the laughter.

'Good luck to the police finding her and her father,' the landlord said.

Kitty decided to do a little Christmas shopping before calling in to see Alice. She didn't want to disrupt her friend during the busy time at the shop, especially if Betty and Rose were there trying to listen in to the conversation. She wasn't sure if Alice would want Betty to know what had happened at the farm.

The shopfronts along Winner Street were all trimmed up for Christmas with enticing offers and tinsel. Kitty had bought quite a few gifts already, but she still had a few last things to get. After posting their acceptance to Mrs Carter's dinner invitation she bought a bottle of eau de cologne and some initialled hand-kerchiefs for Mrs Smith. Then she called at the tobacconists for a gift for Mickey, the handyman at the Dolphin Hotel. He often took care of Bertie for her when she and Matt were away.

After a pleasant hour dawdling around the shops picking up various knick-knacks and small treats for friends, she made her way back to Alice's shop. The weather had closed in again while she had been out and a few snow flurries fell as she hurried along the street.

The shop bell on its coiled brass spring jingled above her head as she pushed open the door and stepped into the welcoming well-lit warmth of Alice's shop. Thankfully it seemed quiet with Betty wrapping a customer's purchases care-fully in brown paper at the till and young Rose folding and restocking baby vests in one of the cabinets.

Alice was counting some of her stock at the haberdashery display but looked up when the bell announced Kitty's arrival.

'Good heavens, you're loaded up with shopping. Did you buy up half of Paignton?' Alice asked with a smile as Kitty wiped her feet on the entrance mat.

'Just a few last-minute gifts,' Kitty said as she greeted Rose and nodded to Betty who was still serving her customer. 'I thought I'd drop in and see how you were after yesterday,' she added in a lower tone to Alice.

'The curtains were definitely a two-person job yesterday,' Alice replied in a louder voice as she shot a meaningful look at Kitty. 'I should have the others finished soon.'

Kitty gathered that Alice hadn't spoken to her cousin or her young assistant about discovering a body at the farm.

'Yes, it was a good thing Matt was there to help us,' Kitty agreed.

Betty finished serving her customer. The woman wished them all a merry Christmas and stepped out of the shop.

'Pop and put the kettle on, Betty, please, it's been so busy this afternoon we could all do with a cuppa,' Alice said.

Her cousin disappeared into the rear of the shop where Alice had a small workroom and a fitting cubicle. She also had a tea-making station there so she and her staff could make a drink when the shop was quiet.

Alice took hold of Kitty's elbow and steered her away from where Rose was working. 'I haven't said anything to Betty or Rose,' she murmured.

'Of course. The chief inspector asked us to keep quiet,' Kitty responded in a similar low voice. She set her shopping down behind the shop counter.

'It's not just that.' Alice stopped when Betty reappeared.

'The kettle's on and the tray's all ready,' Betty announced.

Kitty noticed that Betty had taken a minute to refresh her lipstick and fluff up her hair while she had been in the kitchen area.

'Is your boyfriend coming to meet you?' Alice asked.

Clearly, she too had noticed her cousin's primping.

'Well, you did say as I could finish a bit early. I haven't seen James for a few days he's been so busy, and he promised me we would go out to the pictures tonight,' Betty responded with a bright smile as she adjusted her navy skirt and cream silk blouse to hang properly.

'Of course. It's gone quiet here now so Rose and I can finish up,' Alice agreed.

The kettle in the back began to whistle and Alice sent Rose to make the tea.

'Oh, this is James now.' Betty rushed to collect her winter coat and hat from the pegs just off the shop floor as a black car pulled up outside the shop.

Alice placed a warning hand on Kitty's arm.

'See you tomorrow, Betty, have a lovely evening,' Alice said as her cousin pulled on her black leather gloves and headed out of the shop and into the waiting car.

Kitty frowned at her friend in bewilderment. 'What?'

'Go to the window but take care,' Alice said, the corners of her mouth twitching impishly.

Kitty obeyed, peeking out from behind a display of ladies' gloves and purses.

'Betty's James is Inspector Lewis!' She looked at Alice.

'I know. You could have knocked me down with a feather. I only found out this morning. She's been hinting for weeks about her new bloke, but you know what our Betty's like. Normally they don't last that long, and she's bored with them. She's been proper cagey though about him, not letting on where she met him or what he did for a living. No wonder at it.' Alice shook her head.

Rose returned carefully carrying a small round tea tray with the tea already poured into three china mugs.

'Well, that's a turn up for the books and no mistake,' Kitty said. She didn't normally take sugar in her tea, but she decided a small spoonful now might be good for shock.

CHAPTER EIGHT

'I couldn't believe it this morning when she let slip who she was seeing. I mean she's been talking about him for weeks, you know hinting things and I never twigged,' Alice said.

'Betty's boyfriend?' Rose asked. 'She'd said as he had an important job, and he was working in Exeter.'

'We both know Inspector Lewis quite well. He was seconded to the station there for quite a while but has now returned to Torquay,' Kitty explained.

'Betty says as he's got good prospects,' Rose said before taking a large draught of her tea.

Alice's gaze met Kitty's and they both made non-committal noises.

Once the shop sign had been turned to closed and Rose had been dismissed for the day, Kitty felt she was able to finally discuss everything openly with her friend.

'Betty and Inspector Lewis? I would never have put those two together. It's going to make things a little awkward, isn't it?' Kitty followed Alice into the tiny kitchen area to assist her with washing up the tea things.

'I had wondered why she always looked so smug whenever she mentioned him. She'd said his name was James but, of course, I didn't know the inspector's Christian name. She's been taking an interest in the newspapers more too. You know, reading up on court cases and suchlike.' Alice clattered the cups into the small stone sink and poured in some warm water from the kettle.

'I wonder if he'll tell her about the case he's working on now?' Kitty dried the mug Alice handed her on one of the Irish linen tea towels that her friend kept in the shop.

'You mean what happened yesterday? I haven't said a word to anybody about it. Mother will be proper upset when she hears of it. I were hoping that when the chief inspector said to keep it quiet he would make a quick arrest,' Alice said.

'He still might. When Matt and I were in Dartmouth this morning there were police about in Kingswear. I'm sure they will be asking questions. Matt is trying to find out more information this afternoon.' Kitty dried the last cup and hung the tea towel on the hook under the sink to dry.

'Robert said as he were going to see you both to ask if you'd see what you could find out,' Alice said as she walked back through the shop to double-check the lock on the front door and to change the lighting, so it just showed the fancy goods she had on display in the window.

'He did. He called in on his way home. We're trying to track down the publican, Arthur Maldon, and his daughter, Tilly. The ones the chief inspector mentioned, to find out what they can remember about the case.' Kitty waited for Alice to unlock the small door that led upstairs to her flat above the premises.

'I expect the police will be looking for them too,' Alice said as she switched on the light so Kitty could go up ahead of her.

'Yes, but you'll never guess. Fred Smith, the man that Chief Inspector Greville said had been seeing Tilly Maldon, he's related to my Mrs Smith,' Kitty said as her friend joined her on the landing, and they went into Alice's cosy sitting room.

'Your housekeeper?' Alice frowned as she switched on the electric fire in her tiled hearth and Kitty put on the peach silk-shaded Chinese-style lamp.

'The very same.' Kitty perched on the shabby chintz sofa while Alice swapped her shoes for her slippers with a sigh of relief.

'But Mrs Smith is very respectable and that Fred Smith didn't sound as if he was someone who she would know.' A crease formed on Alice's forehead as she sank down on the chair beside the fire.

'She said he was a distant relative, I assume of her husband's family. I suppose most families have a black sheep,' Kitty grimaced. In her own family it was her father, Edgar Underhay. He was no stranger to the police and the inside of a prison cell.

'Did she tell you where he was?' Alice asked.

'We found him this morning on the ferry crossing the river, but he really didn't say much at all. Then he had gone when we crossed back over.' Kitty's frown deepened. 'It was most annoying. I had several more things I wanted to ask.'

'I appreciate you trying,' Alice said.

'I even called on Mrs Craven to see if she might know something,' Kitty admitted.

Alice burst out laughing. 'Oh dear, Kitty. That is true friendship.'

Kitty was forced to smile herself. 'That's how much I love you,' she responded, grinning.

'Did she know anything? I take it you didn't tell her why you were asking about the case?' Alice asked.

Kitty shook her head. 'Definitely not, you know she can't keep a secret. Funnily enough it was Dora, her maid, who knew most about it all. Mrs Craven was more interested in telling us about the jewel robbery the chief inspector mentioned. She is a friend of the Massey family, of course.'

Alice shivered. 'I don't know, Kitty. This whole business with the farm seems to have been fated since the beginning. First Robert and I almost broke up for good over it, thanks to him just buying it and not telling me. Then he's sunk so much work and every penny he has into the blessed place. And now, all of this. I mean an actual murder. How can I marry him and live in a house where there's been a murder?'

'Lots of houses have histories, Alice. The house is lovely, and you and Robert will make it a real home again. This business with Mr Crabtree was ten years ago, and it seemed from what Doctor Carter said that nothing bad happened in the house itself,' Kitty said.

She could see from the expression on her friend's face that she was not persuaded by Kitty's argument.

'I know all of that, but I still feel, well, I don't rightly know how I feel. I'd just started to come round to it and Robert has had that lovely bathroom done. The curtains and the covers were really making it look nice and then the engineer found poor Mr Crabtree. Or what was left of him.' Alice's lower lip trembled.

'Maybe we should talk to Lord Massey's agent about the history of the house. Who lived there before Mr Crabtree and the tenants who were there afterwards? Perhaps if you knew a family had lived there and been happy you might feel better about it all,' Kitty suggested as she firmly crossed her fingers out of Alice's sight. Surely, there must be some nice history to the house to make her friend feel better. 'I can find out who the agent was and telephone them. See if they can tell us something.'

Alice still looked slightly sceptical, but nodded her agreement. 'Very well, it won't do no harm, and it would make me feel happier knowing as it hasn't always had bad luck attached to it.'

Kitty beamed at her as she glanced around her friend's cosy room. There were Christmas cards hung from strings off the picture rail and a small pine tree in a pot on the tiny dining table. 'Just think, next Christmas you and Robert will be wed, and Midwinter Farm could be as lovely, if not lovelier, than this place. You can have your family to visit and have a wonderful Christmas dinner cooked in your nice big kitchen.'

Alice sighed and gave her a wan smile. 'Thank you, Kitty. I know you think I'm being foolish about all of this.'

'Not at all. Finding a murder victim on your property is enough to upset anyone. My poor aunt and uncle had two people murdered at Enderley Hall and then Lucy and Rupert's best man was murdered at their wedding. At least you're in good company.' She smiled kindly at Alice, hoping her poor attempt at a joke might lighten the mood.

'That's true. I had forgotten that. Yes, you're right. Your cousin's marriage had a dark start, but they are so happy now and the baby is a little smasher.' Alice looked more cheerful at this reminder and Kitty breathed a small sigh of relief.

Kitty glanced at her watch. 'I suppose I should get off home. Matt always worries if I am out in the dark at this time of year in case there is ice on the road. I'll telephone the agent tomorrow and see what I can discover. If Matt has learned anything useful this afternoon I'm sure he will tell Robert or call you.'

'Thank you, Kitty. I just hope our Betty doesn't tell Mother about Mr Crabtree being buried in the piggery afore I have chance to tell her myself or I shall never hear the end of it,' Alice said as Kitty rose and went to collect her hat and coat from the landing.

'It's very odd with Betty walking out with Inspector Lewis. Still, who knows it may be useful. She might learn some titbits about the case which could help us.'

Alice snorted. 'Oh, she'll make a right meal of it when it does become public knowledge. She'll be gloating and hinting at all sorts of things.'

Kitty smiled. 'Chin up, we'll get to the bottom of it I'm sure and then you can have a lovely wedding without any worries.'

Alice let her out through the shop after Kitty had collected her parcels. Kitty waved goodbye to Alice's forlorn figure on the shop doorstep and set off back to Churston. The weather had closed in once more while she had been with Alice and Kitty was forced to drive slowly along the coast road with the wind tugging at her car.

Sleet spattered against the windshield and wisps of low cloud blew across in front of her from the sea, obscuring her vision. She was relieved when she finally made it to the common and turned off onto her drive.

Matt's Sunbeam was parked up with a cover over it so she guessed he must have returned before the weather had worsened. Kitty gathered up her parcels and hurried inside her house, calling out to Matt as she let herself in through the front door.

Bertie immediately came to greet her, wagging his plumed tail joyfully as she deposited her packages beside the hall table while she hung up her hat and coat. She petted her dog and went to find her husband, keen to tell him about what had happened at Alice's shop.

'Hello, darling.' Matt looked up from where he was seated in his usual place beside the sitting room fire. 'I was starting to worry. I could hear the wind blowing about the chimney pots.'

Kitty gave him an affectionate kiss on the top of his head. 'It is turning quite nasty again. I'm glad to be home and I've so much to tell you.' She could see he had a notebook and had been busy writing.

'I've had quite a productive afternoon myself. I was just

jotting some of it down for Chief Inspector Greville. He said he would call in after dinner.'

Kitty perched herself on the edge of the other armchair much to Rascal's disgust since he liked to lie on the seat when Kitty was out. 'Oh, has he made any progress in the case, do you know?'

'He didn't say but I know Inspector Lewis hauled Fred Smith off to Torquay Police Station for questioning at lunchtime.' Matt's eyes twinkled in the firelight as she leaned forward in her excitement to learn more.

'Really? That is interesting. Did you find anything out about Arthur Maldon and his daughter?' Kitty asked.

'It seems that Mr Maldon may be in Paignton and his daughter apparently went to live in Totnes. She has possibly married,' Matt said.

'I suppose she could well be married after so many years. Did you discover anything else?' Kitty had hoped they might have found an address, but she knew it wouldn't be easy. The dead man had not seemed to keep the kind of company that would want to part easily with information.

'There was an odd atmosphere at the pub. I think the men there knew far more than they let on. I had to be careful about how I obtained the information.' Matt looked thoughtful. 'How about you? How was Alice?'

'Alice is all right. She's still dreadfully upset about the whole thing obviously and it's definitely colouring how she feels about the house. I did learn something very interesting, however, and you'll never guess what it is.' She smiled playfully at her husband.

'Go on, I can see you are dying to tell me.' Matt smiled back at her as he spoke.

'The man Betty is walking out with is none other than Inspector Lewis!'

Kitty had the satisfaction of seeing her husband temporarily lost for words.

'Did Alice know?' Matt asked once he'd recovered the power of speech.

Kitty shook her head. 'She had no idea. She said Betty had been cagey about it all, but she always referred to him as James. I had no clue that was the inspector's Christian name, did you?'

'No. Well, that is a surprise. Had Alice said anything to Betty about what happened yesterday?'

'No. The shop has been busy all day, and Alice said she didn't want word to reach her mother before she had the opportunity to tell her herself. You know Betty would have told her.' Kitty looked at Matt.

Betty loved a bit of gossip and Mrs Miller, Alice's mother, would not be happy if she thought her niece and her sister knew something about Alice and Robert's house which she didn't know about first.

Kitty told Matt about her promise to Alice to contact Lord Massey's former land agent to try and learn more about the farm's history.

'That's a good idea. He may also have more information about Thomas Crabtree too,' Matt agreed as Kitty rose to go to the kitchen to start supper.

'Perhaps Chief Inspector Greville can tell me his name and where I can find him when he calls later.' Kitty frowned at Bertie who had sensed that food was in the offing and was already at her heels.

'Good thinking. I wonder what he'll have to tell us,' Matt agreed.

They were just finishing washing up the dishes after a delicious supper of beef casserole in red wine when there was a knock at the front door.

'That will be the chief inspector.' Kitty dried her hands on a tea towel and fluffed up her blonde curls while Matt went to let their visitor into the hall.

'I'm sorry to call so late. It's been a busy day,' the chief inspector said as Matt showed him into the sitting room, after taking the policeman's outdoor things and hanging them on the hall stand.

'Not at all, can I offer you a drink? It's a horrid evening out there.' Matt went to the small drinks trolley while Kitty seated herself on an armchair. The chief inspector took a seat on the sofa and Rascal eyed him warily from under Matt's chair.

The chief inspector accepted a small crystal tumbler of whisky and Bertie settled happily at Kitty's feet. 'Thank you, this is most welcome.' He raised his glass slightly in Matt's direction.

Kitty could see the chief inspector looked tired. Even his moustache seemed a little depressed as he took a sip of his drink. Matt fixed a whisky for himself and a lime soda for Kitty before taking his own seat.

'We heard that Inspector Lewis had taken Fred Smith to Torquay for questioning. We discovered yesterday that he is related to our housekeeper. Not that she gives him a good name. She said he was only recently out of prison,' Matt said as he settled back in his chair.

'That's right. He mainly seems to pick up casual work on the river here and there. He's a bit of a hothead. Gets himself in fights and bother, usually after he's had a drink. He also has sticky fingers and got caught with some items that weren't his. That was the reason for his last stint at His Majesty's pleasure,' Chief Inspector Greville said.

'Did he have anything to say about Thomas Crabtree finally being discovered in Alice's piggery?' Kitty asked.

'He shut up like a clam. Claimed he knew nothing about Thomas being dead and stuck to his story that he had no idea what had happened to him.' Chief Inspector Greville stared at his whisky, watching the firelight twinkling on the cut facets of the glass.

'Who was the last person to see Thomas Crabtree alive?' Matt asked.

'From what we learned at the time he disappeared he was last seen two evenings before down in Kingswear. There was a large crowd of witnesses who saw Arthur Maldon throwing him out of the pub and barring him. Our man, Mr Smith, was also there. It was his argument with Crabtree over young Tilly Maldon that led to Crabtree being barred. There had also been a fight involving someone else. A dispute over a card game. According to the witnesses, Crabtree stomped off to his horse and cart to go back to the farm. He was throwing insults at anyone who cared to listen while Smith and Maldon were making threats,' Chief Inspector Greville said.

'You said before that Crabtree owed his son and daughter-in-law money and they were in dire need. When did they last see him?' Kitty asked.

'Two days before. He was at the market in Dartmouth. William, his son, was seriously ill and laid up in bed at the time. Lavinia, his daughter-in-law, had a go at him in the street telling him he should be ashamed of himself for how he had treated them. Witnesses we spoke to said he brushed her off telling her it was not any of her concern, and she should stick to women's business.' The chief inspector's brows rose as he spoke, mirroring Kitty's own astonishment at the dead man's words.

'And no one else saw Crabtree after he left the pub?' Matt asked with a frown. 'You said he was missed a day or so later? The agent for Lord Massey called at the farm?'

'That's correct. Mr Pettifor was Lord Massey's agent and because of the problems with Thomas he decided to check on things. I think Crabtree was also behind with his rent. He arrived at nine in the morning and the door to the farm was standing open. The dogs were on their chains in the yard, whining with empty water bowls. He went into the house when he got no answer. Crabtree's supper was on the table half eaten and there was no sign of the man. The agent gave the dogs water and went to look for Crabtree and to see to the livestock. He couldn't see any trace of him so came away and called us in,' Chief Inspector Greville said.

A shiver ran down Kitty's spine. Whatever had happened at the farm must have occurred while Crabtree had been eating his supper. Someone had lured him outside and killed him.

CHAPTER NINE

A log crackled in the hearth sending a tiny golden shower of sparks up the chimney.

'There is someone else who we needed to question at the time,' the chief inspector said. 'A man called Joshua Payne. Maldon had told us that this Joshua Payne had fought with Crabtree a few days before Maldon finally barred him from the pub. The men had been in the habit of playing cards together and Crabtree had won a sum of money from Payne. However, Payne had accused Crabtree of cheating and had demanded the money back.'

'What did Mr Payne have to say when he was questioned?' Matt asked.

'That's the thing. He disappeared before anyone could ask him much about anything. Maldon said that Payne was a merchant seaman so it could just be that his ship had sailed just after the time it was noticed that Crabtree was missing. No one seemed to know which line he worked for.' The chief inspector took another sip of his drink. 'You must remember that I was a sergeant back then. It wasn't my place to ask too many questions of my superior and it was a missing persons case, not a murder.'

'I suppose too that if Mr Crabtree was killed out in the old piggery, as we now believe, there would be no physical evidence of him having been harmed in the house?' Kitty looked at the chief inspector. She knew that the answer to this would be very important not only to the case but also to Alice's peace of mind.

'There was nothing. His clothes were still in the wardrobe and in the drawers. Food in the pantry, loose change in a saucer on a shelf in the kitchen. A pair of silver cufflinks in a pot on his dressing table. Nothing seemed to have been touched. Not a thing missing from that house that we could see except Crabtree himself. It was as if he had been spirited into thin air. We searched the farm and outbuildings. We did a field walk looking for him all around the boundaries. No sign of hide nor hair of him,' Chief Inspector Greville said. 'The weather was appalling, driving rain and fog. I did suggest we looked with dogs. We had that offer I mentioned from the kennels master at Lupton House, but my superior felt that was unnecessary.'

'Why do you think the inspector was reluctant to bring dogs into the search?' Matt asked. 'Surely they would have been useful?'

'Lack of manpower basically. There had been those high-profile robberies and we were under a lot of pressure to find the missing jewels and hold someone to account for the thefts. It was winter, coming up to Christmas, and the weather was worse than it is now. You know how the mists come down up there because of the cloud,' the chief inspector explained.

'What happened afterwards, when Crabtree didn't reappear? I presume there may have been a thought that he might simply turn up again like a bad penny, I suppose?' Kitty asked.

'Oh yes, there was an appeal in the paper asking if anyone had seen him. We had a photograph of him which his son supplied. It had been taken at his and Lavinia's wedding. There was no response, of course, except the usual mistaken identities and those from people who like to make themselves important.'

Chief Inspector Greville shook his head in mock despair. 'There was a fair bit of speculation about what might have happened to him in the press. One newspaper had a medium saying as she'd seen him lying drowned in one of the coves in her vision. That sent a pack of idiots endangering their necks climbing over rocks disregarding the tides and winter storms. All on a fool's errand.'

'Then I guess it died down.' Matt took a sip of his own drink.

'There was a bit of a sense of good riddance to bad rubbish. Mr Pettifor and Lord Massey were relieved to be shot of a bad tenant. His son and his wife were relieved not to keep bumping into him and they managed to start to get back on their feet. Maldon was able to keep his licence at the pub. There had been mutterings about revoking it due to the bother. This was all over Christmas and New Year. The farm was emptied and then re-let. That carried on until young Robert Potter bought the place at auction.' Chief Inspector Greville swallowed the last of his whisky.

'Has Inspector Lewis gone through the old files now?' Kitty asked. Much as she appreciated the chief inspector's candour and all the information, she still would have liked to read the notes.

'He has. That's why he pulled in Fred Smith for questioning. The chief constable is keen to get this wrapped up as quickly and discreetly as possible. I've been trying to locate Arthur and Tilly Maldon too.' The policeman set his glass down on the small glass-topped chrome coffee table.

Chief Inspector Greville reached inside the breast pocket of his jacket and pulled out a slim manila envelope which he passed to Matt. 'This contains the important parts from the old files. The interview transcripts with the main suspects. The rest of the files are too bulky and, to be honest, they don't have anything useful in them. I need not remind you that these are confidential and I'm taking a huge personal risk in permitting you to see them.'

Kitty nodded as Matt opened the folder and quickly began to study the contents.

'Thank you, sir. We do appreciate this,' Kitty said.

'Your friend Miss Miller and you have been very helpful over the last few years. I appreciate that the discovery of Crabtree's body is enormously distressing, so the sooner the culprit is apprehended the better for everyone,' the chief inspector said as Matt finished his perusal and passed the notes across to Kitty.

She was surprised he had done with them so quickly but as she looked at the contents she could see why. The interviews were brief and scanty in detail. Each of the main suspects, Crabtree's son and daughter-in-law, Maldon and his daughter, and Fred Smith all claimed they had not seen Crabtree the day he was thought to have disappeared.

The workmen at Coleton Fishacre had all left for the day on the day he had vanished, and no one had seen or heard anything on the track that led to the farm. There was no interview with Joshua Payne. Just a note that he might be a potential witness and the actions taken to try and trace him which had proved unsuccessful.

There was also a short interview with Lord Massey's land agent, Mr Pettifor. This too confirmed what the chief inspector had already told them. Kitty closed the file and handed it back to the chief inspector.

'Do you have a recent address or telephone number for Mr Pettifor at all? I promised Alice that I would ask him about the history of the house before Mr Crabtree took over the tenancy. I think she wants to feel that someone lived there before and was happy. Alice is very superstitious and thinks the house is cursed or under a bad omen,' Kitty said.

'I can understand Miss Miller's worries. I contacted Mr Pettifor earlier today to tell him we had finally found his missing tenant.' The chief inspector took out his notebook and wrote an address and telephone number down for her on one of his cards. 'Mrs Greville is much the same way as Miss Miller; she salutes magpies, won't walk under ladders and all that kind of thing.' He passed the card over.

'I have made a note for you of some of the information we have discovered today.' Matt gave the chief inspector the notes he had been making when Kitty had returned home earlier.

'Thank you, this is much appreciated.' Chief Inspector Greville frowned as he read what Matt had written. 'Hmm, so Maldon may be in Paignton and Tilly Maldon was last known to be in Totnes. At least that may give us a starting point to try and find them.'

'There is one other thing, sir.' Kitty glanced at Matt before diving in. 'Well, it's come to our notice that we are not the only ones with a personal connection to this case. Alice has a cousin, Betty, who works for her in her shop. You may recall Betty, she was a maid previously and provided information on a couple of our other cases. It seems that Betty is the lady walking out with Inspector Lewis.'

The last part of her statement came out in something of a rush. She wasn't sure how the chief inspector would receive this piece of news.

The policeman's eyebrows rose. 'Well, I seem to recall Miss Miller's cousin as being a most presentable young lady. It would seem that the rumours of Inspector Lewis whistling cheerily about the police station may be correct. I had thought them to be a mistake or a result of a burst of Christmas cheer. A young lady in this case is a much more plausible explanation.'

His comment caused Kitty to cough, and she hastily took a gulp of her drink. She tried to picture the usually dour and cheerless Inspector Lewis looking cheerful. His usual expressions when she met him were smug, cross or annoyed. Clearly dating Betty must be having a good influence on his disposition at least.

Chief Inspector Greville smiled at Kitty. 'A most interesting piece of news, Mrs Bryant. I fear that word of the discovery of Thomas Crabtree's body is already getting abroad. We obviously went to see his son and daughter-in-law first before interviewing Mr Smith and various other people. I am hoping that we can resolve this case as swiftly as possible. I know you will be working upon it anyway on behalf of Miss Miller and Mr Potter. Please liaise with Inspector Lewis and I shall instruct him to do likewise with you. The more people there are working to close this affair the better.'

'Thank you, sir,' Matt said and offered to refill the chief inspector's glass.

'No, thank you, tempting as it is to remain here in the warmth, I must get home. Mrs Greville will be waiting, and my boys. Plus, if I am late my dinner will be in the dog.' He stood up as he spoke and smiled at Bertie who had raised his head at the mention of the word dog.

Matt showed Chief Inspector Greville out and Kitty shivered as a blast of cold air swept through the hall and under the door into their snug sitting room. She was quite glad that they didn't have any plans to go anywhere that evening. Still, it made her wonder. If it had been a night not dissimilar to this one, what could have lured Thomas Crabtree away from his supper to his demise in the piggery?

* * *

Matt was downstairs the following morning before Kitty when the telephone in the hall rang.

'Matthew, Dora has just informed me that the body of that missing farmer has been discovered at Midwinter Farm. Is this true?' Mrs Craven's incisive voice sounded through the black Bakelite telephone receiver.

'Yes, Mrs Craven, that's correct. He was discovered the other day.' Matt moved the receiver away from his ear a little and braced himself for the rebukes he knew were coming his way.

Kitty had heard the telephone and was halfway down the stairs.

'Mrs Craven,' he mouthed silently at her and the corners of her mouth twitched upwards. He guessed she had thought it may have been her grandmother calling to let her know she was safely arrived in Scotland.

'Well, I am most disappointed, Matthew, that you clearly knew this man had been found and didn't inform me when you called to ask questions about the case. I mean I expect that kind of concealment from Kitty, but I had thought better of you.' Matt looked up to where Kitty was leaning over the banister listening in to the call. Her slender shoulders shook with suppressed laughter.

'I'm dreadfully sorry, Mrs C. Obviously we would have loved to tell you but at the time Mr Crabtree's family hadn't been informed. Plus, Chief Inspector Greville requested that it was all kept under wraps for a while,' Matt said.

'Well, I suppose if the poor man's family hadn't been told. Still, you both know that I am the very soul of discretion. I think you could have trusted me not to say anything. Dora heard it from the coalman,' Mrs Craven retorted indignantly.

Matt was forced to continue trying to mollify Mrs Craven's injured feelings whilst Kitty continued downstairs to prepare their breakfast. By the time he could escape to join her in the dining room Kitty was already demolishing her second slice of toast and marmalade.

'Mrs C said to remind you about church on Sunday and the tea roster,' he said as he slipped into his chair opposite his wife.

'Oh bother, I had rather hoped she might forget or find a new victim to man the teapot,' Kitty said with a frown. 'I'm rather glad you answered the telephone instead of me though.'

'What are our plans for today with the case?' Matt asked as he poured himself a cup of tea.

'I need to telephone this Mr Pettifor to see if he will agree to meet me and Alice to talk about Midwinter Farm's history. I suppose I should try and arrange it for Sunday afternoon when Alice's shop is shut. She is so busy at the moment and this business of Crabtree's murder couldn't have really come at a worse time with Christmas so close,' Kitty said.

'You could invite him here for tea,' Matt suggested. 'Bribe him with Mrs Smith's home-made mince pies and Christmas cake.'

Kitty grinned at him as Bertie gave a short bark of excitement at the mention of cake, even though he wasn't allowed fruit cake. 'Shush, Bertie.' She gave the dog a corner of toast which he crunched down happily.

'What about you?' she asked, looking at Matt.

He had been giving the matter some thought after the chief inspector's visit. 'I have some contacts in Plymouth at the shipping offices. I'd like to try and discover if Joshua Payne is on any of the payrolls so we can track where he went when Crabtree vanished and where he might be now.'

'That sounds like quite a task,' Kitty said.

'I rather fear it may be, but I doubt the police can spare the manpower to do it and it needs to be ruled out if Payne was involved in Crabtree's death or not,' Matt said.

'Shall you take the train or go on your motorcycle?' Kitty asked.

He knew she worried about him riding in the cold and the sleet but really the bike was the most practical way of travelling to Plymouth. It would only take an hour or so depending on traffic and weather.

'I'll take the Sunbeam. It doesn't seem too bad out. No ice, just cold and rather dreary.' He gave her a reassuring smile.

'So long as you take care,' Kitty warned.

'I will. Scout's honour.' He held up his hand in a mock promissory fashion.

He wasn't sure how well his quest to track Joshua Payne would go but it had to be worth a try. He was the one person who had quarrelled with the dead man that no one had taken any kind of statement from. Rather like the victim, Payne too had disappeared.

* * *

After seeing Matt off, Kitty wrapped up warmly and took Bertie for a brisk walk over the nearby common in an attempt to clear her mind before telephoning Mr Pettifor. The air was cold and moist against her cheeks and her boots squelched across the sodden grass. Bertie romped along sniffing happily after rabbits, often disappearing momentarily from her sight in the patches of mist that were still hanging around.

By the time she had prevented Bertie from rolling in fox poo and had marched him somewhat reluctantly home, she was in need of a fortifying cup of tea. The telephone was ringing again as she put her key in the lock, and she dashed forward somewhat breathlessly to answer it.

'Hello?'

'Kitty, thank goodness. When I called earlier, Mrs Smith said Matt had gone to Plymouth and you were walking Bertie. I need to ask you the most enormous favour.' Alice sounded fraught as she spoke.

'Of course, what do you need?' Kitty hoped something else hadn't gone wrong with the house or with the police investigation.

'I'm so busy here I can't get away and Robert is in Tavistock with one of his tours. Could you possibly collect the key to the house and go up there to wait for the engineer? He's promised to come at two o'clock. I couldn't say no as it may be our only chance to get the telephone sorted before Christmas. The police have given their permission,' Alice said.

Kitty could hear customers' voices and the ding of the shop bell in the background.

'I'll come round shortly and collect the key. I'm just about to contact the land agent. I'll try and get him to come here for tea on Sunday. Would that work for you?' Kitty asked.

'Oh, bless you. Thank you, that'd be marvellous. I must go. See you shortly.' Alice rang off in a hurry.

CHAPTER TEN

Bertie's coat was damp from the mist, so Kitty dried him off with an old towel. Then she made herself a cup of tea before telephoning the number the chief inspector had provided.

'Good morning, is that Mr Pettifor? You don't know me, my name is Kitty Bryant and I was provided with your number by Chief Inspector Greville. I understand you were Lord Massey's land agent and looked after Midwinter Farm as part of the Massey estate?' The voice that had answered her call sounded elderly.

'That's correct, Mrs Bryant. How may I assist you? I presume you are not a journalist?' Mr Pettifor asked.

'No, sir. My friend, Miss Miller, and her fiancé, Mr Potter, were the purchasers of the farm at auction. Now with all that has happened recently my friend is worried about the property and wondered if you might be able to come to tea on Sunday and perhaps tell us more about the history of the farm?' Kitty explained.

Mr Pettifor sounded a little surprised by her request but agreed to call when Kitty gave him the address.

'I can certainly give them some history to the farm if you feel it would help,' he said.

'Oh, thank you, Mr Pettifor. We shall expect you on Sunday at four then. Miss Miller and Mr Potter will be most grateful.' Kitty replaced the receiver.

That was one task off her list. She hoped Matt had made it safely to Plymouth ready to start the laborious task of trying to track down the elusive Joshua Payne. She decided to pack herself a picnic lunch to take with her to Alice's home, as by the time she had collected the keys and driven back it would be rather a rush. Alice's house would be cold, and she wanted to get a fire going in case she was waiting a while for the engineer.

Her plans made she said goodbye to her housekeeper and her pets and jumped in her car to head to Alice's shop. When she arrived, the shop was full of customers all selecting gifts for Christmas or collecting gowns that Alice had repaired or altered.

'Oh, Kitty, I am so grateful to you.' Alice handed her the keys to the farm. 'The kindling should all be there and a fire laid ready to be lit. Robert always leaves it that way since we've been working up there.'

'Thank you. Now, Mr Pettifor is coming on Sunday at four so you can ask him anything about the house,' Kitty said as she dropped Alice's keys into her black leather handbag.

'Thank you. Robert and I will be there. It makes me feel much better about things.'

Alice was called back to the counter by Rose and Kitty slipped out of the shop ready to drive back up to Hillhead and Coleton to the farm. Low misty cloud closed in on her as she drove up the hill past Lupton House. The sounds of the hunting dogs in the kennels baying echoed eerily and she was glad when she had cleared the woods and started further towards Coleton and Alice's house.

The road was deserted with no other cars, horses, or vehicles passing her as she drove carefully along the narrow lanes. Bracken, brown now and dripping with water from the fog, brushed against the red paintwork of her car in the narrowest parts of the road.

Midwinter Farm loomed up ahead, a dull dark-grey stone shape in the mist. Kitty halted the car to unlock the wooden gate to the entrance so she could drive through. Freezing air greeted her as she stepped out of her car and she hurried to unfasten the padlock. At least it seemed there were no journalists or nosy parkers prowling around.

She could see why Alice and Robert were so keen to get the telephone installation completed. The farm was isolated at the end of the track and without cheerful lights shining from the windows and smoke coming from the chimney it looked like a very forlorn place indeed.

Kitty drove through the now open gate, leaving it standing aside for the engineer's arrival, and parked on the gravel near the old piggery. It looked as if the new pole and materials had been delivered already. Robert must have let them in before departing to Tavistock. She shivered as she unlocked the front door and stepped into the hall, taking care to wipe her feet on the mat.

The air inside the house was not much warmer than the air outside. Kitty carried her handbag and her lunch into the kitchen and placed it on the table, before removing her gloves ready to light the fires.

Alice had been right about Robert leaving the house prepared. She decided to just light the one in the kitchen but went through to the sitting room and dining room to turn on the lights. At least then anyone approaching the farm could see it was occupied. She also took the precaution of locking the front door again. She rather regretted her decision to leave Bertie at home as at least he would have kept her company while she waited.

She kept her coat on until the fire was well ablaze, and she had boiled the kettle to make a cup of tea to have with her sandwiches. With the lights on and the house feeling warmer, she began to feel more cheerful.

Mrs Smith had packed her some delicious cheese and pickle sandwiches, along with a sliver of pork pie and a couple of mince pies. Seated at the table drinking her tea and eating her lunch she could see what a lovely home the farmhouse could be. Alice's curtains were bright and cheery, and the rooms were spacious.

Once her lunch was finished and she had cleared away she prepared a tea tray ready for the engineer's arrival. If they were working outside erecting the extra telegraph pole then she was sure they would be glad of a hot drink.

It was quarter to two, so she expected the engineers to arrive at any time. She had taken the precaution of placing her latest library book in her handbag to pass the time, so she settled her seat near the kitchen fire to read.

A noise outside in the yard disturbed her before she had read very far and she placed her bookmark inside the book. She went to the sitting room to look through the window to see if the workmen had arrived. Her car still stood alone on the gravel with no sign of any other vehicle.

The fine hairs on the nape of Kitty's neck prickled as she peered cautiously around the edge of Alice's smart new curtains, looking for anything which may have made the noise she had heard.

While she was standing there she heard a sound she did recognise. Someone was trying the handle of the back door to the scullery. Her heart thumped in her chest, and she quietly picked up the iron poker from the stand at the side of the fire.

Kitty crept silently out into the hall where she could lurk in the shadows and observe the back door without being immediately obvious to anyone looking in. She saw the metal door handle jiggle again and through the small piece of frosted glass she could just make out the blurry shape of what seemed to be a man in a dark coat.

She wondered if she should turn off the lights but decided that would alert whoever was out there to her presence. The movements at the back door ceased and Kitty blew out a breath of relief. She stayed motionless in the hall listening for any indication of where the intruder may have gone.

The sudden movement of the front door handle made her jump, sending her heart racing once more. She was glad now that she had locked the door when she had entered the house. The movement ceased when whoever the man was found that the door was secure.

Kitty was about to slip back into the sitting room to try for a better look at the would-be burglar when the black metal letter box rattled. She froze in place as the flap on the inside of the door was slowly lifted and someone tried to peer inside.

Without pausing to think of the consequences, Kitty rushed over to the door and rapped the metal poker down smartly on the man's fingers where he was holding up the flap to look inside.

The man released the flap amidst a shower of colourful curses and there was a frantic scrabbling of feet on the gravel as Kitty ran into the sitting room to try and get a better look at the man who was running away from the house, nursing his hand. All she could see was that he wore a dark coat and trousers with his cap pulled low on his head.

Kitty's own hands were shaking as she went back into the kitchen and sank down onto the sturdy pine chair. She placed the poker on the table, adrenaline still coursing through her veins from what had just happened.

Who was the man? How had he got there? She wondered if he might have had a vehicle parked in the lane in one of the passing places. He could have been a reporter she supposed, just trying his luck, but then why not knock on the door? The lights were on, and her car was clearly visible through the open gate.

She supposed he may not have been sure of who was in the house, but it still didn't explain what he had been doing. Whatever he had been up to, she was sure it was nothing good. At least Alice had not been with her. It would have added to her bad feelings about the place.

Once she felt more settled, Kitty went back to the sitting room and placed the poker back in the stand. She would need to let Chief Inspector Greville or Inspector Lewis know about what had just happened. She also needed to tell Matt and Robert. Perhaps they could then help her warn Alice.

A rumble of a small lorry alerted her to the imminent arrival of the telephone engineers. A dark-blue van appeared out of the mist and entered the yard to park alongside her car. She recognised the man from the other day and this time he was accompanied by a tall, broad-shouldered younger man dressed as a labourer.

Relief flooded through her as she hurried back into the kitchen to fetch the keys to unlock the front door.

'Afternoon, miss.' The engineer tipped the brim of his cap to her, looking a little surprised by her prompt arrival on the front step.

'Good afternoon. You didn't just pass anyone in the lane did you on your way here? Either a man on foot or a vehicle?' Kitty asked.

'There was a fool in dark clothes on a bicycle with no lamp, almost knocked him off the thing. He was weaving all over the road. I suppose he must have been drunk or something,' the engineer said.

The labourer came over to stand next to him. 'It looked like he was steering with one hand. It was pretty reckless if you ask me, he nearly went into a ditch.'

'Were you expecting someone?' the engineer asked.

Kitty shook her head. 'No, I thought I saw someone in the yard earlier, that's all.'

The engineer explained what they needed to do to set up the pole before he could run the cable into the hall for Alice and Robert's telephone. An additional cable was being run to the barn but not connected just yet until Robert had his office properly set up.

Kitty returned to the kitchen to make them both a mug of tea while they set about their work. With any luck the mystery man would stay well away from the house after his encounter with the poker. She could only hope that either Inspector Lewis or the chief inspector could find out his identity. If he had cycled to the farm he had to be local.

Kitty made the engineer and his labourer mugs of tea and was kept busy while they set up the new pole and strung the cables to the house to connect up the telephone in the hallway. She was glad of the fire in the kitchen, since much of the work necessitated having the front door open for periods of time, letting in the icy winter air.

It was dark by the time the men were finished and had tested the new telephone. Kitty made a note of the number and followed them out of the farmhouse, locking it up behind her. She also secured the gate knowing that Robert would double-check it when he returned with his touring coach later on. After the earlier incident she had no wish to stay in the house alone, telephone or no telephone.

The mist had thickened, and Kitty drove slowly back along the narrow lanes following the engineers' van until they reached the main road. Then the engineer headed towards Kingswear and the ferry, while Kitty turned off to return home. She hoped that Matt would be back so she could tell him what had happened before she called Chief Inspector Greville.

* * *

It had taken Matt longer than he had anticipated to reach the docks and the shipping offices. The weather conditions had meant he had to ride more slowly than usual since the visibility was poor all the way to Plymouth.

The shipping offices were all situated in a large red-brick building with the names of the various companies on brass plates beside their doors. He knew from past experience that as well as the public-facing parts of the company, which sold berths for passage to different countries, there was also a commercial section.

The commercial areas were where he hoped he might find some clue of who Joshua Payne may have been employed by and where the man could have shipped to. The dates he had probably left when Crabtree had vanished were in Matt's notebook and he thought that might be a good starting point.

He had contacts in a few of the merchant offices and decided to try the largest of those fleets first. He parked the Sunbeam and drew off his leather gauntlets, stowing them in the box on the back of the bike before heading to the commercial end of the building.

The silver-haired elderly lady behind the desk peered at him through her black metal-framed glasses as he approached the counter.

'Matthew Bryant, as I live and breathe. It's been a while since we last saw you. What can we do for you today?' Behind her he could hear the buzz of voices and clatter of typewriters as the clerks in the offices sorted out shipping orders.

'Hello, Marjorie. You're always a treat for the eyes.' Matt grinned at her. Marjorie Robinson had provided him with useful information many times over the years.

'Humph, same old silver-tongued rascal, I see. I suppose you've come looking for information rather than just the pleasure of seeing me?' She gave him a quizzical look, and he could see the twinkle in her eyes.

'Much as I love seeing you, Marjorie, I'm afraid I'm working on a case. I need to look at some records from ten years ago.' Matt smiled as he spoke. He liked Marjorie, she was a nice lady and was an expert at her job.

'Ten years hmm, then you'd best come upstairs to the archive room.' She lifted a hatch in the polished wooden counter to allow him access and led the way to a narrow wooden staircase at the rear of the reception area.

He followed her as she led the way up and unlocked the door of a large store room lined with shelves filled with leather-bound ledgers. The shelves were marked with dates. In the centre of the room was a small plain deal table and a couple of chairs.

'Here are all the records. Make sure you put anything back in the right place that you take out. I suppose too that you'd like a cup of tea while you're looking?' Marjorie asked.

Matt knew that she didn't usually allow many people to access the shipping records and definitely didn't offer tea to just anyone.

'Thank you, tea would be very welcome. It's been a long, cold ride to get here today.' He unfastened his heavy leather greatcoat and hung it on the hook at the back of the door, before removing his cap and muffler.

'Are you after something in particular?' Marjorie asked.

'A farmer went missing ten years ago near Dartmouth and has now reappeared as a murder victim. A man called Joshua Payne, a merchant seaman, was known to have quarrelled with the victim before he disappeared. At the time the police had no cause to look very deeply into the matter and the man was thought to have left the country shortly afterwards. I need to know if he did sail and where he went. This might help us find where he is today as the police wish to speak to him,' Matt explained.

'I see. Then try the shelves in the back left corner, third from the top. Those should cover that time period. I'll bring a biscuit with your tea,' Marjorie said and departed, leaving him to his quest.

Matt grinned as he headed towards the spot the shipping manager had suggested. He soon saw that as usual Marjorie's records were impeccably filed. He checked the dates he was looking for in his notes and saw there were at least five ships' ledgers which could have departed the port around the time Crabtree had vanished.

The shelving labels indicated a span of five years for each section. There were several ships' books filed alphabetically so he guessed he would have a lot to wade through to discover exactly what he was after. He had just hauled the first of the books to the table when Marjorie returned bearing a cup of tea with three biscuits balanced on the saucer.

'Here you go, warm you up a bit.' She set the pale-green china cup and saucer down carefully at a distance from the now open ledger. 'Are you sure he was on one of our ships?'

'No, but I thought since your company was the largest it was the best place to start. If I can't find him here then I'll go and see Mr Northcott of the Blenheim Line and see if he was working for them,' Matt said, his eyes already scanning the pages looking for the right set of dates.

'You know he's not as pretty as me and he won't give you tea.' Marjorie winked at him.

'Then let's hope my man is in here somewhere,' Matt responded with a grin. He always enjoyed Marjorie's teasing.

'Good luck, and if you need assistance, I'm just downstairs,' Marjorie offered.

'Thank you.' Matt settled to his task. The first three ledgers were a blank with no sign of Joshua Payne's name appearing amongst the crew on any of the sailings of those particular ships around the date of Crabtree's disappearance.

Marjorie reappeared with fresh tea and more biscuits just as he was starting on the last of the ships' ledgers that fell in that period.

'Any luck yet?' she asked as she put the cup down on the table.

'This is the last one of your ships that was sailing out of here at that time. I know it's like looking for a needle in a haystack, but I thought it was worth a shot. The police don't have the manpower to spare to do this,' Matt said, frowning at the neatly written columns.

Marjorie turned on the large Anglepoise lamp that stood at the side of the table. 'You'll strain your eyes, it's getting dark already outside today.' She picked up the empty cup from earlier ready to return downstairs.

'That's better, thank you. Wait! I think I have him.' Matt reached for the lamp to angle the shade to throw more light onto the bottom of the page.

CHAPTER ELEVEN

Marjorie came around the table to peer over his shoulder. 'Is that your man? Joshua Payne?'

'That looks as if it's him. He's the only one I've found,' Matt said.

'Right.' Marjorie put down the cup and took out a tiny notepad and pencil from her cardigan pocket. 'That number in the column there is his CR 10 number. All merchant seamen have them. It's his licence to work for us. We'll have all his details on file downstairs including his next of kin and home address when in port. I assume that's what you'll want?' she said as she jotted down the number from the register. 'Come down when you've finished your tea and tidied up. Bring the cups,' she instructed and disappeared back to her office.

Matt drank his tea and ate the biscuits to quiet the rumblings in his stomach that reminded him that he had skipped lunch. Once the ledger was back in place and the room was tidy he carried his crockery back downstairs to find Marjorie.

The older woman had a tiny private cubby hole under the stairs where she could observe the front desk and work in peace at the same time. She beamed at him as he deposited the cups on her desk.

'I have your information for you. Joshua Payne, aged thirty-two, currently aboard the *Regardless* and due back into Plymouth on Saturday when he'll be due for two weeks shore leave. Here's the home address we have for him. It looks as if he lives with his mother when he's on shore leave. She's listed as next of kin at the same address in Paignton.' Marjorie pushed a piece of paper towards him.

Matt read the address and tucked the paper safely inside the notebook in the breast pocket of his jacket before donning his heavy leather greatcoat and his leather cap. 'You are an absolute gem, Marjorie. I owe you for this one.'

The elderly lady dimpled, her cheeks pinking. 'I bet you say that to all the girls. Give my love to Kitty and take care riding back. There's sleet starting to come down again.'

Matt said his farewells and set out to walk back to his motorcycle. The lights were all on in the various shipping offices and he could see the passenger ticket offices looked busy. He guessed a good many people would be trying to obtain one of the last crossings to get over the Atlantic to America in time for Christmas.

He and Kitty had been in just such a position last year. He climbed onto his bike after retrieving his heavy-duty riding gauntlets from the box where he had placed them earlier. A man leaving the passenger ticket office and striding away into the murky fading light caught his attention.

There was something oddly familiar about the figure. A sense of déjà vu came over him and a shiver ran up his spine. He had spent too long studying those ledgers. His eyes must be deceiving him. He looked in the direction where the man had gone but there was no sign of him now.

Matt started his motorcycle and tried to shake off the eerie feeling that had come over him. He had experienced just such a feeling last January when he and Kitty had disembarked in the port. Then, he had seen a man who he had believed dead and buried years earlier.

The same man he just thought he had glimpsed once again. Redvers Palmerston had since gone on to make a career of deceiving single women by promising marriage and fleeing with their money and jewellery.

The wanted posters were torn and faded now in the various police stations around the county, but Matt was almost sure he had just glimpsed him once more. He switched on the bike's headlamp. He must be mistaken. It was probably just that he was back in almost the same place where he had first seen him. A man of a similar build and way of walking, that was all.

Kitty was on the telephone in the hall as he let himself into the house. Bertie came to greet him, enthusiastically wagging his tail and snuffling against his pockets in the vain hope that a treat might be in the offing.

It was clear that Kitty had only just returned herself. She was still wearing her thick woollen coat with the sable collar and matching hat.

'No, I'm afraid I didn't get a look at his face at all. Neither did the telephone engineer when they passed him in the lane.' She looked at Matt and mouthed, 'Inspector Lewis.'

Matt took off his own coat and cap and hung them on the hall stand. His feet and hands were freezing from the long ride home from Plymouth. He was anxious to warm himself by the fire and get a hot cup of tea. He was also curious to discover what Kitty was talking about with Inspector Lewis.

'I see, of course. Thank you.' She replaced the receiver on its stand.

'Was there a problem?' Matt asked as Kitty took off her coat and hat, adding them to the hooks beside his own apparel.

'Let me go and put the kettle on and make us a drink and I'll tell you all about it.' She stretched up to kiss his cheek. 'Brr, you feel frozen. Go and sit by the fire.' She shooed him into the sitting room while she went and made tea.

Mrs Smith had banked up the fire before she had finished for the day and had drawn the curtains and switched on one of the silk-shaded lamps giving the room a cosy, snug feel. More Christmas cards had been added to the ones already on display and the scent of pine from the Christmas tree lingered in the air. Matt put on his slippers and moved Rascal from his seat.

Kitty returned a few minutes later bearing a small wooden tray set with tea things and slices of Christmas cake.

'Did you manage to get any lunch?' she asked as she poured him some tea.

'No. Marjorie kept me well supplied with biscuits though. What did Inspector Lewis want?' Matt asked as he selected a slice of cake.

'Well, after you left I organised a meeting with Mr Pettifor for Sunday tea at four. Then Alice called to ask a favour.' Kitty went on to explain what had happened at the house.

'You hit his fingers with the poker? Ouch, no wonder he was all over the road afterwards trying to steer his bicycle.' Matt chuckled but then sobered. 'Seriously though, darling, that is quite worrying. Have you told Alice or Robert yet?'

Kitty shook her head as she stirred her tea. 'No. I'd just got in when you came back and I called Inspector Lewis straight away.'

'They'll need to know.' Matt could see that Kitty was concerned, and he guessed that she was probably worried about Alice's reaction.

'I know. I have to return Alice's keys too and give her and Robert their new telephone number,' Kitty said.

'It's Saturday tomorrow. They will both be busy. It's Alice's busiest day in the shop and Robert is taking his tour bus out to

Saltash Christmas market over the border in Cornwall,' Matt said.

'Robert is keeping his vehicles at the farm, so he'll have gone back there tonight already, and he'll be there early tomorrow morning.' Kitty looked worried. 'Suppose whoever it is comes back? I would hate Robert to be hurt.'

'I'll call Mr Potter, Robert's father, and warn him you saw a prowler. That should set him on his guard. It may simply be someone nosing around.' Matt finished his cake and brushed the crumbs from the lapel of his jacket.

Bertie immediately pounced to gobble them up from the Turkish carpet. 'Inspector Lewis said the same thing. He said he'd make a note of it and see if anyone seemed to fit the description I gave. Not that I could give him much since I never saw the man's face. Just his eyes and then a hand reaching in through the letter box.' Kitty shuddered.

'Well, I don't suppose he'll try that again in a hurry.' Matt smiled at her. 'I'll call Mr Potter and ask him to let Robert know what happened.'

* * *

Kitty finished her tea while Matt made the call to Robert's father. She knew that Alice would probably telephone her as soon as she had eaten her supper after work to make sure everything had gone smoothly with the engineer.

She wasn't looking forward to telling her friend what had happened at the farm. It would undoubtedly make Alice's feelings about the house even worse. Matt returned to the sitting room as she was gathering up the crockery to take the tray to the kitchen ready to begin supper.

'Mr Potter will tell Robert about the prowler, and he says Robert will explain to Alice. He asked us to keep the key until we see them both on Sunday. Robert has his own set of keys for the house and the outbuildings.'

Matt followed her into the kitchen to assist her in washing up the tea things. She lit the oven and placed the casserole inside that Mrs Smith had left for their supper. While they were completing their domestic tasks, Matt told her what he had learned while he was in Plymouth.

'That's good if we have an address for Joshua Payne and even better that his ship is due in to dock tomorrow. I daresay Chief Inspector Greville will wish to speak to him too,' Kitty said as she cut some bread from the fresh crusty loaf and buttered the slices ready for them to have with their meal.

'It is. It'll be very interesting to hear what his recollections of Mr Crabtree are like and what happened in their argument.' Matt carried the cutlery into the dining room to set the table before returning to the kitchen to put Rascal's food and Bertie's supper in their respective dishes.

With everything prepared for supper, they returned to the sitting room while the casserole heated. Matt poured them both a pre-dinner glass of sherry.

'I wonder what your intruder was looking for today?' Matt mused as he sipped his drink.

'It's rather queer, isn't it? The house has had several tenants since Thomas Crabtree vanished, and it's been empty quite a few times. While Robert has been working on it these last few months there have been lots of opportunities to look around,' Kitty replied thoughtfully.

'You said you had the lights on and the fire burning. Your car was parked outside too. He must have known someone was inside so why not knock on the door?' Matt's frown intensified and she could see his thoughts were similar to her own.

'I can only think that perhaps he didn't recognise my car and wanted to try to see who was there first. He may have been feeling through the letter box hoping to find a key on a string,' Kitty suggested.

'It's a good thing you locked the door while you were waiting for the engineers,' Matt said.

'I wished I had taken Bertie with me, but I thought he might be a nuisance barking at the workmen.' Kitty took another sip of her drink. Normally sherry wasn't her favourite aperitif but there was something about Christmas that always made sherry and port taste so much nicer than at other times in the year.

Bertie lifted his head from where he had settled to snooze at her feet and gave her a baleful look.

Matt chuckled. 'You're probably right. There was something odd that happened to me too just as I was coming away from the docks today.'

'Oh?' Kitty looked at him. She sensed from the slightly uncertain note in his voice that he had been debating if it was something worth sharing.

'It was dark and quite misty with bits of sleet coming down when I said goodbye to Marjorie. I'd just reached my bike when I glanced over towards the passenger ticket office for the transatlantic liners. The office looked busy as you can imagine with everyone wanting to secure a last-minute berth.' He paused and lifted his gaze to meet hers. 'I don't know if it was a trick of the light or my mind playing me for a fool, but I thought I saw Redvers Palmerston.'

'Redvers? He was last seen in Plymouth when there was that fire and you were called back from Paris,' she said. Matt had been compelled to briefly return to Devon to identify a body found in a burning lodging house. The dead man had Redvers's family ring, but the body wasn't his. Since then things had gone quiet.

'I can't be certain that it was him. I didn't see his face and the mist was drifting about. It was just something about his frame and the way he was walking.' Matt's expression was troubled.

Kitty nodded. 'I understand. It must have felt most unnerving.'

'He had vanished into the mist before I could call out or get off the motorcycle to try and follow him,' Matt said.

'It doesn't sound as if there was anything you could have done. Like you said, it may well not even have been him. It could just have been a perfectly innocent stranger.' Kitty glanced at her watch and sniffed the air. 'Supper should be ready, it smells delicious.'

The telephone rang just as they finished their dessert of cherry pie and custard.

'I'll wager that will be Alice,' Matt said as Kitty dumped her linen napkin down on the tablecloth and went to answer.

'Kitty, Mr Potter has told Robert what happened at the house today.' Alice's anxious voice reached her as soon as she lifted the receiver.

'It was nothing much. I gave his fingers a good rap with the poker so I doubt he'll try that again in a hurry. I let Inspector Lewis know and he thinks it may well be a journalist snooping about trying to add some colour to a story about Mr Crabtree's death.' Kitty tried to sound matter-of-fact and calm.

'Well, it's a blooming cheek, that's what it is. It must have been proper frightening for you. I'm so sorry as you had to experience that,' Alice said.

'It was fine. The engineer arrived soon afterwards. Oh, I have your new telephone number; do you have a pencil?' Kitty gave her friend the new number for her telephone at the farm. 'At least that is all connected now.'

'And just in the nick of time from the sounds of it. I've told Robert to keep a sharp eye out when he's up there. He's at the farm early and late taking the buses in and out and locking up. It's a bit worrying,' Alice said.

'Inspector Lewis felt it probably was just someone being nosy rather than someone wishing to cause harm,' Kitty reassured her.

'Well, I hope he's right. I don't want my Robert getting hurt,' Alice said.

Kitty tried her best to reassure her friend some more before ending the call with the reminder that they were talking to Mr Pettifor on Sunday.

She just hoped as she went into the kitchen to help Matt with the supper dishes that the inspector was right for a change. And that the snooper was just someone being nosy and not Thomas Crabtree's murderer.

CHAPTER TWELVE

The following morning dawned bright and clear with a white frost on the lawn that quickly started melting under the winter sunlight. Kitty shivered as she let Bertie into the garden and Rascal blinked at her from his snug spot in front of the kitchen range.

Matt had been restless in his sleep during the night. She had heard the bed creaking as he had tossed and turned. She hoped the experience at Plymouth hadn't triggered his recurring nightmares about his time in the Great War. At least it seemed he had not been up and wandering about the house refighting long-gone battles.

He entered the kitchen just as she closed the back door and Bertie seated himself expectantly in front of the stove.

'Morning, darling.' Kitty scanned her husband's face for signs of weariness as she lit the gas beneath the cast-iron pan and prepared to fry some bacon and eggs for their breakfast.

'Morning.' He bent to fuss Bertie. 'Is it this evening that we are expected at the Carters' house?'

'Yes, six thirty for pre-dinner drinks and dining at seven

thirty. It should be fun.' Kitty concentrated on her pan as the fat was beginning to spit around the bacon.

Matt carried the kettle to the tap and filled it ready to make their morning coffee. 'I wonder if they have invited Inspector Lewis?'

'And Betty?' Kitty added with a smile. 'That would be interesting.'

Matt laughed. 'I still can't believe that the inspector is walking out with Betty. If they are at dinner Alice will be very prickly about it. You know she holds strong views on the propriety of things.'

'Oh dear, she does, doesn't she? No doubt she will think her cousin is getting above her station.' Kitty drained the bacon and transferred it into a covered dish before cracking a couple of large, brown-shelled eggs into the hot pan.

Poor Alice was having quite a difficult time of things lately. The world was changing and although Alice had now become a businesswoman, she still held on to some of the old-fashioned values her mother had instilled in her.

Matt made the coffee, and Kitty carried the dish with their breakfast into the dining room. Mrs Smith came later on Saturdays after visiting the market to order their groceries for the week. She would then prepare their lunch and meal for Sunday before finishing for the day. Sunday was her housekeeper's day off.

The newspaper rattled onto the doormat as they were about to sit down so Matt went to collect it from the hall.

'It seems that the discovery of Mr Crabtree's remains is on the front page of the national press,' he said as he resumed his seat opposite Kitty.

She glanced at the newspaper. 'At least it isn't headlines. Although I suppose it will be in the *Torbay Herald* later today. Perhaps that man who was snooping around the farm was a journalist after all.'

'It's possible but it still seems strange that whoever he was didn't knock at the door but tried to peer inside the house instead,' Matt said as he helped himself to eggs and bacon from the dish.

'True.' Kitty poured her coffee. The incident had left her feeling unsettled and concerned. She could only hope that the police would make an arrest in the case soon and everything would settle down again.

They passed the rest of the day peacefully. Matt gave the information he had found in Plymouth to Chief Inspector Greville and said they looked forward to seeing him and Mrs Greville at the Carters' house later.

'You did get some flowers for us to give to Mrs Carter?' Kitty asked her husband as she finished tidying her hair ready for their evening out.

'There is a bouquet of pink roses in the kitchen sink,' Matt assured her.

'I have their Christmas gifts all wrapped and ready.' Kitty checked her appearance in the dressing-table mirror before turning on the stool to assist her husband with his cufflinks. She had some chocolates for Mrs Carter and a box of his favourite cigars for her husband.

Matt obediently held out his hands so she could insert the gold cufflinks into his shirt. 'Wonderful, it should be a nice evening. The Carters always host good parties. They have an excellent cook.'

'I just hope that Bertie behaves himself while we are out,' Kitty remarked drily as she completed her task.

When they pulled up near Doctor and Mrs Carter's house in Torquay a little later the drive was already full of cars, and the street parking was also quite crowded. Kitty managed to squeeze her small car into a spot and joined Matt to cross the road, linking her arm through his.

She was relieved she had elected to wear her sable fur coat over the thin ruby silk evening gown as ice was already beginning to form on the edges of the leaves in the shrubbery.

A smiling uniformed maid met them at the door to take their coats before they carried on through to the large drawing room at the rear of the double-fronted Victorian villa. Kitty handed over the bouquet Matt had bought and the carefully wrapped Christmas gifts.

'Matthew, Kitty, how wonderful to see you both. You shouldn't have brought gifts too.' Mrs Carter swept towards them as they entered the busy drawing room. Her round, pretty face wreathed in smiles as she kissed their cheeks and encouraged them to go to the cocktail bar in the corner of the room to get drinks.

The room was decorated for the season with gaily coloured paper chains suspended from the high ceiling, and sprigs of mistletoe hanging up around the room. A large Christmas tree stood in the corner near the French windows. The branches were barely visible through the layers of tinsel and baubles.

There were a few couples there who they had met before at other parties given by the genial doctor and his wife. Kitty greeted several of them, wishing them a merry Christmas as they went to claim a cocktail from their host.

Chief Inspector Greville was standing beside the gilt trolley which was laden with bottles. He was sipping a brightly coloured concoction somewhat morosely through a straw.

'Ha, Kitty, my dear, and Matthew, what can I get you?' Doctor Carter rubbed his hands together gleefully as they approached.

'A negroni would be delightful,' Kitty suggested as their host picked up the smart silver cocktail shaker.

'And for me too, please,' Matt added. 'Chief Inspector, that looks a fascinating drink. Is Mrs Greville here with you this evening?'

The chief inspector shook his head. 'I'm afraid that Mrs Greville is unable to attend. Her mother is unwell so isn't able to stay with the boys.'

'Oh dear, what a shame,' Kitty said sympathetically as Doctor Carter rustled up their drinks and served them with a flourish.

'Is Inspector Lewis attending?' Matt asked as he surveyed the party enjoying the music from the gramophone in the far corner of the room.

'Yes, indeed. He's bringing his young lady tonight too.' Doctor Carter beamed at them from his station behind the bar trolley.

'Yes, I believe he is walking out with my friend Miss Miller's cousin, Betty,' Kitty said.

As she spoke Inspector Lewis entered the room with Betty on his arm. Betty was dressed to impress in a midnight-blue satin gown and faux pearls around her neck. Inspector Lewis appeared somewhat self-conscious. Mrs Carter greeted them both and dispatched them in Matt and Kitty's direction to collect drinks.

'Ah, Inspector Lewis, and Betty, is it?' Doctor Carter smiled happily at his new guests. 'What can I get you both?'

Kitty and Matt greeted the new arrivals while Inspector Lewis requested a whisky and water for himself and a negroni for Betty. He looked askance at the drink in the chief inspector's glass as Doctor Carter busied himself once more with the cocktail shaker.

'You must be exhausted, Betty. I suppose you've been on your feet all day at Alice's shop,' Kitty said sympathetically.

'Not half. I think every mother in Paignton has been in to buy baby garments or to pick up mending or alterations. Our Alice will be seeing ribbons dancing in front of her eyes tonight she's hemmed that many party frocks,' Betty replied with feeling.

'How long have you been walking out with Inspector Lewis here?' Kitty asked as Doctor Carter handed Betty her drink.

'Oh, me and James have been seeing each other for about three or four months now. It's been a bit tricky with him being in Exeter for a while but now he's back in Torquay it'll be easier,' Betty said with a smile.

Inspector Lewis accepted his whisky and water looking even more self-conscious at being the subject of the conversation.

'How did you both meet?' Matt asked.

'You'll laugh at this,' Betty said, nudging the inspector's arm gently with her elbow. 'I was in Exeter near the cathedral on the green when all of a sudden this blooming great pigeon flies at me out of nowhere. I was completely taken by surprise and tried to bat it off with my handbag. James here was walking past, and I accidentally clocked him right in the face. I was that embarrassed, but he was ever so nice, calmed me down and took me for a cup of tea in one of the cafés. I knew we'd met before but it took us a while to recall when it was. It was when the beauty pageant was on in Dartmouth for the Jubilee.'

'Quite a knight in shining armour.' Kitty was enjoying the spread of pink appearing across Inspector Lewis's face as Betty told her story.

'How are matters progressing in the Crabtree case?' Doctor Carter asked. 'I see it made the newspapers today.' He glanced at the two policemen.

'It's taking some time to track down the people from the original case files who were interviewed when he first went missing,' Chief Inspector Greville said.

'I can't believe as you found a body at our Alice's house. I said to James here as my aunt would go spare when she found out,' Betty remarked, before taking a large gulp of her cocktail. 'I had just started in service when it happened and that Mr Crabtree went missing. I was working for Lord and Lady Massey at Seacliffe House. I started there just after the robbery. You know when all those jewels was pinched.'

'Goodness, Betty, I didn't know that,' Kitty said.

'Oh yes, it was the talk of the place. The servants' hall was full of it. The rumour was that the bloke what went missing had something to do with the robbery. Horace, his lordship's valet, he said he'd heard as Lord Massey wanted Thomas Crabtree out and had asked the land agent to deal with evicting him. That's when they found as he'd done a bunk. Except he was lying dead as a doornail all this time in our Alice's old piggery,' Betty said. 'Horace reckoned as Crabtree had double-crossed the others what had stolen the jewels and they was probably hidden somewhere around the farm.'

'A most interesting theory, my dear.' Doctor Carter's eyes were twinkling with amusement.

'It'd be a lark if our Alice were to find them as well after all these years,' Betty said, giving Inspector Lewis's elbow another playful nudge.

'It would indeed,' Chief Inspector Greville agreed.

'Do you think as they could be hidden someplace around there?' Betty asked. 'I mean they haven't ever turned up, have they?'

'No, the jewels and silver are still missing and unfortunately no arrests for the robberies were ever made,' Chief Inspector Greville said.

Mrs Carter approached them. 'I do hope you aren't all talking shop. Poor Kitty and Betty will be bored rigid. Now, I rather think dinner will be ready so we should start to go through, my dear.' She looked at her husband.

Doctor Carter gave them all an apologetic smile and joined his wife to lead their guests into the dining room.

The dinner table had been pulled out to its full extent for

the evening and was immaculately dressed in crisp white damask table linen with a large poinsettia centrepiece. The silver candelabras were trimmed with red-berried holly around the bases and red crepe-paper crackers were at every place setting. The silverware gleamed in the light of the fat white wax candles and the glittering crystal chandelier.

Matt and Kitty were seated opposite Inspector Lewis and Betty, while Kitty had Chief Inspector Greville on the other side of her. Once they were all seated Doctor Carter tapped a spoon against his crystal water glass to gain the attention of everyone at the table.

'Welcome, dear friends, to our annual pre-Christmas dinner. I have been instructed by my good lady wife to lead you all in saying grace.'

Once the short and simple grace had been said, the Carters' servants began to serve the first course of French onion soup. Chief Inspector Greville's morose mood appeared to have lifted at the sight and scent of the aromatic cheese-topped first course.

'Inspector Lewis informed me that you had an unpleasant encounter yesterday with someone at Miss Miller's farmhouse.' Chief Inspector Greville glanced at Kitty as he smothered creamy-yellow butter in a thick layer on his bread roll.

'Yes, I didn't see his features, unfortunately, but hopefully he has sore fingers.' Kitty kept her tone low to match the chief inspector's as she inserted her silver spoon into the fine-china soup bowl.

'So I understand. A poker was involved, I hear.' Chief Inspector Greville's lips twitched upwards beneath his moustache and Kitty's cheeks pinked.

'Perhaps it might make him easier to find with an injured hand,' she suggested.

CHAPTER THIRTEEN

The rest of the dinner party passed off in a pleasant manner. The food, as always, was delicious, a perfectly roasted joint of pork with apple sauce followed by flambéed bananas, which had Kitty fearing for the safety of the paper chains. Although Matt was forced to come to her rescue when she was cornered by one of the junior doctors who worked under Doctor Carter. She had endured twenty minutes of a lecture on the intricacies of pathogens when Matt spotted her distress.

By this stage everyone was back in the drawing room and the furniture had been rearranged to permit dancing. Kitty gratefully accepted Matt's hand and they joined Betty and Inspector Lewis and another two couples on the compact makeshift dance floor.

Kitty made a mental note to tell Alice how enamoured the inspector appeared to be with her cousin. Certainly, she was seeing a very different side to the often rude and snappy policeman this evening. He was almost jovial under Betty's mellowing influence.

It was late when they returned home, and she had been

concerned that Bertie might well have been up to mischief whilst they had been away. Although he was calmer now than when they had first acquired him, he was still prone to destroying things if left unattended for too long. The last victims had been a feather-filled new cushion in the sitting room and one of her slippers.

This time, however, all seemed well, and she went upstairs to prepare for bed while Matt saw to their pets. It had been an enjoyable evening and thanks to Betty and her colourful employment history she had learned a little more of what had been happening around the time that Thomas Crabtree had been murdered.

There was no time for too much speculation though since she would need to be up bright and early to assist at the church. She hopped into bed with a sigh and snuggled up to her hot-water bottle. How had she allowed Mrs Craven to talk her into this again?

* * *

Sunday morning dawned gloomy and dull. There had been some rain overnight and even the evergreen bushes in the garden looked wet and depressed as she ate her toast and marmalade.

'I had better get going,' Kitty said, before swallowing her last mouthful of tea. 'We have to set out the cups and things before the start of the service. As soon as the congregation exit the door of the church, they circle around like a cloud of locusts to collect tea and cake.'

'Never mind, darling. It's Christmas after all.' Matt grinned at her from over his newspaper.

'It's all very well for you. You get to stay here and walk Bertie. I have to smile and pour tea and hope that perpetual dewdrop on the end of Mrs Hartlebury's nose doesn't land on the mince pies.' Kitty rose from the table as Matt burst out laughing.

'Poor Mrs Hartlebury. It is an unfortunate affliction the poor woman seems to have.'

Kitty humphed as she hurried into the hall to put on her coat and hat. Normally she enjoyed the services in the run up to Christmas. This was one of her favourite times of the year with the lighting of the candles and countdown to the big day. This morning, however, was likely to prove something of a trial. It was a popular service as it was the last Sunday in Advent and there would be a larger group than usual wanting tea.

She drove her car down the hill and crossed the river on the ferry, before parking as near to the ancient church as she could. Since she was early everywhere was quiet and the bell-ringers hadn't yet started to summon the worshippers to church.

Kitty took the opportunity to slip down the side of the church and into the graveyard. She had visited her mother's grave the week before and had left a small posy of creamy Christmas roses tied up in red tartan ribbon on the grave. She spent a minute or two there, comforted by the visit, before heading for the hall.

Mrs Hartlebury was already there, wrapped in a large floral pinafore as she set out the utilitarian pale-green cups and saucers. Mrs Craven was there too with two large tins, which Kitty guessed contained the baking that Dora had done for the occasion.

'Kitty, dear, there you are.' Mrs Craven's tone implied that somehow she was late, which Kitty knew was definitely not the case.

'Good morning,' Mrs Hartlebury greeted her with a smile.

'Now, Kitty, please arrange the biscuits, cake and mince pies. I have brought some of my own festive china from home to display them on so make sure that they are returned to me afterwards, won't you?' Mrs Craven thrust the tins she was carrying at her.

Kitty could see the plates already on the table waiting for the baked goods. They were painted with wintry scenes of robins and holly and looked expensive. 'Of course, I shall do my best.'

'Splendid. Now I have arranged for another couple of ladies to assist you after the service. The children will require orange juice and biscuits. Don't let the Pinkerton boy steal more than his fair share.' Mrs Craven adjusted the collar of her fur coat, the diamond brooch on her lapel on show as usual. 'I shall see you after the service. I must just go and have a word with the vicar.'

Mrs Craven trotted off leaving Kitty and Mrs Hartlebury to finish their tasks as the bells started to peal, signalling that the service would be starting shortly. Once the cakes, biscuits and mince pies were set out and the kettles filled, Mrs Hartlebury locked the door to the hall and they hurried into the back of the church.

Once seated on a pew at the rear of the church Kitty relaxed and breathed in the timeless scent of flowers and candles. Near the altar a large, decorated Christmas tree stood beside the advent scene. The painted wooden figures were placed on the straw-strewn floor patiently awaiting the arrival of baby Jesus in a few days' time.

The church, as she had expected, was full. Small children fidgeted and were shushed by their parents as the vicar delivered the readings. Timeless festive hymns suitable for the advent period were sung and the last candle lit on the advent crown. Just before the final dismissal, Mrs Hartlebury touched her arm, and she accompanied the older woman back to the hall.

Once inside, the kettles were boiled and they both donned pinafores ready for the arrival of the congregation. The door to the hall opened and a group of small children rushed in, clearly eager to ensure they got their share of the treats.

Kitty dispensed orange squash and biscuits while more people filed inside creating a buzz of chatter. It was all getting quite busy when another woman, thin faced with dark hair and a harassed expression, came to join them behind the counter.

'Hello, Lavinia, my dear, I didn't think you were helping us today?' Mrs Hartlebury said as the new arrival hung up her coat and put on an apron.

'I weren't going to. It was supposed to be Peggy, but she's got something come to her throat and that Craven woman grabbed hold of me in front of the vicar. I could hardly say no, could I? Not after all the church has done for us in the past.' The woman started to refill the milk jugs and make conversation with the customers at the table.

Kitty was intrigued. Lavinia was the name of Thomas Crabtree's daughter-in-law and the reference to the church having helped her in the past set her wondering. She was prevented from asking any questions for the time being since they were rapidly running out of clean cups, so she had to go around and collect crockery to wash it up in the kitchen.

Another older woman arrived to assist at the counter, breathless and apologising for being late. Lavinia came to help dry the clean cups and saucers.

'Phew, it's busy out there today,' Kitty remarked conversationally as Lavinia picked up a tea towel.

'I swear as half of them weren't in the service. They just come for the tea and cake,' Lavinia said.

'The run up to Christmas is always busy.' Kitty deposited more clean saucers onto the wooden draining board.

'I'm glad to be in here as they can't all be asking questions and nosing about,' Lavinia said as she stacked some freshly dried cups.

'Oh, about your father-in-law, you mean?' Kitty asked.

Lavinia shot her a look. 'You've heard about it an all then. I think most of Dartmouth has by now. They found his body at last buried in the old piggery at his farm. He could have stayed buried there for all I care. Best place for him. Now I suppose we'll be put to the expense of a funeral. More money as we don't have.'

'You didn't get on then?' Kitty kept her tone casual.

'Get on! With that miserable, dishonest old skinflint. He nearly sent us to the poorhouse and made me a widow. If I knew who'd killed him, I'd shake them by the hand and give them half a crown.' Lavinia spat the words out. She paused as if to collect herself. 'That doesn't sound right Christian, does it? But he was a terrible man.'

'It must have come as a dreadful shock, him being found after all these years,' Kitty said as she placed more soapy cups on the board.

'It certainly was. My poor husband went as white as a sheet. I thought he was going to pass out when the police came to the door,' Lavinia said.

'Do they know who may have killed him?' Kitty asked as she released the plug from the sink.

'There's probably a queue stretching from here to Paignton. He owed some folks money and then, of course, everyone thinks as he was involved in those robberies.' Lavinia shook her head. 'He were a right bad lot.'

The hall was starting to thin out now, and the plates of baked goods were empty. Kitty gathered them up and washed them, carefully setting them aside to return to Mrs Craven. Lavinia went out with a tray to fetch more of the dirty crockery while Kitty ran fresh water into the sink. Mrs Hartlebury set a cup of tea and a mince pie down beside Kitty and put one for Lavinia.

'I saved us all one of these. Dora is a wonderful hand with pastry, and I don't see why those greedy gannets should have ate everything and the workers have nought,' Mrs Hartlebury said, the dewdrop wobbling perilously on the end of her nose.

'Thank you, that's very kind.' Kitty smiled gratefully at her fellow volunteer.

The other lady had already departed and Mrs Hartlebury started to wipe down the tables as she talked to the stragglers. Lavinia returned with a heavy tray of crockery.

'That's the last of the crocks,' she said, her eyes lighting up at the sight of the tea waiting for her.

'Mrs Hartlebury saved us a mince pie,' Kitty said.

'She's a good egg.' Lavinia ate her mince pie like a starving woman as Kitty plunged her hands back into the sink.

'Have mine too if you like, I prefer fruit cake but don't tell Mrs Hartlebury. I don't want her to feel I didn't appreciate the thought,' Kitty said. She did like mince pies, but she suspected that money and food was tight in Lavinia's household, and a home-baked mince pie was a rare treat for the woman.

'Oh, ta ever so.' Lavinia pounced on the pie and ate it with relish before resuming drying the remaining crockery and stacking it in the cupboards. 'I didn't catch your name.'

'Kitty, Kitty Bryant.' She smiled at Lavinia.

'You from the Dolphin Hotel?'

'Yes, I used to work there for my grandmother,' Kitty confirmed.

'I thought as I knew your face. Did the Craven woman get you to do this as well? I don't think I've seen you in here before?' Lavinia asked.

'She did and I have helped out in the past but usually she collars me for jumble sales and summer fêtes,' Kitty said with feeling as she washed the milk jugs.

'I'm not posh enough for them jobs.' Lavinia gave Kitty a sympathetic smile.

'I don't think I am really,' Kitty admitted. She certainly never felt as if she was, even if her cousin was a lady. Kitty had been just a hotelier and was now a private investigator, which reminded her she should ask more questions.

'It was queer what happened to your father-in-law. When did you and your husband last see him alive?' Kitty asked.

Lavinia gave a short laugh. 'William was in bed seriously ill. His old man had been to see him about two weeks before he went missing. I found out after the crafty old devil had taken every last penny we had in the house. He already owed us money and that was the last straw. I mean robbing a family when a man could have been on his deathbed. I weren't well myself and our Ginny, our eldest, she was only two months old. I saw him two days before he disappeared. The police reckoned I might have been one of the last ones to see him alive. I run into him at the market. I had the baby with me. I begged him for the money back as he owed us. Told him how sick his son was and we had nothing in the house...' Lavinia's voice tailed off and she blinked unshed tears from her eyes, before dabbing at them with the corner of the linen tea towel.

'I'm sorry,' Kitty said. 'I didn't mean to distress you.'

Lavinia shook her head. 'No, it's all right. I mean everyone knows as I yelled at him. Told him he was a worthless piece of a man. I said how I wanted to kill him for what he had done to us.'

'That must have been awful.' Kitty could only imagine how distressed and desperate the woman must have felt.

'It was. So, I've told William his father can have a pauper's funeral. He got enough from us when he was alive. I'll not spend a brass farthing on him now he's dead no matter what anybody thinks.' Lavinia dried the last of the crockery as Kitty pulled the plug from the sink once more.

'I can understand how you feel.' Kitty dried her reddened hands on Lavinia's tea towel, before the woman folded it ready for Mrs Hartlebury to take with her.

'It's not like we've spare money lying around. There's four children in the house now and William's work is slow this time of year. Then he bloomin' well went and injured himself on a job yesterday.' Lavinia removed the apron from around her narrow waist.

Kitty could see that the woman's dress, although clean and pressed, bore the signs of mending on the cuffs and wear on the waist.

'What does your husband do?'

'Gardening and handyman repairs. Spot of painting and carpentry. He hurt himself getting a tree root out.'

'Are we all done?' Mrs Hartlebury bustled in as Kitty removed her own pinafore and went to collect her hat and coat from the hooks.

'All finished,' Lavinia said.

'Splendid. Thank you both so much for your help.' Mrs Hartlebury beamed at them.

'That's all right,' Lavinia said.

'Now, I saved a few biscuits for your children, my dear.' Mrs Hartlebury thrust a small package into the pocket of Lavinia's shabby coat.

The woman blushed. 'Thank you, Mrs Hartlebury. You're too kind.'

Kitty gathered up Mrs Craven's fancy china festive plates and followed the other two women out of the hall. She wondered where Mrs Craven had gone. No doubt she would expect Kitty to deliver her crockery to her house.

Lavinia said her farewells and started off down the cobbled slope towards a thin man in a cap standing nearby surrounded by a group of children.

'Bless his heart, he always comes to meet her,' Mrs Hartlebury said, her gaze travelling in the same direction as Kitty's.

The children surrounded their mother, and she delved into her coat pocket to distribute the biscuits that Mrs Hartlebury had saved for the family.

'She seems a good mother,' Kitty said as the little family turned to walk into the town towards the river.

'Heart of gold,' Mrs Hartlebury said. 'And loves those kiddies and that man of hers more'n life itself.'

Kitty watched the little family walking away. The youngest child holding his mother's hand. A cold shiver ran along her spine as she realised that William Crabtree's right hand was heavily bandaged. Had he hurt it pulling out a tree stump? Or was it a poker-inflicted injury?

She barely heard Mrs Hartlebury wishing her a merry Christmas as she said goodbye. Her thoughts were whirling in a jumble in her mind. If it had been William Crabtree looking around his late father's old home, then what had he been looking for?

Mrs Craven's plates slipped in her leather-gloved hand bringing her sharply back to reality. If those plates landed on the cobbles and broke she would never hear the end of it. She secured them more firmly in her grip and made her way slowly towards her car.

Dora answered the door of Mrs Craven's house at the first fall of the door knocker.

'Mrs Bryant, I'm afraid the missus isn't home just yet,' she said on seeing Kitty on the step.

'That's all right. I called to return her plates. Thank you for the lovely baking, by the way. It was greatly appreciated.' Kitty handed the china over to the maid.

Dora's cheeks flushed with pleasure. 'Thank you, that's right nice of you to say so.'

'I thought I should bring these back straight away in case of accidents. I was washing up with Mrs Lavinia Crabtree, the daughter-in-law of the man who went missing at Midwinter Farm,' Kitty said.

'I heard he had been found at Mr Potter and Miss Miller's new house. Terrible thing, although not too surprising I suppose since no one had heard of him after all this time.' Dora clicked her tongue.

'Do you know much about his son, William?' Kitty asked. She knew Dora knew most people in Kingswear and Dartmouth. Since Lavinia had said William was a gardener and handyman it seemed sensible to think Dora might know more about the family.

'He's different from his father. A quiet sort of a chap. Never been very healthy, does bits of gardening and such. Lavinia is the one who keeps them all together. She takes in washing, hard-working girl she is.' Dora shivered as she spoke, and Kitty suddenly became conscious that she was keeping the maid on the doorstep.

'Thank you, Dora. I'm sorry to keep you out here in this beastly cold. I'd better be off before Matt wonders where I've gone.' Kitty said goodbye and drove back to Churston in a thoughtful mood.

CHAPTER FOURTEEN

Robert and Alice arrived promptly at Kitty's house at three thirty. Robert, smart in his grey Sunday best suit and navy tie, looked apprehensive. Alice was in a neat pale-green coloured two piece which she had designed and made herself. Her auburn hair was confined in a neat bun and her eyes wide in her pale face.

'Let me give you a hand with the sandwiches,' Alice said as she followed Kitty into the kitchen.

'Borrow Mrs Smith's apron then, your clothes are too lovely to get jam or meat paste on them,' Kitty said.

Robert had accompanied Matt into the sitting room and Kitty could hear the low rumble of masculine voices as they talked. Bertie had naturally joined Kitty and Alice in the kitchen with the hope of a tasty treat falling his way from the tabletop.

'I hope as this Mr Pettifor can tell us some good things about the house,' Alice said as she carefully cut the crusts from the sandwiches and placed the dainty triangles on the tiered china stand.

'I'm sure he will. He sounded very pleasant on the telephone,' Kitty said.

'I don't know, what with whoever that man was that tried getting into the house and a body in the grounds. It just keeps playing over and over on my mind.' Alice shrugged her shoulders unhappily.

'I think I may know who it was that tried to peer in through the letter box,' Kitty said as she finished preparing the last of the savoury goods.

'Oh? Was it somebody from the newspapers like the inspector thought?' Alice asked, her attention clearly caught by Kitty's words.

'No, I believe it may have been Thomas Crabtree's son, William.' Kitty added a few slices of pork pie to the stand. She told her friend everything she had discovered at church that morning as they set the dining table with a pretty embroidered festive tablecloth and napkins.

'But what would he have been doing up there? After all this time?' Alice asked as she placed the teacups on their saucers and arranged the milk jug and sugar bowl.

'I don't know but I intend to try and find out,' Kitty said.

'But he couldn't have killed his father, could he? You said his wife told you he was on death's door in bed when his father disappeared.' Alice stood back from the table to admire their handiwork.

'That's true. Chief Inspector Greville said the same thing. Unless, of course, Lavinia was lying to cover for him.' Kitty frowned and placed her decorated yule log centrepiece on the table to give their tea the finishing touch.

'I suppose that's possible. Do you think she was telling you the truth?' Alice asked as she untied her apron.

'She seemed to be. She was certainly very frank about her dislike of her father-in-law.' Kitty also removed her own apron, and they went back to the kitchen to fill the kettle and warm the teapot ready for Mr Pettifor's arrival.

'Robert's being very good about all of this, but I know he's as worried as I am really. I don't mean he's superstitious but if there are people prowling about the farm, what if they set fire to the sheds or damage his coaches?' The frown on Alice's forehead deepened.

'I don't think that would be the case. I just wonder if perhaps there is something in this story about the stolen jewellery. Perhaps they believe it's hidden on the farm somewhere. Finding Thomas Crabtree's body could have stirred up speculation,' Kitty suggested.

'That's what our Betty said. You know she was in service with the Masseys at the time. She were barely fourteen though, like young Rose who works for me. It was her first job. I was only a nipper back then.'

There was a knock at the front door and Alice immediately started to smooth down her skirt and tweak her top. Matt went to the front door to greet their guest, showing him into the hall and taking his hat and coat.

Once he was in the sitting room, Kitty and Alice went to join Robert and Matt. Mr Pettifor was a small rotund gentleman in his late sixties. His grey flannel waistcoat strained slightly at the buttons and he had a cream rosebud in his lapel. He took a seat after shaking hands with them all.

'Well, this is most delightful, if unexpected. What a charming home you have, Mrs Bryant.' Mr Pettifor beamed at Kitty while Bertie investigated the newcomer's shoelaces. 'A spaniel. I used to have a couple of those. Wonderful gundogs but remarkably inattentive when they choose.'

Mr Pettifor didn't seem to mind Bertie, and Kitty immediately warmed to her guest. The kettle whistled in the kitchen and Alice excused herself to go and make the tea.

'Thank you for accepting our invitation, sir,' Matt said. 'My friend Mr Potter here and his fiancée Alice have purchased Midwinter Farm.'

'So I believe. A jolly good purchase, a very solid building if in need of some restoration,' Mr Pettifor said just as Alice returned to the room.

Robert appeared relieved to hear the land agent's opinion of the farm. 'My fiancée is naturally worried about the history of the place given the recent discovery of Mr Crabtree's body. We were hoping you could tell us more of the history of the place and your recollections of what happened when Mr Crabtree disappeared,' Robert said.

'It would give me some peace of mind.' Alice slipped her hand into Robert's.

'Well, let us all go through to the dining room and have some tea and then perhaps, Mr Pettifor, you could tell us what you can recall,' Matt suggested.

Once they had all seated themselves at the table and tea had been served, Alice raised the first question.

'Had Thomas Crabtree held the tenancy of Midwinter Farm for long?' she asked as she arranged her sandwiches on her plate.

'I think he was there for five years altogether. Before that the tenancy was held by the Davies family. They lived there for a long time, his father had the farm before him. Mr Davies sadly lost both his sons in the Great War and when his wife passed away, he no longer had the heart to stay. His health wasn't good, arthritis I believe, and farming is a hard job. He went to reside with his sister in Tiverton, I think.' Mr Pettifor had filled his own plate with food and appeared to be enjoying himself enormously.

Alice's expression lightened a little on hearing that her home had once been a settled family place.

'How did Thomas get the tenancy?' Robert asked. 'There's usually a lot of competition for farms, or so I've heard.'

Mr Pettifor nodded, his cheeks bulging like a happy hamster. He chewed and swallowed before replying. 'Indeed, however Lord Massey always made it a priority to give tenancies to local men and veterans. The Masseys lost their youngest son, Bertram, in the Great War and were very empathetic to others who had suffered. Thomas Crabtree fulfilled both of those criteria and had the money for the deposit and first quarter rent.'

Kitty glanced at Matt when Mr Pettifor said that Thomas Crabtree had been a veteran.

'Did he move there alone, or did he have family when he took the farm on?' Kitty asked, helping herself to a fruit scone from the stand.

Mr Pettifor frowned as he tried to recollect who had moved to the farm initially. 'Thomas was a widower, his late wife had died a few months earlier. I think the deposit was money from an insurance policy. His son, William, was there but he moved out after two years to marry Lavinia. The daughter also left to get married.'

'Oh, I didn't know there was a daughter,' Kitty said. No one had mentioned that William had a sister.

'Yes, a lovely girl, the daughter. She married a man from Ireland, and they returned there. It was rather tragic as she died in childbirth about six months before Thomas disappeared. Her demise was partly why we didn't issue eviction notices sooner. Lord Massey was a very good man. He had a kindly disposition,' Mr Pettifor said, before taking a sip of his tea.

'So, Mr Crabtree was to be evicted?' Alice said.

'Yes, my dear. That was why I had gone to the farm that day. We had been unhappy for some time. The rent was late, the land not being tended properly. The property not being kept up. Then, of course, there were incidents in the village. We had strict behaviour rules written into the tenancy agreements.

Lord Massey was anxious that his tenants should be respectable and well regarded.'

Kitty could see why Thomas Crabtree would have failed in all of those criteria. 'I see. Did he know his livelihood and home were at risk?'

'Oh yes, he had been given several warnings. I believe any other landowner would have evicted him much sooner.' Mr Pettifor selected another slice of Christmas cake from the stand.

'It must have been quite shocking for you to discover the farm abandoned,' Matt observed.

'It was. The dogs' water dishes were quite empty when I entered the yard. I knocked at the front door with no reply, so I went around the back. My thought was to obtain water for the dogs if Thomas was out on the land. There is an old well in the orchard. The back door was slightly ajar, so I knocked and called Crabtree's name. Obviously I didn't get a reply, so I pushed the door open thinking it was odd. It was a cold dreary day, and I realised there had been no smoke coming from the chimney as I had approached.'

Kitty saw Alice shiver and look anxiously at Robert as Mr Pettifor recalled what had happened that day.

'The fire was out, and the inside of the house was freezing cold. The table in the kitchen had supper half eaten, the knife and fork left on the plate and half a cup of tea still there as if he had just popped out for a minute. Except it had to have been longer than that for the fire to be out. I called out and went upstairs. I thought perhaps he had been taken ill, pneumonia or something. Everything upstairs was in its place. His razor in the bathroom, his clothes in his room. Nothing appeared out of place at all except Mr Crabtree was missing.' The crease that had formed on Mr Pettifor's forehead deepened.

'What did you do next?' Kitty asked.

'I then thought that maybe he had gone out to some emergency and might be lying injured someplace on the farm. I went back downstairs to fill the dogs' bowls with water and to give them some biscuits I found in the pantry. I realised then that the coat and cap Crabtree usually wore were still on a hook on the back of the kitchen door. Once I'd seen to the dogs, I went out and up to the highest point to look over the fields. It being winter the land was bare, and most trees and hedges had lost their leaves, so it was easy to see the lie of the land. I could see no sign of him anywhere, so I went off to find a telephone. I had to go to a house just off the hill going down to Kingswear. Then I telephoned the police and Lord Massey to let them know what I'd found.'

'I see,' Matt said.

Kitty thought the former land agent's account tallied well with what Chief Inspector Greville had told them and what they had seen in the reports.

'The police came and obviously I told them what had happened. They searched the farm and the grounds but could find no trace of the man. The weather was appalling by then, torrential rain and mist. There was still a small sum of change on top of the mantelpiece and nothing seemed to have been taken.' Mr Pettifor paused and looked at Alice. 'I hope this is not distressing to you? There was no clue that he might have been killed. Nothing gory or horrid anywhere in the house or outside. I suppose I assumed that perhaps he might have been overcome in some way and either met with an accident or perhaps done away with himself and we had not found him. There are a lot of wild places around there.' Mr Pettifor shook his head sadly.

'No, not at all. It's very helpful and it was nice to know that Midwinter Farm had been a loved and happy place in the past,' Alice reassured him.

'It was indeed, my dear. The Davies family were very happy there and it always had a very homely feel,' Mr Pettifor assured her.

'May I ask, Mr Pettifor, we discovered Mr Crabtree in the ruins of the old piggery. The stone wall had partially collapsed. Was it in use when he disappeared?' Matt asked.

'Not for pigs, no. Mrs Davies used to raise a couple of piglets a year in there for meat years ago. It was in a perilous state then. No, it was already going to rack and ruin when Mr Davies left but Crabtree had his chicken coop in there,' Mr Pettifor explained.

Kitty looked at Matt. If chickens had been kept there then Crabtree could have been lured from the farm by someone disturbing the hens. The farmer may have thought there was a fox, but then he would surely have taken his gun out with him.

Matt's thoughts were clearly running on the same lines as her own.

'Did Mr Crabtree own a shotgun?' he asked.

Mr Pettifor's brows rose. 'Why, yes, he did but the thing was he'd had it confiscated a few days before after a huge drunken row down in the village. Words had been said and there was some pushing and shoving. Arthur Maldon, the pub landlord, banned Crabtree from the premises. Crabtree went to his cart and produced his gun, waving it around. A shot was fired into the air and the constable took it from him. Told him he was going to hang on to it and he would have to go before the magistrates to see about getting it back. I discovered all this later when the police came to see Lord Massey.'

This was all news to Kitty. No mention had been made anywhere in the reports about Crabtree having his gun confiscated. That must have been a big thing for a farmer.

'Oh dear, it sounds as if Mr Crabtree had a great many enemies,' Kitty said.

'I don't doubt it, Mrs Bryant. He even treated his son very poorly. The lad was gravely ill at the time he disappeared, and I heard that he had borrowed money the family could not afford to lend, then refused to pay it back. Lavinia was ill herself and their eldest was only a few months old. I understand the church took up a collection for them and saved them from eviction. Lavinia comes from a poor but respectable family, and they tried their best to assist them.'

'I take it there was no sign that you noticed of the ground being disturbed in the old piggery?' Matt asked.

Alice bit her lip and Robert looked troubled.

'No, there was nothing. The ground was muddy and churned up. It was a wet autumn leading into winter. I suppose too that one good push on those old stone walls would have easily collapsed more rubble on top of any disturbed soil. No one imagined that he could have been buried there.' Mr Pettifor looked apologetically at Alice.

'No, I suppose they wouldn't. It certainly stirred up a lot of attention in the newspapers at the time,' Kitty said.

'Oh yes, it was quite the nine days' wonder. People comparing it to those poor missing souls from the *Mary Celeste*. One journalist tried to have a medium come to the farmhouse to do a séance. Lord Massey was livid and banished the lot of them. He'd not been happy with them since the theft of the family jewels and silver a few weeks before. He said they asked intrusive questions and tried to make out the robberies were an inside job. All nonsense, of course. There had been a number of thefts from high-class houses in the area. The police felt a London gang may have been involved,' Mr Pettifor said.

'Really? We had heard that people whispered that Thomas Crabtree had been involved in some way,' Matt said.

'I believe that was the rumour after he vanished. As a land agent I talked to a good many people as I visited the farms and cottages. The story I heard was that he was what was known locally as a "bagman". Someone who held on to any stolen goods until the heat had died down and then later received a cut of the proceeds for his trouble. He didn't steal himself nor did he sell any stolen goods. He merely minded them for a time,' Mr Pettifor explained.

Kitty shifted uncomfortably in her seat. It sounded all too like the kind of things her own father, Edgar Underhay, had served time for in the past. Unlike Thomas Crabtree, however, her father had never engaged in any kind of violence or threatening behaviour. Usually, he simply charmed people into giving him things or doing him favours.

'What happened after Thomas Crabtree vanished? To the farm, I mean? It was let again, wasn't it?' Alice asked.

'It was, my dear. A couple of gentlemen took it on. A Mr Warrender was the first tenant. He had quite a struggle trying to turn a profit. The economy was not good, and Crabtree had let the land go to rack and ruin. He gave it up and a Mr Horsely took it on. He did his best, but I don't believe he was cut out for the farming life. When he too gave up the lease it was just as I was due to retire. Lord Massey passed away unexpectedly, and Lady Massey needed money to pay death duties. She was also not minded to keep so large an estate. The loss of her youngest son had stayed with her and her eldest, Lord Massey's heir, Algernon, spends most of his time in London. That's why the farm went to auction.' Mr Pettifor looked kindly at Alice. 'It really is a very solid investment, my dear, and apart from Crabtree it was a lively, happy home for many years. I have no doubt that you and your fiancé will return it to that happy state once more.'

Kitty sincerely hoped he was right.

CHAPTER FIFTEEN

Mr Pettifor took his leave shortly after tea was finished. Robert and Alice also left as they had promised to visit Alice's parents to allay her mother's concerns about the house.

'Thank you for asking Mr Pettifor to tea. He seems such a nice man and my mind feels a bit easier now. I just hope as I can calm Mother down. She's been having conniptions ever since she heard about Mr Crabtree's body being found,' Alice said as Kitty showed her friend and her fiancé out.

'I'm sure Robert will help you to reassure her.' Kitty kissed her friend's cheek and waved them off from the step.

Once their guests were gone, Matt helped Kitty to clear the table. They then set about washing all of the crockery so that Mrs Smith would arrive to a clean and tidy kitchen early the next morning.

'Phew, that was a lot of information.' Kitty handed her husband a tea towel.

'It certainly was. Mr Pettifor appeared a nice gentleman and at least now Alice feels a little happier knowing the history of their house,' Matt agreed as he waited for Kitty to wash the first of the plates.

'It's all so strange though, don't you think? The way this business about the jewel thefts keeps cropping back up.' Kitty looked thoughtful as she plunged the delicate teacups into the sudsy water.

'It's hard to know after all these years if that's something that may have become muddled up with Thomas Crabtree's disappearance simply because the two events were close together. Plus, our Mr Crabtree was known to be a wrong'un and neither case has been solved.' Matt dried the saucers and stacked them neatly back on the shelf in the dresser.

'I see what you mean. At least we know the background more fully now about why Crabtree was not discovered straight away or in subsequent years. It's only since Robert acquired the farm and started to clear that area ready for the siting of the telegraph pole. If he hadn't done that it may have been a lot longer before anything came to light. I don't suppose anyone had cause to move anything there before.' Kitty placed another pile of clean crockery on the small draining board.

'No, the subsequent tenants obviously left everything as it was. I'd like to know what William Crabtree was doing though prowling around the farm and peering in through the letter box. There seems little doubt in my mind that it was him. Mr Pettifor said he had left home some eighteen months to two years before his father vanished. Then there has been ten years of other tenants in the house as well as other short vacant spells. So why now? What was he looking for?' Matt frowned and clinked the cups together drawing a look from Kitty.

'Don't break my china. Those were a wedding present from your parents,' she reproved.

'Sorry.' Matt grinned at her as he apologised.

'I don't know. The only thought I had is that Robert has been renovating the place and somehow that might be why,' Kitty suggested.

They completed the clearing up and retired to the cosy warmth of the sitting room, setting thoughts of the puzzle to one side. Rascal curled up beside the fire and Bertie settled at Kitty's feet. Matt switched on the radio as there was a concert they both wished to hear. Kitty relaxed in her chair and Matt resumed the final clues in his crossword.

* * *

They had only been settled for about an hour when there was a knock at the front door. Matt put his paper aside and went to see who was there. He hadn't heard any voices so he thought it was unlikely to be carol singers.

Instead, when he opened the door he discovered Chief Inspector Greville on the step.

'I do hope I'm not intruding, but something has occurred today which I thought you should know about.' The chief inspector's expression was grave under the shadow cast by the brim of his hat.

'No, not at all, come inside. It's bitter out there.' Matt ushered him into the hall to take his outdoor things. The evening air was icy and tendrils of mist had curled around the policeman when he had been on the step. 'Go through to the sitting room.' Matt hung up the chief inspector's hat, coat and scarf.

Bertie let out a lazy woof followed by the steady thump of his tail in welcome as Chief Inspector Greville entered the room.

'Chief Inspector, good evening.' Kitty switched off the radio as the policeman took a seat on the end of the sofa.

'Can we get you a drink? Some refreshments? We have some sandwiches in the pantry,' Kitty offered.

The chief inspector looked tired, Matt thought.

'That would be most kind, Mrs Bryant. I must admit I haven't stopped since about eleven o'clock this morning.'

Kitty gave a slightly alarmed look at Matt and went back to the kitchen to prepare a plate and a hot drink for the chief inspector.

Matt waited until Kitty returned bearing a loaded tray of supper which she placed on the policeman's lap before asking any questions.

'Now, do tuck in, Chief Inspector. You look exhausted.' Kitty's voice held a note of concern as she retook her seat beside the fire opposite Matt.

'We were called late this morning to an incident at Totnes. A resident had reported hearing a man and a woman quarrelling loudly near their house. They reported hearing screams and then a splash. An hour later, another resident reported seeing what appeared to be a woman's body caught up in the reeds near the riverbank. The local police there attended, and it was discovered after a while that the dead woman was Tilly Maldon. She had been throttled and shoved into the Dart.' Chief Inspector Greville paused to take a large bite of his sandwich.

Bertie, who had changed his position to sit with his nose near the chief inspector's knee, looked hopeful at this break in case a sliver of pork pie might land his way.

'Tilly Maldon?' Kitty looked at the chief inspector.

'It took a little time to determine her identity as being a person of interest in the Crabtree case. She was well known to the local constabulary in Totnes but there she went by Tilly Swann. She was a lady of the night,' Chief Inspector Greville explained.

'I see. That explains why she was hard to trace,' Matt agreed.

'It was assumed at first that the quarrel that had been heard could have been Tilly arguing with one of her customers. It was only when one of the constables who had known her from her time in Dartmouth confirmed that she was in fact Tilly Maldon that we were called.' Chief Inspector Greville picked up his tea, wrapping his hands around the cup as if to warm himself up.

Matt saw Kitty shiver as if a chill had run along her spine.

'We are still trying to track down her father to complete the formal identification of her body. There is no doubt that it's her though. I recognised her when I saw her. A sad end.' The chief inspector shook his head in sorrow.

'Did anyone else see or hear anything that could identify who may have attacked her?' Kitty asked.

'We've been interviewing people all day. There weren't many people around in that part of town.' Chief Inspector Greville took a large draught of his tea, smacking his lips as he placed the cup back on the tray.

'Do you think her death is connected to the Crabtree murder?' Matt asked.

'It's hard to be absolutely certain but it seems a rum coincidence that she's killed now just after his body has been discovered.' The chief inspector took pity on Bertie and allowed him a tiny crumb of Scotch egg.

'That's true.' Kitty seemed to be thinking about what the policeman had just told them.

'Did the person who overheard the quarrel hear anything that could lead to the identification of the killer?' Matt asked. There was something about the chief inspector's demeanour and his sudden arrival at their house that made him think there was more to the story.

The policeman dabbed the ends of his moustache with the linen napkin Kitty had provided and put the now empty tray aside. Bertie subsided with a huff of disappointment as the chief inspector pulled out his trusty notebook.

He flicked through the pages until he reached the one he wanted. 'The witness says he heard rising voices as if the couple were drawing closer to his house. His cottage is situated beside the river. Only a footpath separates it from the water, but the building is side on, so to speak. There is only the landing window that overlooks the path. The voices grew closer and he became aware it was a quarrel.' He broke off to clear his throat before continuing. 'Do excuse me, a crumb of your housekeeper's most excellent pork pie. Now, the witness said he heard a woman's voice say, "I know as you done it. You thought he had done you down." The man then said something like, "You know nothing and had better say nothing." By this stage the couple had moved further along the path, so the next sound was that of a woman screaming and a loud splash as if something or someone had gone into the water. The witness rushed out of his house onto the path to see if he could see anyone. He obviously feared the worst. The path was empty at this point. There are several tracks there that lead into the alleys of the town,' the chief inspector explained.

'That was when he reported it to the police?' Kitty asked.

'Yes, he met one of the constables patrolling the town centre, and they headed back towards his home and looked together. Of course, the current had carried her downstream a little way by then until she was caught in the reeds. The tide is quite high at this point in the year when there's been a lot of rain on the moors. She was caught up by some tree roots. Otherwise, she would have been carried much further down and possibly out into the estuary,' Chief Inspector Greville said.

'And shortly after this first incident someone else spotted her body?' Matt asked.

'That's correct.' Chief Inspector Greville closed up his notebook and tucked it back inside the breast pocket of his jacket.

'The content of that conversation is certainly most suggestive in the light of recent events,' Matt said. He knew it didn't definitely connect Tilly's death to Crabtree's murder, but it certainly increased the possibility of a link.

'Inspector Lewis has increased his efforts to find Arthur Maldon and he has taken in Fred Smith once more for questioning,' Chief Inspector Greville said.

'I suppose that is sensible. It will be interesting to see if he has an alibi for this morning,' Matt said.

'Then there is William Crabtree,' Kitty added. 'He was not in church this morning so far as I know. Lavinia was assisting us with the tea after the service, and he came to meet her at midday with the children. His hand is bandaged, and I believe he may have been the man I hit with the poker when whoever it was tried the doors of the farm.'

'If his hand is injured though, he is less likely to have been able to choke Tilly Maldon to death. I imagine she would have put up a fight,' Chief Inspector Greville said. 'I take your point, however, Mrs Bryant. He may be working in collusion with others.'

Kitty appeared relieved that the chief inspector was prepared to consider her suggestion.

'There is one other thing. Joshua Payne's ship has docked. He disembarked at 06.00 yesterday morning,' Chief Inspector Greville said.

Matt's brow rose at this. That was plenty of time for Payne to have arrived back at his mother's home. No doubt there would be a good many people eager to inform him of the discovery of his old enemy's body. But then what? Where did Tilly Maldon fit into it all?

'I assume Inspector Lewis will also be interviewing Mr Payne?' Kitty asked.

'He is on our list,' Chief Inspector Greville confirmed.

* * *

Kitty carried the chief inspector's empty tray back into the kitchen while Matt offered the policeman a tot of whisky. She was glad of a few minutes alone to clear up and to work through what they had just been told.

What had the murderer thought Tilly had meant? It had sounded as if the murder was connected to Crabtree and that Tilly had known who had killed him. It had also sounded as if the motive for Crabtree's murder might have been connected to the jewel thefts. The reference to being 'done down' suggested that Crabtree had once again swindled someone. Then again, if it were Joshua Payne or even William Crabtree then she could have been referring to the money both men were reportedly owed.

She went back into the sitting room still mulling everything over in her mind. The chief inspector, having declined the whisky, was preparing to take his leave.

'Thank you for your hospitality, Mrs Bryant. It's most appreciated. I had better get off or Mrs Greville will be concerned.' The chief inspector rose and headed for the hall.

Matt followed after him to hand him his coat and hat. 'Thank you for keeping us informed on the case, sir. We appreciate it. I know Alice and Robert do too.'

'Not at all. I am anxious to get this business resolved. I dislike having an unsolved case on my record even though I was only a sergeant back then. Let's hope we can get to the bottom of the whole thing soon.' Chief Inspector Greville put on his hat and tucked his thick dark-blue woollen scarf around his neck. 'I'll keep you abreast of any further developments. If you learn anything new please make me or Inspector Lewis aware.'

Kitty and Matt agreed and waved the chief inspector off as he trudged out into the bitter cold mist to his car.

'Brr,' Kitty shivered as the door was closed, and she was glad to scuttle back to the warm comfort of her fireside.

'That was quite a turn up for the books.' Matt dropped back down in his favourite armchair.

'What did Tilly know? And is it connected to Thomas Crabtree's murder?' Kitty asked as Bertie resettled himself near her feet.

'I'm not certain. It may well be connected. It certainly appears that way to me. The timing of her murder may be coincidental but we both know not to trust coincidences in these kinds of cases,' Matt said.

'That's true. The other thing is do we tell Robert and Alice about Tilly's death?' Kitty asked.

Her friend had seemed much happier after tea with Mr Pettifor. It would be awful to start her fretting again.

'The newspapers probably won't report the murder until the police locate her father and tell him what's happened. Chief Inspector Greville and the other constable have provided the identification for the coroner. The papers may even report it using the name she was living under. What was it again?' He looked at Kitty.

'Tilly Swann. I wonder why she chose that as her name?' Kitty mused.

'To preserve her reputation in other places perhaps? She may have wanted to keep her lifestyle from her father. Or she may have married or been living with a man called Swann at some point and taken his name,' Matt said.

'So do you think it better not to say anything to Alice for now, until we know more?' Kitty asked.

She disliked the idea of keeping something from her friend. However, she had no wish to unsettle Alice if it turned out that Tilly's demise wasn't anything to do with Thomas Crabtree's murder.

'I'll tell Robert if you like and discuss it with him. We can always let Alice know when we find out if her death is connected to Crabtree's murder,' Matt suggested.

Kitty nodded. Robert could decide if he thought Alice would wish to know right away or if they should wait. It seemed to her that Alice should and would be told, the question was when would be the most opportune time. They just had to hope that Inspector Lewis didn't say anything to Betty in the meantime about the case.

CHAPTER SIXTEEN

Kitty was still turning everything over in her mind the next morning when her housekeeper arrived to begin the week's work.

'Good morning, Mrs Bryant.' Mrs Smith had already started preparing breakfast by the time Kitty got downstairs. Bertie and Rascal had both been fed and attended to and the scent of bacon and coffee was in the air.

'Good morning.' Kitty could see that the mist from yesterday had cleared and the grass beneath the apple tree was dusted white with frost.

It occurred to Kitty that Mrs Smith might know something of Tilly's history since Fred Smith had once courted the young woman. She tried to keep from under the housekeeper's feet while thinking of a way to broach the subject.

'Is there something as you want, Mrs Bryant? I've placed the orders for the Christmas groceries so that's all in hand.' Mrs Smith looked enquiringly at her as Kitty hovered in the kitchen doorway.

'No, well, yes. I suppose so. Oh dear, that sounds dreadfully muddled. Yesterday evening the chief inspector called here at the house. He had some bad news about a woman called Tilly Maldon. I think you mentioned that your disreputable relation used to court her back when Thomas Crabtree disappeared,' Kitty said.

'Oh yes?' Mrs Smith continued to keep her attention on the frying pan, expertly cracking two fat brown-shelled eggs into the sizzling fat. 'I wouldn't be surprised if you were to tell me as she'd come to a bad end.'

'I'm afraid that is exactly what has happened. Did you know her then?' Kitty asked.

'I met her once or twice when I caught the ferry and she was hanging about after Fred. That was a good many years ago, mind you. She'd only be about seventeen or eighteen. Very pretty she was in a commonplace sort of way.' Mrs Smith lifted the bacon out of the pan to crisp while she finished frying the eggs.

'Why did you think she would come to no good?' Kitty was curious to find out more. 'Had you seen her or heard anything of her since then?'

'Well, for a start she was hanging after Fred, which no respectable lass would ever do. There was always something a bit knowing about her. Her father didn't have the best of reputations neither and she'd been brought up in public houses with just him to look after her, poor lass. Then after Crabtree went missing and Fred was questioned, she seemed to cool things with him. Not long after that I heard that her father took over the running of another public house. I heard a bit of gossip in the town as she was always with a different man.' Mrs Smith slid the eggs into a dish ready for the table and started on the toast.

'She was murdered yesterday in Totnes. The police said she'd been living under the name Tilly Swann,' Kitty said.

'Tilly Swann, hmm, yes, that was a name as she went by when she wanted to be on the stage. She wanted to be an actress at one time, Fred reckoned as she could sing too. I'd forgotten all about that. Like I said I haven't seen or heard nothing of her for about six years now.' Mrs Smith cut the toast and placed it in the chrome-plated toast rack just as Matt came down the stairs.

Kitty helped carry the breakfast things through into the dining room while Bertie trotted back and forth clearly hoping some bacon might find its way under the table. The house-keeper wished Matt a good morning and returned to the kitchen to allow them to eat their breakfast.

'You look very thoughtful,' Matt observed as he placed his linen napkin across his knees and helped himself to bacon.

'I was asking Mrs Smith what she could recall of Tilly Maldon. She said Tilly had aspirations to be an actress and that Swann was a stage name.' Kitty told him everything Mrs Smith had said while she poured her coffee and added marmalade to her toast.

'Well, that's one question answered.' Matt added one of the eggs to his plate and started to eat.

'And dozens more still unanswered,' Kitty said. 'I feel so stuck at the moment. I feel as if we should be doing something to try and solve this case, but the police seem to have all the angles covered and we are not party to anything they discover.' It really was most frustrating. It was good of Chief Inspector Greville to keep them informed but she longed to be out, talking to people and trying to put the pieces together herself.

'I know what you mean. Perhaps we should leave the murder to the police for now and focus our attention on the jewel thefts. It would be useful if we could prove or disprove a link between the two,' Matt suggested.

Kitty immediately brightened up. 'You clever old thing. Yes, you're right. I wonder who we could speak to about those.'

'Betty said she joined Lord Massey's household shortly after the thefts. She would know the names of some of the staff at the house. Perhaps we could track some of them down and see what they recall.' Matt smiled at Kitty's enthusiasm.

'Betty usually has Mondays off. She will probably be at home. We could call there after we finish breakfast. She is not an early riser when she doesn't have work so I daresay we will find her in.' Kitty started to feel much more positive now they had something to work on.

They drove across the river into Dartmouth and parked near Betty's parents' home on the opposite side of town to the Dolphin Hotel. Here the houses were a jumble of whitewashed cottages that led up the hillside, linked by steep alleyways.

When Betty had left her last service post to go and work for Alice she had moved back to live with her parents. Since she was an only child and the apple of their eyes this was not an unwelcome move. Betty's parents' house was a neat white cottage in the centre of a row with a holly wreath fastened to the door. Kitty raised a leather-gloved hand and rapped the polished-brass door knocker.

After a minute or two Betty answered, dressed in a smart blue dress and standing sleepy-eyed in the doorway.

'Kitty, Matt, this is a surprise. What brings you here? Is Alice all right?' Alarm flitted across her pretty face.

'Alice is fine. This is about another matter that we thought you might be able to assist us with,' Kitty said.

Relief replaced panic on the girl's face and she invited them into the house. 'Come inside. You had me worried for a minute there.'

'We're sorry about that. We've been thinking about what you told us at Doctor and Mrs Carter's dinner party the other evening,' Matt said as Betty showed them into a tiny front parlour room which Kitty suspected was kept for best.

Christmas cards jostled for space on the crowded mantelpiece alongside various pieces of Staffordshire china shepherdesses. Silver-framed photographs of Betty at various stages of her childhood were grouped on the many highly polished tables. A small Christmas tree stood on a crimson velvet clothed table in the window and the air smelt of pine and beeswax.

'Oh, what was that then?' Betty asked as she perched on one of the overstuffed chenille-covered armchairs.

'You said your first job was at Lord and Lady Massey's house and you were there just after the robbery. The one where the jewels were stolen and the silver,' Kitty said.

'That's right. I was fresh out of school, just turned fourteen. It was still the talk of the servants' hall when I started. The Masseys had offered a big reward, but no one hadn't come forward,' Betty said.

'Do you know which staff were in the house when the robbery occurred?' Matt asked.

Betty's brow crinkled. 'The Masseys were away in London and had took their valet and Lady Massey's maid and... oh and the governess with them. If I remember right there was only the butler, old Mr Hodgett, and Mrs Clark the cook in the house. The maids lived out then and the gardeners obviously had cottages nearby. Mrs Clark was as deaf as a post, so she wouldn't have heard nothing. Mr Hodgett claimed as he didn't hear nothing neither. He said as he found the safe open and the silver missing the next morning.'

'Wasn't there a rumour that the robbery could have been an inside job? Do you know if the police believed the staff?' Matt asked.

'Well, they was both still working for the Masseys when I went there so I suppose they must have been telling the truth, or they'd have given them their cards. They was both very respectable people and good to me. I don't know how it could have been an inside job. One of the gardeners told me as the glass had been broke on the back door to the scullery and that's how they got in. I don't know how they managed to crack the safe though. I was only a kid when I was there.' Betty gave an apologetic shrug.

'Do you know if Mr Hodgett still lives locally? I presume he is retired from service now that Lady Massey lives mostly in London?' Kitty asked.

'Yes, he lives just down the road from you in one of the workers' cottages near the windmill on the far side of the common. Lady Massey gave him a life tenancy when he left her service. He'd been with them for forty years. I saw him not long ago in town and spoke to him,' Betty said.

Kitty thought that if the robbery had been an inside job then Mr Hodgett was an unlikely suspect. The Masseys clearly hadn't blamed him for the robbery. Betty provided a description of which cottage belonged to the former butler.

'Here, does my James... I mean Inspector Lewis know as you're looking into this robbery?' Betty asked suddenly.

Kitty looked at Matt.

'Chief Inspector Greville is aware we are working on Alice and Robert's behalf, and we have his full blessing and permission to find out whatever we can that could help the police,' Matt replied.

'I can see why our Alice is uncomfortable about moving into that house if this murder business doesn't get sorted,' Betty admitted. 'The wedding's not that far away now and it'd be nice if it was all wrapped up by then. Do you think that man's death was to do with this robbery? Is that why you're asking questions about it?'

'We don't know and neither do the police. There may be a connection, or it may just be a story that someone at the time dreamt up,' Matt said.

'Oh well, we all know what gossip can be like around here,' Betty agreed with a slightly superior air.

'Thank you for your help. I know Alice appreciates

everyone who is working on this.' Kitty rose ready to take her leave. Matt followed suit.

Kitty was eager to track down this Mr Hodgett to hear his recollections of the robbery. Perhaps there might be a clue to link it to Mr Crabtree and Tilly Maldon's deaths.

Betty stood too, ready to walk them to the door. 'Well, I hope she does. My James is so busy working on all of this I've hardly seen him except at Doctor Carter's house and one trip to the pictures. I hope as he gets some time off at Christmas. Mother has asked him to dinner.' She smiled as she spoke, her tone vaguely triumphant.

'That sounds lovely. I expect otherwise he would be on his own in his lodgings. His family is all still in Yorkshire I assume?' Kitty said. They had first met Inspector Lewis at her cousin Lucy's wedding in that county.

'That's right, although the chief inspector had asked him to theirs. He went there last year.' Betty led the way to the front door.

'Is it serious then, you and Inspector Lewis?' Kitty asked archly as she stepped out onto the pavement.

'It's early days but I think he might be Mr Right.' Betty blushed as she spoke.

Matt had followed Kitty out and he raised a slightly enquiring eyebrow in Kitty's direction. Kitty had heard this from Betty before about various gentlemen she had courted. Betty had two previous engagements under her belt already that she had ended but she smiled at the girl.

'I do hope so.'

They said goodbye and walked back to Kitty's car, shivering in the icy wind blowing in from the river.

'Back to Churston to track down Mr Hodgett then?' Matt said as she started up the car engine.

'Let us hope he is at home and is willing to talk to us,' Kitty said as she drove towards the ferry once more.

She knew the row of cottages that Betty had been referring to. They bordered the Churston estate and she had always assumed they were part of that manor. According to what Betty had told Matt, Mr Hodgett's cottage was the end one, furthest from the road.

Kitty parked her car, and they climbed out to crunch their way along the narrow dirt track that led to the houses. The cottages were ancient limewashed cob houses with thatched roofs. Each one had a tiny pocket-handkerchief-sized garden out front bordered by a low stone wall. She guessed it probably looked very pretty in summer.

The low front door was situated under a tiny, thatched canopy held up by two thick wooden posts hewn out of tree trunks. A holly wreath with a tartan bow hung from the brass door knocker. Matt rapped on the door, and they waited to see if anyone was at home.

After a moment Kitty thought she detected the sound of shuffling feet on a stone flag floor before the door was cracked open and a small, wizened elderly man peered suspiciously up at them.

'Whatever you're selling I am not buying any,' he said in a quavery voice.

'We aren't selling anything, Mr Hodgett. We came to see if you could help us with some questions about your employment with the Massey family,' Kitty said as Matt produced one of their business cards and handed it to the former butler.

The old man squinted at the card. 'My eyes aren't what they were,' he grumbled.

'We are private investigators based in Torquay. We have been asked to talk to anyone who remembers the theft of some jewels from Lord Massey's home about ten years ago. One of the young maids, Betty, she said you used to be Lord Massey's butler and said you could probably help us,' Kitty said.

'I don't know what I can tell you really. It was a long time ago now and very upsetting,' Mr Hodgett said.

'I can imagine,' Kitty sympathised.

'You've probably not worked in a household with a servants' hall, miss. The gossip and suspicion and upset.' The elderly former butler looked quite distressed, and Kitty was worried he might close the door and refuse to speak to them.

'No, I haven't but my grandmother and I own the Dolphin Hotel in Dartmouth, and our staff are much the same,' she said.

'The Dolphin? Are you Gwen Treadwell's granddaughter? A fine woman your grandmother. You should have said so right away, come in, come in.' Mr Hodgett's demeanour changed immediately to one of welcome and he ushered them inside.

They stepped into a tiny front parlour with a roaring fire in the hearth. The heat hit them as their host invited them to remove their coats and take a seat on the high-backed old-fashioned sofa. A miniature Christmas tree stood on a green-velvet tablecloth surrounded by a handful of Christmas cards.

'You must be Elowed's girl, Kitty?' Mr Hodgett studied her with rheumy eyes. 'My, you look like your mother.'

Since Mr Hodgett appeared to know her and her family Kitty tried to recollect if she had met him before. Nothing sprang to mind, however, as she introduced Matt and assured him of her grandmother's health.

'I used to court your grandmother years ago, before she married your grandfather. A lovely lady, I have such happy memories of her and her friend Millicent,' Mr Hodgett said.

Kitty glanced at Matt. It seemed to her that not only did Mr Hodgett know her grandmother, he also knew Mrs Craven.

'Grams is in Scotland at present for the holidays with her sister, but I'll be sure to remember you to her when she comes back,' Kitty said.

'Thank you, my dear. I recall her sister too, a lovely young lady. May I get you both some tea?' Mr Hodgett looked as if he were about to leap into action.

'No, thank you,' Kitty declined gracefully, not wishing to put their host to any extra work. 'We hoped you could tell us more about the robbery at Seacliffe House. Betty said that there was just yourself and the cook at home at the time. Is that correct?'

'Lord and Lady Massey were away from home. They had gone to London to their house there, taking some of the principal staff who usually lived in. Miss Noon, the governess, Pridmore, the valet, Minette, her ladyship's maid, and Emerson the first footman. The London house only kept a cook there usually and the rest of the staff would travel between the households. Usually, I would have gone too but there was a lot to do to prepare for Christmas and his lordship had commissioned some remedial repairs to the orangery. The other household staff all lived out at the time so there was only the two of us on the premises when the robbery occurred,' Mr Hodgett explained.

'Do you think the burglars knew this? That there would only be the two of you in the house?' Matt asked.

Mr Hodgett frowned as if he hadn't thought of that before. 'I don't know. I suppose they may well have done. It was something the family did every year. They would go to London, take in a show, attend some pre-Christmas parties and concerts, buy presents and then return home.'

'Could you tell us what happened the night of the robbery?' Kitty asked, feeling rather warm in the hot little room.

'Well, the workmen had been and repaired the broken glass and replaced some of the putty in the orangery. I saw them off the premises and cleared up. Then I took supper with Mrs Clark, the cook. We listened to the radio while I cleaned the silver and went through some of the menus with her. We finished around ten o'clock then I made my rounds of the house ensuring the lights were off and the doors and windows all secured. The silverware was locked in my pantry just off the scullery and the jewels were in his lordship's safe in the study. Usually, the Massey tiara would have been in the bank vault but it had been cleaned ready to wear to one of the festive balls. His lordship didn't have time to return it to the vault before leaving for London.' The butler shook his head sorrowfully at the memory.

'Did you hear anything during the night? Betty said that Mrs Clark was quite deaf,' Kitty said. She wished she could open the door since she was beginning to perspire in the heat from the fire.

'Yes, indeed she was, bless her. A most wonderful cook, however, such a delicate hand with a soufflé. No, neither of us heard a thing. We slept at the top of the house you see, so there was a floor between us and where the robbery took place,' Mr Hodgett explained. 'The first thing I knew was at five thirty the next morning when I went downstairs to light the fires and open the door for the maids. That was when I saw the broken glass in the scullery back door.'

CHAPTER SEVENTEEN

'That was how they broke into the house then?' Matt asked.

'Yes, the glass was smashed and then they had reached through to force the lock. The lock to the silver cupboard had also been broken and every piece was gone.' Mr Hodgett's lower lip quivered at what was obviously a traumatic memory. 'I went straight to the safe in the study, fearing the worst. I was horrified to discover my fears confirmed. Some kind of cutting tool had been used along with a crowbar. The door was open and the jewels, including the tiara, were gone. I telephoned the police straight away and then I had the dreadful task of informing Lord and Lady Massey.'

Kitty shifted uncomfortably in her seat as Mr Hodgett produced a crisp, white handkerchief and blew his nose loudly.

'What did the police say when they came?' Matt asked when the elderly man had somewhat recovered himself.

'Oh, they went all over everything with a fine-tooth comb. Asking all the questions, you know, had we heard anything? Seen anything? Who was in the house?' Mr Hodgett sighed and looked downcast.

'It sounds like it was a dreadful ordeal,' Kitty said sympathetically.

'It was, my dear, it was. I blamed myself. I should have heard something or been more alert. Mrs Clark was most distressed too. It took months before her pastry was back to its usual high standard. Lord Massey returned early from London to talk to the police and to deal with the insurance and all of that. At least the family did not hold me or Mrs Clark to blame in any way. Indeed, his lordship was kind enough to say that he was glad we had not heard them and ventured downstairs. We might have been injured or killed. All the same I still feel terrible about it all even to this very day,' Mr Hodgett said.

'I really don't think you should blame yourself at all,' Kitty said. 'It sounds as if you had done everything that was expected of you. It was just unfortunate the robbery happened when it did. It would have been so much worse had the family been home or if someone had been hurt.'

'Thank you, my dear. I believe that is what his lordship felt too,' Mr Hodgett said.

'Did the police find any clues to who may have been responsible?' Matt asked.

Mr Hodgett shook his head. 'A few boot marks, I believe, in the flower bed near the back door. Nothing of use.'

'That's a pity.' Kitty looked at Matt.

'His lordship offered a most generous reward for information leading to the recovery of the jewels or the conviction of the thieves. It made no difference. The jewels have never been recovered or anyone held to account over the robberies,' Mr Hodgett said.

'There were other robberies before then, weren't there? In the local area at other large houses?' Matt said.

'Yes, ours was the last. I believe the police said there had been four others, all using the same method. I rather think they stopped then. Perhaps the thieves thought the police were onto them. I suppose they could have moved on to a different area.' Mr Hodgett looked thoughtful.

'I would have thought the tiara would have been hard to get rid of, even if it was broken down, as it had a number of distinctive stones,' Matt said.

'Indeed, it was most unusual. Queen Victoria herself is said to have admired it,' Mr Hodgett agreed.

'Why do you think there were rumours later about Thomas Crabtree being involved in the robbery in some way? Or that it may have been an inside job?' Matt fidgeted in his seat and Kitty thought her husband was looking a little flushed thanks to the heat in the small room.

'I presume you are referring to that farmer who disappeared? I suppose Mr Crabtree's disappearance occurred only a few weeks after the robbery. I heard his body had recently been recovered at Midwinter Farm. As for it being an inside job, I can't say unless it was because the family were known to be away and there was only myself and the cook in the house that night.' Mr Hodgett suddenly looked alarmed. 'I do hope no one has ever believed that I may have deliberately set out to rob his lordship? Any guilt I feel is over my failure to have heard the miscreants breaking in. At least they didn't steal the guns from the gun cabinet.'

'No, I suppose by an inside job the police may have thought that someone informed the robbers that the house was almost empty or that the tiara had not gone back to the bank, that sort of thing. The Masseys clearly valued your service. Betty said that you had been gifted this cottage for your lifetime,' Kitty hastened to reassure him.

'Yes, indeed, a very thoughtful gesture. I am most comfortable here and Lady Massey always ensures that I have enough coal and wood for the fire.' Mr Hodgett beamed with pride as he surveyed the orange and red flames still leaping in the grate.

'That is very kind of her. We have disturbed you long

enough I fear, and our housekeeper will be expecting us back for lunch.' Kitty shook hands with the former butler and prepared to make her escape from the hot little room.

'It was my pleasure, my dear. Do remember to give my best wishes to your grandmother and her friend too, of course. Perhaps I should take the ladies to tea in the new year?' Mr Hodgett said as they donned their coats and hats once more in the tiny hallway.

'That sounds lovely. I'm sure they would enjoy catching up with you,' Kitty said.

Mr Hodgett waved them off from the front step before disappearing back inside his cottage.

'Oh dear, I am so hot and thirsty now,' Kitty said, sighing with relief as the cold winter air hit her face during the short walk to her car.

'It was a little stuffy in there,' Matt agreed with a grin as she started the engine ready to drive them home.

'I thought I should pass out at one point.' Kitty turned her car around and a couple of minutes later they were back outside their house.

Kitty switched off the ignition and Matt jumped out to open her door for her.

'Captain and Mrs Bryant?' Kitty swung around at the unexpected voice. She clutched at Matt's arm as a familiar-looking man peeled himself from where he had been sheltering from the wind under the beech trees and approached them.

'Fred Smith?' Matt too had clearly recognised the man.

'I came to see you to ask for help, but my aunt shut the door in my face and said to sling my hook as you were out.' He inclined his head towards their house. 'I decided to hang about in case you come back. I'm desperate see.'

Kitty could see the fear in the man's eyes. 'How long have you been waiting?' she asked.

'Over an hour. I walked up here from Brixham and I haven't

got the money for the bus to get back and then come back again. I lost my job on the ferry because the police keep coming after me.'

'Well, I suppose you had better come inside and get warm. You'll catch pneumonia hanging around out here in the wind.' Kitty looked at Matt and he gave a barely discernible nod of approval to her suggestion.

Mrs Smith's expression darkened with disapproval when Matt requested she delay lunch for half an hour and asked for a tray of tea.

'I told him to clear off, Captain Bryant. You be careful, he'll rob you as soon as looks at you.' She glared at her troublesome relative.

'I assure you we shall bear your warning in our minds, Mrs Smith. If you could spare a sandwich for our guest too, I should be most grateful,' Matt asked.

Bertie woofed as Fred sat gingerly on the edge of one of the armchairs.

Kitty took her seat on the sofa while Matt had his usual place near the fire. Rascal jumped up beside Kitty to survey Fred with unblinking green eyes.

'Now, why do you need to speak to us so desperately?' Kitty asked.

Mrs Smith clumped in and placed a tea tray down on the table with a sniff of outrage. A couple of thick cut cheese sandwiches had been added to the tray.

'Thank you, Mrs Smith,' Matt said as their housekeeper stalked back to the kitchen.

Kitty proffered the sandwiches to Fred who fell on them like a man half starved. Which, Kitty reflected, he probably was. She poured the tea and waited for Fred to finish his first sandwich before asking again.

'What can we do for you, Mr Smith?'

Fred looked her squarely in the face. 'I ain't no angel, Mrs Bryant. I've been inside a few times, but I don't want to be hung for something I haven't done.'

'Do you mean the murders of Thomas Crabtree and Tilly Maldon?' Matt asked as he stirred his tea.

Fred nodded miserably. 'That Inspector Lewis is like a dog with a bone. I'd have still been in the cell now if it weren't for the chief inspector saying they hadn't got enough evidence to charge me yet.'

'Perhaps you could tell us why Inspector Lewis believes you are responsible for their deaths? And bear in mind that if you want us to assist you then we need to know everything, even if you think it puts you in a poor light,' Kitty said.

Fred ladled sugar into his tea, his hand trembling above the sugar bowl. 'Crabtree and me had a fight over Tilly a few days before he disappeared. He'd been pestering her, never leaving her be. Dirty old man. He was old enough to be her grandfather. I'd been walking out with Tilly for a few months. She was seventeen then and pretty. Turned heads everywhere she went she did. Her father had warned him off as well, told him to leave her alone. She was too young for him.'

'You hit Mr Crabtree?' Matt asked.

'Yeah, it was all a lot of shoving and pushing really. A few of the lads pulled us apart before I could land a good punch. Crabtree fired off his shotgun and had it took by the constable. Arthur barred him from the pub. He barred me as well for good measure as the magistrates were reviewing his licence. I told Crabtree if I saw his face again trying it on with Tilly I'd finish him.' Fred's expression clouded as he recalled the past.

'When was this exactly?' Kitty asked.

'Three days before they found out he was missing. This was on the evening time about eight o'clock. I'd finished working the boats and gone for a pint of cider and to see Tilly. He was in the bar giving it some old chat about winning money at cards. Tilly walked past and he smacked her on her bottom and made some lewd remark. I just saw red.' Fred paused and looked shame-faced. 'I've always been a bit hasty like.'

'I see. I suppose since people had to separate you a good many people would have heard you threaten Mr Crabtree?' Matt asked.

Fred hung his head. 'Yeah. That was why I got hauled in the first time, when he disappeared. Then, of course, they found his body up at the farm and I got pulled in again. You and Mrs Bryant come asking questions as well while I was working on the ferry.'

'You can hardly blame Inspector Lewis for wishing to speak to you again after Crabtree's body was found?' Kitty said. 'They have been trying to find all of the people they interviewed back then and also to speak to some of those who may have been witnesses to altercations between Crabtree and other people.'

Fred picked up his second sandwich and took a large bite, eating it quickly as if half expecting it to be snatched away before he was finished. He chewed and swallowed. 'I suppose so. I know they spoke to William, his son, and Lavinia. They had about the same love for his old man as I did.'

'William was very ill when his father vanished. Lavinia told me she thought he might die and her father-in-law owed them a great deal of money. They needed it back as William wasn't able to work and the rent was overdue.' Kitty watched Fred closely as she spoke.

'That's right. It took William a good three months to recover and get some work. The church people come to their aid and Lavinia sold some of the old man's things from the house when he didn't come back. They had no money for food, rent or fire-wood. Lord Massey wanted the farm emptied and another tenant in so Lavinia took care of everything,' Fred said.

'Do you know a man called Joshua Payne?' Matt asked. He too was watching Fred carefully.

'Only his name and that he was a merchant seaman. He was the one who lost at cards to Crabtree. Arthur said as he didn't take it well, he lost a pile of money. He kicked the table over and accused him of cheating. He made all kind of threats. Arthur barred him as well. He went back to sea though. I dunno where he is now.' Fred finished the rest of his sandwich.

Kitty frowned. 'Mr Crabtree had a large sum of money from the card game, and he had borrowed money from his son. Do you know what he planned to do with the money? I don't recall seeing any mention of money in any of the reports after his disappearance.'

Fred shrugged. 'He was behind with his rent, and he needed feed and stuff for the farm. He said that Lord Massey's agent wanted him out. I don't know where his money went. I suppose he must have paid the rent and his other bills and things with it.'

Mr Pettifor had said that Crabtree had owed rent, so he clearly hadn't received it when the man had vanished. It had been one of his reasons for calling at the farm. Lavinia and William had help from the church to keep their home and feed themselves. They had sold what they could from the farm and obviously the money hadn't been in Crabtree's effects. There had been no mention of money being found with Crabtree's body either. Where had it gone?

'Inspector Lewis took you in for questioning after they discovered Tilly's body in the river. Why was that? Did you know she was in Totnes? Had you been to see her?' Matt leaned closer to Fred, causing the other man to shrink back slightly in his chair.

'I knew as she were in Totnes. She'd been there for a while. Her old man, Arthur, he threw her out a few years ago. I was in prison at the time, but I heard she got pregnant and wouldn't tell him who the father was. Then she lost the baby. She always wanted to be on the stage Tilly did. She had a voice like a nightingale.' Fred paused clearly lost in memories of happier times in his youth. 'There was a music hall there and I think she went to try her luck.'

'Did you ever contact her? Go to see her?' Kitty asked.

'I was going to a few years ago. Then I heard she was living with some rich bloke. I left it, no point if she were happy and settled.' Fred slurped up his tea and Kitty refilled his cup with what was left in the pot.

'And recently?' she asked as she placed the now empty teapot back on the tray.

Fred fidgeted uncomfortably.

'We need to know the truth. The inspector would not have taken you to the police station if he didn't believe you had not seen or heard from Tilly in years.' Matt's tone was stern.

'When I was inside this last time, I shared a cell with a bloke from Paignton. We got talking and Tilly's name come up. He said she was down on her luck and turning tricks in Totnes. I didn't believe him, but he swore on his mother's life he were telling the truth. Ever since I got out I wanted to go and find her, see if it was right, what he'd said.' Fred stared miserably at his teacup.

'Did you go to see her?' Kitty asked.

'I used the last money I had to get the bus to Totnes. I asked around and found she was using her old acting name, Tilly Swann. She had some cheap lodgings in a low part of the town.' Fred stirred sugar into his tea as if hoping it might fortify him for what came next.

'When was this?' Matt asked.

'Saturday. I got there mid-afternoon. I tried to save some money by walking part of the way and taking the bus for the last part. The bus driver might be able to vouch for me.' Fred's expression brightened a little at this thought.

'And you saw her?' Kitty could see that Fred was struggling with his story. She wasn't sure if it was emotion or guilt.

Fred nodded, a dark expression on his face. 'I found her at her lodgings. She was shocked to see me. I felt the same seeing her. She looked ill, haggard and hard. Not like the Tilly I knew. She asked me why I'd come. I said I'd heard how she was turning tricks and she said as she had no choice. It was that or starve. She told me everyone had abandoned her.'

'How long were you there at her lodgings?' Matt asked.

'A few hours. I had to get back before seven or else I would be on the streets. I had a bed at a mission in Brixham,' Fred explained.

'I take it your meeting was cordial, once Tilly had recovered from her surprise at seeing you?' Kitty eyed him curiously.

'Yes, it was. She made us a cup of tea, and we just sat and talked. She didn't know anything about Crabtree's body being found. That shocked her,' Fred said.

'Did she say anything about him and what happened all those years ago?' Kitty asked.

Fred scratched his head, his brow puckering. 'Only as she couldn't understand it. She had thought he'd gone away. She said that was what she'd been told.'

Kitty was puzzled. 'Why did she believe he had gone away even if someone had said that to her? I know it was a suggestion at the time, but he had left everything behind at the farm, just abandoned.'

'I asked her that. I sort of joked with her and she said, well, he had the goods. She seemed thoughtful like she was remembering things.'

'The goods? Did she mean the money from his son and the card game?' Matt jumped on Fred's words.

'I don't know. She was sort of cagey, but I don't think so. She shut up like a clam then and changed the subject. I don't know quite what she meant,' Fred said.

'But you knew Tilly's father sometimes stored stolen goods in the cellar of his pub and then sold them on? Was Crabtree part of that? Were goods left in his care before they could be passed on?' Matt's tone hardened once more.

CHAPTER EIGHTEEN

Matt's question seemed to hang in the air. Kitty's heart thumped in her chest as she waited for Fred to answer. The man's gaze flitted towards the sitting room door and back again. For a second she wasn't sure if he might make a run for it rather than give an incriminating reply.

'I don't think I quite catch your meaning, Captain Bryant,' Fred eventually said.

He looked decidedly shifty now and Kitty's dog moved closer to her knee.

'I rather think you do know exactly what I mean. I'd like to remind you there is the shadow of the noose hanging over you. Now is not the time to worry about past misdemeanours if you wish to save your skin.' Matt was firm.

'I don't know...' Fred looked wildly around the room as if trapped and Bertie gave a low warning growl.

'Let us assist you.' Kitty placed her hand on her dog's collar. 'Mr Crabtree was what I believe in criminal parlance is called a bagman. Any goods that were too hot to be sold on at that moment in time were left in his safekeeping. They were then taken by the original thieves who would pay him a fee once the goods were disposed of. Arthur also had stolen goods but he was the person who found buyers for them. A fence, I believe is the term. I think Mr Crabtree may have been holding on to the goods stolen from Lord and Lady Massey a few weeks before. Maldon couldn't risk having them at the pub so an isolated place like Midwinter Farm was the perfect spot to keep them.'

Fred exhaled. A huge gusty sigh. 'All right, yes, so Crabtree would mind stuff sometimes. Usually, bits that fell off the back of a boat or a lorry. I wasn't one of them who robbed the Massey house. Robbery isn't my game. I only knew what Tilly told me back then. She would often hear stuff, living in the pub and I think Arthur had her on a few jobs. She knew better than to say anything to anyone though. Her old man is handy with his fists, and he'd often catch Tilly one if she didn't dodge out the way in time.'

'Oh dear. Poor Tilly. She had a hard life,' Kitty said. 'Was Joshua Payne part of this gang who robbed the Massey house?'

Fred shook his head. 'Honest, Mrs Bryant, I don't know. Him and Arthur was quite thick though back then. There was a lot of shady stuff going on. I know when Arthur barred me and Crabtree from the pub, Crabtree told him he'd regret it. That it would be a costly mistake.'

'Do you think that he may have been "minding" the goods from the Massey robbery at time he vanished?' Kitty said.

'It's possible.' Fred swallowed the last of his tea in one big gulp.

'It's also possible that when you told Tilly that Crabtree's body had been found she may have remembered something about the robbery. She could even have come up with a name for who may have killed Crabtree,' Matt said.

Fred looked stricken. 'I didn't hurt Tilly. I would have never harmed a hair on her head. If she did remember something about all that she didn't say anything to me.'

'Did you tell Inspector Lewis all of this when he questioned you?' Kitty asked.

Fred again became shifty, avoiding her gaze. 'I answered all of his questions.'

'In a word, no, you didn't. Really, Fred, you are making things worse for yourself. I presume people saw you call on Tilly?' Kitty felt quite exasperated.

'Yes, the nosy woman who lived below her saw me going up to her place and she banged her broom handle on her ceiling at one point because we laughed a bit too loud.' Sadness clouded his features once more. 'Tilly said as the woman didn't like her and wanted her out.'

'Did anyone see you leave? Do you have an alibi for Sunday morning when Tilly was killed?' Matt asked.

'I don't know. Maybe the bus driver will remember me counting out coppers for the conductor to get back to Brixham Saturday evening. Then the hostel can say I spent the night there,' Fred said. 'I didn't have enough money to go back to see her on the Sunday morning. It's too far to walk and there wouldn't be enough trucks and things going in that direction for me to try for a lift.'

'You could have taken a boat?' Kitty suggested as her dog stirred restlessly under her fingers.

'No one would have loaned me one and I'd have had to have got to the river and rowed against the tide. No, I stayed in Brixham on Sunday morning. I walked round the harbour hoping I might get some casual work for Monday. Wait, the fishermen there, they might remember me. They were sat by the walls fixing their nets.' A gleam of hope appeared in Fred's eyes.

'I presume the inspector asked if you had an alibi. Did you mention any of this to him?' Kitty asked. His story sounded pretty thin to her and why would he only now recall talking to the fishermen at the time Tilly was killed?

'I don't know what I told him. I was so shocked when he

said that Tilly was dead. That someone had murdered her. One of the last things I said to her before I left was telling her to be careful. She said she always was. I panicked I suppose when he was talking to me. My mind just went blank. All I could think about was her lying dead, floating in the river like a bit of rubbish.' Tears appeared in Fred's eyes, and he dashed them away swiftly with the back of his grimy hand. 'She didn't deserve that.'

Kitty could see his sorrow and anger at Tilly's death was real. The news of her murder had obviously affected him deeply.

'The police have been trying to find Tilly's father. We know after leaving the pub in Kingswear he went to keep the Dolphin pub in Dartmouth by the market for a while. Someone thought he had gone to Paignton. Do you know where he is?' Matt asked.

'He dropped out of the pub trade for a while. I heard he had arthritis and couldn't manage it no more. He was in Paignton, but I think he moved away up towards the moors. Ashburton I heard. He's probably lying low if he's heard the police found Crabtree,' Fred said.

'Do you think he could have killed him?' Kitty asked.

'I think he were capable of killing him but then if he did, who killed Tilly? Her old man wouldn't have killed her for all he threw her out over the baby. I got the feeling the police didn't think it was one of her customers that murdered her. Not from the way they was asking me questions. And what happened to the stuff from the Masseys' house? It didn't seem as that was found. There's been nothing in the papers.' Fred seemed to be telling the truth, Kitty thought.

She exchanged a glance with Matt. Inspector Lewis had obviously been careful not to play all of his cards about Tilly Maldon's murder.

'So, you may have an alibi for Tilly's murder but that still doesn't put you in the clear for Thomas Crabtree's death,' Matt said.

'That's why I came here. You were asking questions about it all and this bloke I knew from prison, he said as you were good at your game. His uncle works for Mrs Bryant.' Fred turned his gaze to Kitty.

She knew who he was referring to. Her hotel manager's errant nephew who seemed to be in and out of trouble as often as Fred himself. She knew Mr Lutterworth would have happily disowned him years ago but a loyalty towards his dead sister meant he felt an obligation towards his nephew.

'We will obviously pass on what you've told us to Inspector Lewis and Chief Inspector Greville. Our advice would be to stay quietly in Brixham. If you discover anything new or hear something, no matter how small, then you must let us or the police know. Whoever killed Thomas Crabtree may have killed Tilly.' Matt gave Fred one of their business cards.

Kitty found a few shillings from her purse and passed them to Fred. 'This will get you the bus and cover you for some food for a day until you can get some work.'

Fred's eyes lit up as he pocketed the coins. 'Ta ever so, Mrs Bryant. You will try and get the police from off my back? I swear as I didn't kill anybody.'

Matt got up from his seat to usher Fred out of the house. 'We will do our best to discover who is behind the murders.'

He walked Fred into the hall and closed the front door behind him, while Kitty watched discreetly from behind the curtains in the sitting room to see that he left the premises.

Mrs Smith promptly appeared as soon as she heard the front door close. 'I hope as you don't come to regret letting him in here, Captain Bryant. Light fingers he's got. You can't trust him no further than you could throw him. Now, your lunch will be spoiled if you don't come to the table.' She wiped her hands on her apron and went back to the kitchen to dish up their food.

Kitty and Matt went into the dining room to eat. Mrs Smith had made a hearty winter vegetable soup with fresh crusty bread. Kitty's stomach rumbled as she sniffed appreciatively at the full china bowl in front of her.

Matt picked up his bread. 'We shall have to telephone the police station and update them with everything we've discovered this morning.'

'Including Fred's alibi for Tilly's murder. If he was in Brixham looking for work I don't see how he could have been the person arguing with Tilly in Totnes that morning.' Kitty blew on the soup on her spoon to try and cool it down. Mrs Smith had clearly kept their lunch very hot while they had been talking to her nephew.

'True, but we also can't rule out that he may have been working in partnership with someone,' Matt pointed out.

'He did seem to be genuinely upset about Tilly's death.' Kitty dabbed a bit of her bread in her soup.

'Maybe. We only have his word for it too what he and Tilly spoke about.' Matt looked thoughtful.

'Everything he said seemed to fit with what the chief inspector told us. Do you think he was still holding something back?' Kitty asked.

'Perhaps. Those jewels and silver are still missing, and Tilly seems to have known something about it all from all the pieces of evidence we've gathered so far.' Matt spooned up the last of his lunch.

'If she did, she evidently only seems to have put the pieces together after she talked to Fred.' Kitty placed her spoon down in her empty dish.

'Or is Fred himself now in danger if someone realises he's spoken to Tilly?' Matt looked at Kitty.

'Well, if he's not the murderer, that does seem to be a possibility,' Kitty admitted. 'We really need to track down this Arthur Maldon if the police haven't found him yet.'

Matt dabbed at the corners of his mouth with his napkin before depositing it on the table beside his dish. 'I'll telephone the police station now and see if I can speak to the inspector or chief inspector. I'll tell them what we know and see if they have found Arthur Maldon.'

He disappeared into the hall as Mrs Smith came to clear the crockery and serve their dessert of home-made blackberry and apple crumble with thick creamy pale-yellow custard.

'Is Captain Bryant telephoning the chief inspector?' the housekeeper asked as she gathered up the soup dishes.

'Yes. Fred has an alibi for Tilly Maldon's murder,' Kitty said.

Mrs Smith gave a disparaging sniff. 'Well, I hope he has. He's a rogue and no mistake but I wouldn't want him to swing for something he hadn't done.'

Matt reappeared when Kitty was halfway through her dessert. He slid into the seat opposite her and picked up his spoon. 'I've passed on all the information. They haven't found Maldon yet, but I think they were still making enquiries in Paignton.'

'Did they say anything about Joshua Payne?' Kitty asked. She wondered if they had spoken to him since he had disembarked.

'No, I spoke to Inspector Lewis but as usual he wanted all of our information without giving away much of his.' Matt smiled at her as she scowled at her dessert.

'Honestly, that man is so infuriating. I really don't know what Betty sees in him,' Kitty said.

They finished their desserts and Kitty wrapped up warmly to take Bertie out for his walk. Matt opted to accompany her since they had currently reached an impasse in the investigation for a moment.

Once they stepped outside the house mist enfolded them, cold and damp.

'Why don't we go down to Kingswear and walk Bertie there?' Matt suggested. 'The mist might not be as bad by the river if this is just low cloud.'

Kitty looked at him as he bundled Bertie into his usual place on the back seat of her car. 'Do you have something else in mind while we are in Kingswear?' she asked.

She knew her husband well and he was up to something.

'We might run into your new chum, Lavinia Crabtree,' he said as she started the car engine.

'Hmm, or better still the elusive William. We could at least establish if he was my Peeping Tom at Alice's house. The police have been so busy with Fred Smith and hunting for Arthur Maldon that no one seems to have checked up on William Crabtree lately,' Kitty remarked as they drove across the common and up towards Hillhead.

Matt's smile widened. 'He may avoid us if he recognises your car.'

* * *

Matt asked Kitty to leave her car in the railway station car park, and they walked the short distance across the road and then up towards the main centre of the tiny village. His suggestion that the fog might prove less dense near the river had proved right. Their house being much higher often was affected by low cloud at certain times of the year while the rest of the bay was clear.

Kingswear was surprisingly busy with people taking the ferry across the Dart or boarding the train. The small collection of shops were also doing a brisk trade. Their windows were decorated for the festive season and Kitty stopped frequently to peer at the brightly lit displays.

This did not please Bertie, who while enjoying a new place to sniff, was keen to get going. Matt kept a sharp eye open as they strolled along the narrow streets for any sign of either Lavinia or William Crabtree.

Eventually they walked back downhill again in the direction of the river and the local yacht club. This time, since they were approaching from a different direction, they heard the sound of shovelling and spotted a man with a spade digging out the remains of a decaying tree stump from the ornamental gardens near the entrance to the club.

The grubby bandage on the man's hand and the slightly awkward way he was holding the shovel told Matt that they had found William Crabtree at his labours. As they drew nearer, the man straightened up to ease his back and to wipe his brow with the back of his good hand.

'Mr Crabtree, good afternoon,' Kitty greeted the man and Bertie paused to give the rotten stump a good sniff.

William touched his cap with his hand. 'Afternoon.' His voice and his gaze were wary.

Matt could see that he had obviously recognised Kitty, probably from their last meeting.

'Having some trouble with that stump?' Matt asked as Bertie continued his own investigations.

'Aye, it's a bit stubborn.' William frowned at the tree roots which had been chopped off with an axe but which still appeared to be firmly attached to the ground.

'I do hope your hand is improving? Your wife said you had injured it.' Kitty inclined her head in the direction of the bandages which the man seemed to be attempting to conceal behind his back.

'Yes, it's much better, thank you.' William dropped all eye contact with Kitty.

'Just what were you doing up at Midwinter Farm when you injured your hand?' Matt asked in the same conversational tone he'd used when asking about the stump.

'I don't know what you mean, sir.' William picked up his shovel again as if ready to return to digging out the tree roots.

'Really? I would have thought being cracked across the knuckles by a poker while you were peering through the letter box would have been quite memorable,' Kitty said.

William startled and stepped back from her as if afraid she might have another poker concealed about her person.

'I see you do remember. Now, perhaps you could answer my question. What were you doing up there and what did you hope to find?' Matt asked.

For a split second he thought the man was going to refuse to answer.

'Nothing, like I said. I was just curious to see what had been done to the place.' William's reply was barely audible, and he kept his head down as he spoke.

'What, since you and your sister lived there with your father?' Kitty asked.

This caused William to raise his head to stare right at Kitty. A red spot had appeared on each of his sallow, sunken cheeks and his dark eyes gleamed with something akin to anger.

'Don't go bringing my sister into this. She's long gone,' he said.

'I know, I heard that she passed away a while ago in Ireland. That must have been hard.' Kitty's tone softened, and Matt saw some of the tension leave the man's body at her sympathy.

'She was a lovely person, my sister. There's not a day goes past when I don't think of her. Lizzie, my youngest, is her spitting image.' William leaned on his shovel.

'Why go to Midwinter Farm now? After your father's body was discovered there? You didn't knock on the door, even though you must have seen the smoke from the chimney and Kitty's car parked outside near the barn,' Matt said.

'I didn't know who was there. It could have been the police for all I knew or the people who'd bought the house. I just wanted to see inside a bit and see what had been done,' William said.

'You never went to look inside when either of the tenants who had the farm after your father were there?' Kitty asked. 'Why was that?'

'I think I know why.' Matt looked squarely at William. 'They didn't do any work to the place.'

CHAPTER NINETEEN

Matt continued to speak, ignoring the people passing them by on the pavement. 'The other tenants didn't do work. They just moved into the farm and went about their business. You knew Robert had builders in making all kinds of alterations. Did you think they might have found your father's secret hiding spaces?'

Kitty waited for William to speak. He stood silently, his uninjured hand clenching and loosening over and over around the handle of the spade as if trying to come up with a response.

'I didn't know what the inside of the house would be like after the work. When Father disappeared, the money he'd borrowed from us were gone. There was other money too, what he'd won at cards that we heard about. The land agent, Mr Pettifor, said he hadn't received it in rent. Father also, well, he looked after things for people.' William looked shifty.

'He handled stolen goods until the fuss had died down before passing them on to Arthur Maldon who disposed of them through his contacts at the pub,' Kitty said.

The spots of colour on William's cheeks grew larger and he scowled down at his spade. 'I was proper ill when Father vanished. Lavinia didn't even tell me what had gone on until after my fever broke. By then the police and everybody had been over every inch of the farm. He'd been missing nigh on a week by then. They didn't find anything, no stolen goods and no money, except a few bob in loose change.'

'This surprised you?' Kitty asked. 'What did you think might be there?'

Again there was the sense that William was choosing his words carefully. 'I don't know. Definitely the money he'd took from us and his winnings at cards, that should have been there. Like I said, Father wasn't the most honest of men. He might have had some stolen stuff on the farm but if he did, they didn't find it. The police and Mr Pettifor had told Lavinia though that nothing in the house had been disturbed. There was even his best cufflinks left in his bedroom. No signs of anyone looking for something. That was when I thought as mebbe he had just took off. Got scared or decided the temptation of whatever he were minding was too much and he'd double-crossed them all. Vanishing like that would throw them off the scent.'

'Where did your father usually hide the things he was minding?' Kitty asked. 'In the house? Or in one of the outbuildings?'

She was curious about Thomas Crabtree's secret hiding places. Clearly there must have been some in the house or why would William want to see what Robert and his builders may have done?

'It depended on what it was and how long he was supposed to keep it. Simple stuff like a picture or a bit of whisky or summat he would hide in the barn under the straw up in the loft. But he had some places that I didn't know of. I allus thought as mebbe they was in the house but I never found them. I checked all the floorboards downstairs once when he was at the market. This was before I married Lavinia and moved out. I didn't find nothing, not even a mouse's droppings. There weren't a cellar and the loft door had been nailed shut for as long as I could remember.' William raised his gaze to look at Kitty. 'I thought if the house were empty of furniture mebbe I might see something. The builders obviously hadn't found anything or else the police would have said, wouldn't they?'

'Were you hoping to discover the missing money somewhere? Or the jewels and silver stolen from the Masseys?' Matt asked.

William ran his tongue over his lips as if his mouth had grown dry while they had been talking. 'I don't know anything about the robbery. I thought if he had been minding that stuff then whoever killed him probably had taken it. The money though, Father was crafty. He could have hid that someplace small inside the house and mebbe as no one had found it yet. Me and Lavinia, he owed us, and we could use that money now. My work is slow, and the children are growing.'

'You frightened Kitty half to death, prowling around, peering through windows, trying the doors.' Matt's tone was stern. 'You could have just knocked on the door.'

'I were only trying to find what's rightfully mine. I didn't intend to scare no one.' William scowled at Matt.

'It seems my poker put paid to your prowling in any case,' Kitty remarked, looking pointedly at William's bandaged hand. 'I suggest you stay well away from Midwinter Farm. I have no doubt that should Robert or Alice discover anything untoward then they will inform the police.'

She did feel a slight twinge of sympathy for the man since he and his family were clearly struggling. However, she had no wish to encounter William or anyone else snooping around the farm on the off chance that something of value might still be hidden there. Alice would be horrified by all of this when she found out.

'I presume you have heard the news about Tilly Maldon?' Matt asked.

'Tilly? The old landlord's girl. That's a name I've not heard for a while. What of her?' William looked blank.

'She's dead. She was killed on Sunday. They found her strangled and floating in the river at Totnes,' Matt said.

Kitty suspected her husband was speaking bluntly on purpose to try and shake any information from William that he could.

'I hadn't heard anything about no murder. What happened to her?' The colour receded as quickly as it had appeared from the man's face and he appeared genuinely shocked by the news.

'The police aren't sure. They don't know if it's connected with what happened at Midwinter Farm or if it's a separate murder,' Kitty said.

'That's a shock all right. I don't see how as Tilly being killed could have anything to do with Father's death. Not now, not after all this time,' William muttered almost as if talking to himself.

'Before he vanished your father fought with a man called Fred Smith over Tilly Maldon. She was walking out with Fred at the time.' Kitty watched William closely.

'Aye, he were barred from the pub, him and the other man. Lavinia told me as the constable had confiscated his shotgun. Father had an eye for a pretty face so that was no surprise when I heard he'd been in bother. I knew it wouldn't last long though, him being barred. Maldon were wary of losing his licence so he had to make a stand of it.' William still seemed to be processing the news of Tilly's death.

'When did you last see Tilly?' Kitty asked.

'I haven't seen her. Not for years. They moved across the river to Dartmouth to keep a pub there and then Arthur went to Paignton. I heard how Tilly got herself in trouble and he threw her out. That was all a long time ago. I don't even know where she went. I've not seen or heard of her for years now.'

William's response seemed genuine to Kitty. 'What of her father, Arthur Maldon?'

'Again, I don't know. You hear rumours like, from time to time. The last thing I remember was that he was ill and had gone to bide up on the moors.' William's reply appeared to fit with what Fred Smith had said.

'One more thing. Do you know a man called Joshua Payne? He lost money gambling at cards with your father at Maldon's pub,' Matt asked.

'I know he lost a lot of money and were right angry about it. Lavinia told me when I was recovering from my fever. She'd had it from the police when they were looking into Father's disappearance. We talked about it when we wondered what had become of Father's money. I can't say as I know him at all though. I heard he was a merchant seaman and had gone back to sea.' William gave a small shrug and lifted his spade to continue his task.

Kitty could see they would get little else of value from William, so they said goodbye and continued to walk with the now very restless Bertie, back towards Kitty's car.

'Do you think there is more that he knows that he isn't telling us?' Kitty asked as Matt stowed Bertie on the back seat of the car.

'Undoubtedly, but I think when we told him Tilly had been murdered, he was frightened,' Matt said as he opened the passenger door to get in beside Kitty.

'That was my thought too,' she said as she turned on the ignition once more. 'Where shall we go next? I really want to talk to this Joshua Payne or to Arthur Maldon.'

'I agree, but speaking to either of those two gentlemen may prove difficult. Maldon seems to have gone to ground, and I don't know if Payne has been seen by the police yet. Although I would have expected the chief inspector to have called on him by now. Especially after they fished poor Tilly's body out of the river,' Matt said.

'Then it seems we are at an impasse. I suppose if we were to call at the address your contact in Plymouth provided for Mr Payne, Inspector Lewis would not be at all pleased,' Kitty said thoughtfully.

'When did you worry about upsetting Inspector Lewis?' Matt asked with the hint of a chuckle in his voice.

'I don't usually but now he has become James and is walking out with Betty everything feels a tad more personal,' Kitty said.

'Murder is a very personal business. Most people are killed by someone they know well,' Matt reminded her.

'I take it that a trip to Paignton is in order then?' she asked.

Bertie emitted a long-suffering sigh from behind her as Matt nodded his agreement.

Kitty had a rough idea where Joshua Payne's mother lived in Paignton. She was sure the road was one that led off from Palace Avenue. Matt had the address in his pocket, so she drove slowly along the street while her husband looked at the numbers on the doors of the houses.

'It's that one, over there, Kitty,' Matt said.

She pulled to a stop. The street was growing quite dark now and the children were out of school. The small ones were escorted by weary-faced mothers either pushing a pram or hefting a basket of shopping. The children laughed and giggled as they skipped along. Snatches of carols and Christmas songs filled the air.

Joshua Payne's mother's house was in darkness. Most of the other tall narrow terraced houses had a light in their window or the shimmer of a decorated tree standing proudly in the front bay. The house they had been looking for appeared shut up and deserted. There was no wreath on the door, and the brass was dull and unpolished. Kitty had a foreboding feeling in the pit of her stomach.

'It looks empty,' Kitty said, looking at the weeds which had pushed their way around the front doorstep.

'Stay here. I'll go and knock.' Matt was out of the car before she could stop him.

She watched from the car as he crossed the street and up the short path leading to Joshua Payne's front door. Matt raised the round brass knocker and rapped it loudly on the faded-blue door.

There was no reply that she could discern from inside the house and Matt tried again.

'There isn't anybody living there, mister. The old lady died and it's empty.' A small boy of about ten was at the top of the path regarding Matt with a curious gaze.

Kitty wound down the car window so she could hear what was said more clearly.

'What about the gentleman who was living there?' Matt asked.

The boy folded his arms and tilted his head to one side studying Matt's appearance. 'Are you with the police? Because they were here the other day and they were looking for him as well.'

'We are private investigators and need to speak to Mr Payne. He works on the ships,' Matt said.

The boy's eyes widened at the mention of private investigators. 'Like in the films?'

'Sort of. Have you seen Mr Payne here at all recently?' Matt asked.

The boy nodded. 'I live over there.' He half-turned and pointed to a well-kept property across the street. Kitty was fairly sure she saw the curtains twitch and guessed someone in that house was keeping a watchful eye on the lad. 'He was here a few days ago. He had a big bag with him. Mum came over and told him about the old lady.'

'That must have been a shock for him,' Matt said.

The boy nodded. 'He was upset and went in the house for a bit. Then he went away and I haven't seen him again. The policeman asked Mum if he'd been home but he hadn't, not since then. Is he in trouble? Is he a bad man?'

'No, I don't think so. It was just a few questions about something that happened a long time ago. I'll leave him a note through the door.' Matt whipped out a card and Kitty saw him scribble a few words on the back before pushing it through the grimy letter box.

'Do I get a reward for helping? They give rewards in the films!' the boy asked.

Matt grinned. 'You have indeed been most helpful.' He reached into his pocket and Kitty saw him give the boy a shilling.

The boy's eyes grew very wide at the sight of such largesse, and he flew off across the road with a shouted, 'Ta, mister,' presumably to inform whoever was behind the curtain of his riches.

Matt made his way back to where Kitty was waiting and climbed back into the passenger seat. 'I take it you heard all of that?'

Kitty wound her window back up. 'I did. It seems we have drawn another blank. How awful though if the poor man was at sea to come home and discover his mother had died and no one had been able to let him know. It must have been the most dreadful shock.'

'Indeed,' Matt agreed as he glanced at the house once more. 'I wonder where he has gone.'

'It doesn't seem as if he was able to face staying here. Perhaps he has gone back to Plymouth,' Kitty suggested.

'It's a strong possibility. He may be staying with a fellow shipmate until his next sailing,' Matt said.

'It seems there is nothing more we can do here at any rate.' Kitty restarted her car. She couldn't help feeling disappointed that two of their main suspects still hadn't been interviewed as far as they knew.

The mist had lifted slightly by the time they arrived back at their home although it was now quite dark, and the temperature had already begun to fall again. Matt collected Bertie from his seat in the back of the car and Kitty unlocked the front door. Their housekeeper had finished for the day and had left their supper in the oven to keep warm.

Kitty took off her outdoor things and turned on the lamps before drawing the curtains. Matt stirred up the fire and added more wood. The house felt cosy and snug, and Rascal mewed his delight at their return as he wound his way lovingly around Matt's legs.

More Christmas cards and another couple of anniversary cards had arrived in the post. Kitty duly admired them and added them to the others on display. Matt settled himself in his usual seat beside the fire and picked up the newspaper ready to begin the daily crossword.

Kitty went to the kitchen to make a cup of tea. She had just filled the kettle when there was a loud knock at the front door. She put the kettle on the hob and went to see who was there.

'Chief Inspector, do come in. I'm just making some tea.' Kitty ushered their guest into the hall to take his hat and coat before sending him through to the sitting room to Matt.

She hurried back to the kitchen and added an extra cup and saucer and a plate of mince pies to the tray. Hopefully the chief inspector might have some news he could share with them about Tilly's murder and what had happened at Midwinter Farm.

Perhaps, he may even have made an arrest.

CHAPTER TWENTY

When Kitty returned to the sitting room carrying the loaded tray she discovered both men were waiting for her arrival.

'I've just told the chief inspector of our adventures this afternoon in Kingswear and Paignton,' Matt said as she slid the tray onto the coffee table.

Chief Inspector Greville's expression brightened at the sight of the mince pies. 'Most useful information, as indeed were the things you told us at lunchtime. We have been kept busy following up on all the information you provided. Checking Fred Smith's alibi for a start and then moving our search for Arthur Maldon to Ashburton and the area around Bovey Tracey on the moors.'

'It's so frustrating that we haven't been able to speak to the two people most concerned with the murders. Especially Mr Maldon. If he is not involved then he may well be unaware that his daughter is dead,' Kitty said as she poured out the tea and offered the plate of mince pies to the policeman.

'Believe me, Mrs Bryant, we share your frustration. Mr Maldon is, however, a very slippery fish. He has managed to escape prosecution by the thinnest of margins many times during the course of his life. I have no doubt that even if he were not involved in Thomas Crabtree's death, he would be anxious to avoid revisiting that period of time with us,' the chief inspector said dryly.

'Is that because he was involved somehow in the robberies, including the one at Seacliffe House, the Masseys' home?' Matt leaned back in his seat and balanced his cup and saucer on the black leather arm of his chair.

'Precisely.' Chief Inspector Greville helped himself to another mince pie. 'As part of our investigations into both Thomas Crabtree and Tilly Maldon's deaths we have also been reviewing all the information that we hold on the robberies that took place at that time. Especially the one at Seacliffe House.'

'Were there any more robberies after the one at Seacliffe House? Or was that the last one in this area?' Kitty asked.

'It seems to have been the final one. It was right in the middle of November. Thomas Crabtree vanished at the end of the first week of December. The next report of a robbery of any significance in the area didn't occur until the following June. A diamond bracelet and various other pieces were stolen from the Countess of Dunberry while she was visiting her god-daughter in Torquay for a tennis event,' the chief inspector said, before popping the last bite of his mince pie into his mouth.

'That's quite a gap. Do you think the countess's jewels were stolen by the same villains as before?' Matt asked.

'It would seem their method was the same and naturally they too were never caught, although the bracelet did reappear some years later at one of the London auction houses. It appeared to have been bought quite innocently from a dealer. We followed the trail, but of course it led nowhere.' Chief Inspector Greville looked longingly at the final mince pie and Kitty offered him the plate once more.

'And there were no reports from other areas of the country

with a similar rash of robberies fitting the same style?' Kitty asked.

The chief inspector shook his head, scattering pastry crumbs on to the floor to be cleaned away by Bertie who was loitering near the tray. 'No, there were thefts in London, and a cat burglar in the spring but the mode of entry was different and he was caught.'

'It's interesting that there was a break. Were there any others after the last one in Torquay?' Matt asked.

'No, it all came to a halt at that point. I can only assume the gang moved on or perhaps something happened to one or more of them,' the chief inspector said.

'You don't believe the thefts were carried out by one person acting alone?' Kitty said.

'No, the very few witness accounts we have and statements leading up to the thefts and from what was noted in evidence is that it was at least two people working together and possibly three. The third is believed to be someone who went in on the "inside" to look around the property and ascertain the security arrangements within the house. There was also believed to have been someone acting as a lookout for a couple of the thefts.' Chief Inspector Greville picked up his cup and saucer to drink his tea, having finished all of the mince pies.

'And you believe that Arthur Maldon was somehow involved or had knowledge of who was involved in the robberies?' Matt asked.

'Oh, I'm sure he did, but knowing something and proving it are two very different things as you well know. The robberies halted after Maldon moved to the Dolphin public house near the market square in Dartmouth. It was further from the river and there were more people living around there than there were in Kingswear. I think it got too difficult for him to continue with things on the same scale as before. Then, of course, he moved to Paignton which is where he disappeared from our notice.' Chief

Inspector Greville drained his tea and set the cup and saucer down on the tray.

'Do you think you will find Arthur Maldon soon?' Kitty asked.

'My men are going from house to house. They have left messages at all the local hostelries too in case he calls in. They have been told it is a matter of urgency on family business that he contacts us. I can only hope we can flush him out. He may well be living remotely somewhere though. There are a good many isolated cottages and small hamlets on the moors.' Chief Inspector Greville's moustache drooped a little at the scale of the operation.

'What of Joshua Payne? He seems to have vanished after discovering his mother's death,' Matt asked.

'More manpower is being spent in Plymouth in case he has gone there. It seems likely he may be staying at a boarding house or with a shipmate until his next sailing,' the chief inspector said. He settled back a little in his seat. 'Which brings me to the other purpose of my visit.'

'Oh?' Matt looked surprised.

'Captain Redvers Palmerston.' The policeman cleared his throat. 'There have been a couple of possible sightings of him in Plymouth just lately near the docks. It's thought he was attempting to secure a passage aboard a ship sailing in the new year to America. He is obviously using an assumed name, but the physical description appears to fit.'

'Do we know what ship and when?' Matt said.

'That is not yet confirmed. It's just a possibility since he has made enquiries about berths at the ticket office. He hasn't yet confirmed a booking. We are obviously looking out for him,' Chief Inspector Greville said.

'Thank you, sir. I didn't mention it before because I wasn't certain if I was imagining things but when I was in Plymouth tracking down Joshua Payne, I too thought I caught a glimpse of him while I was at the docks,' Matt confessed.

'Hmm, it seems as if he is preparing to flee the country.' Chief Inspector Greville stroked his moustache thoughtfully.

'Let us hope you can intercept him before he can do so. I can only wonder at him choosing to try to leave from Plymouth. After the fire in the summer at the lodging house, he must surely know you are searching for him,' Kitty said with a frown.

She would have thought he might have travelled north to Liverpool and gone from there or one of the other major ports that had regular sailings across the Atlantic.

'It's been six months, he might believe the coast is clear. There is always though the possibility that he has one big fraud he is expecting to profit from before the new year and the intended victim lives in this neck of the woods,' the chief inspector said.

Kitty hadn't considered this possibility, but the chief inspector's theory made perfect sense. Despite the warmth in the room, she shivered and hoped he was mistaken. Too many people had already suffered loss and heartache at Redvers Palmerston's hands.

The chief inspector declared he would not keep them from their evening's pursuits and took his leave. Matt saw him out and sent their regards to Mrs Greville.

'Well, that was a surprise visit,' Kitty said as Matt closed the front door behind their guest. 'I wasn't expecting to hear more about Redvers Palmerston. I thought that perhaps the police would have found and interviewed Arthur Maldon and Joshua Payne.'

'I'm relieved in a way that I didn't imagine seeing Redvers that day when I was at the docks. With the fog and all the boxes being unloaded at the docks in the gloom it was hard to be certain. I wish they could catch him though. He is as slippery a fish as Arthur Maldon it seems.' Matt accompanied her to the kitchen as she carried the tray through and began to clear up ready for supper.

'Do you think the chief inspector is right when he suggested that Redvers may be planning one last con job and then fleeing abroad?' Kitty said as Matt opened a tin of pilchards for Rascal's supper.

'Unfortunately I do think it seems to be a very plausible explanation. He must be feeling confident again if he has returned to Plymouth,' Matt said as he set the cat's dish down on the tiled floor before starting on Bertie's supper dish.

Kitty slept poorly that night. Her dreams were full of colourful images of Redvers Palmerston interspersed with snippets of the interviews they had conducted with Fred Smith and William Crabtree.

The next morning dawned gloomy and cold and her head felt stuffy as if filled with cotton wool. Mrs Smith had made porridge for breakfast, followed by toast and marmalade. Bertie was very fond of porridge and was mightily pleased to discover he had a small dollop in his dish.

Matt intended taking his motorcycle into Torquay to visit their office. Although they were technically closed until after the New Year there might well be post from prospective clients. Kitty opted to remain at home. There were some letters she wished to write, and a couple of Christmas presents to wrap if she were to get them in the post in time for Christmas.

Armed with a mug of hot chocolate, she turned on the radio once Matt had set off. She started to wrap her presents in the sitting room, hindered by Rascal who wanted to play with the spool of ribbon she was using. There seemed to be little they could do on the Crabtree case until they received more information. It also appeared that there was nothing to be done about

Redvers Palmerston either. It was, she decided as she added some ribbon curls to her parcel and placed the reel out of her cat's reach, most unsatisfactory.

She also wanted a good heart-to-heart with Alice. Her friend needed to know what had happened since the discovery of Thomas Crabtree's body in her old piggery. She also needed to be made aware of Tilly Maldon's murder. Kitty added a label to her present and frowned unseeingly at the perky-looking robins on the paper.

There was the risk that Alice might be made even more anxious about starting her married life at Midwinter Farm, but it had been bothering Kitty that her friend may not be in possession of all the facts. If the murderer thought there was still something hidden at Midwinter Farm then they might try there again.

Alice would be very busy in her shop all day but tomorrow was her friend's day off. Probably her last free time before Christmas Day itself. Kitty resolved to telephone her later to see if she would be free for lunch. There was also the matter of them finishing the job of hanging the rest of the curtains at the farm. Although she wasn't sure how Alice might feel about going back there just yet with the case not yet solved.

* * *

Matt parked his motorcycle on the main street near their offices. They rented a couple of rooms above a gentleman's outfitters, sharing the landing with a company that manufactured dentures. The office was a good place to meet prospective clients, store paperwork and provided a mailing address for their business.

Much of their work now came via word of mouth from the various businesses around the seaside towns of Torquay,

Paignton and Brixham. Torquay was very much still a popular resort for wealthy visitors who enjoyed the milder air, palm trees and sunny vistas across the bay. Many titled and well-known people owned villas in the area, and the harbour attracted those who enjoyed yachting.

This plethora of wealthy holidaymakers also attracted those who wished to prey on them, thieves, rogues and conmen. Hoteliers were keen to maintain their security and guests often wished matters to be handled discreetly and swiftly. All of which meant that Kitty and Matt's services were much in demand.

Kitty had posted a notice on the office door stating they were closed until January. It had been their intention to take a few weeks off since it was usually a quiet time of year and their wedding anniversary fell on Christmas Eve.

The office felt cold as he unlocked the door and scooped up the small pile of post from the mat. He carried it through to the inner office and quickly sorted through it all. There were the usual advertising circulars. A couple of Christmas cards from businesses who had used their services in the last year and a letter from a potential client who wished to discover if her husband was being unfaithful.

They didn't deal with those kinds of cases so he tucked it into his pocket knowing Kitty would send the woman one of their standard letters declining the case. Satisfied there was nothing that merited their attention he locked everything back up and set off again.

His route was to take him past the police station as he wanted to collect something he had reserved for Kitty as an anniversary gift. He called in at the gallery and collected the small, beautifully wrapped parcel from the gallery owner before departing again.

The traffic near the police station was surprisingly busy and as he slowed down ready to weave his way between a horse-drawn cart and a sleek dark-blue Rolls-Royce he saw two policemen escorting a man into the police station. He recognised him right away from the photograph Marjorie had shown him in Plymouth when he had been searching the files.

His curiosity immediately piqued, he pulled over at the side of the road and parked his bike behind one of the police vehicles. It seemed too good an opportunity to miss so before giving himself time to think he hopped off his motorcycle and went inside the police station.

'Captain Bryant, we've not seen you for a while.' The desk sergeant was an old friend, having grown used to Kitty and Matt's frequent calls to see Chief Inspector Greville over the years.

'No, it's been a good six weeks or more I think.' Matt smiled affably at the older man. 'Um, I thought I just saw two constables escorting Joshua Payne inside the building.'

'Did you indeed, sir?' The sergeant gave a half smile, his thick grey eyebrows twitching upwards.

'I don't suppose Chief Inspector Greville is in at all?' Matt asked.

The sergeant picked up the receiver to his desk telephone and dialled an internal number. 'Captain Bryant is in reception, sir. He is asking about our latest visitor.' The sergeant listened to the reply.

'No, sir, Inspector Lewis is gone to Ashburton this morning,' the sergeant replied to whatever the chief inspector had asked. 'No, sir, we aren't expecting him back for some time.' He listened for a moment. 'Very good, sir.'

The policeman replaced the receiver on its stand and raised the hinged portion of the polished wooden desk to permit Matt to go through.

'I take it you know your way to the chief inspector's office by now, Captain Bryant?' the sergeant asked as he unlocked the door to a small corridor which led into the heart of the police station where the offices and the cells were situated.

'Yes, thank you.' Matt smiled his thanks at the sergeant and made his way towards the chief inspector's office.

CHAPTER TWENTY-ONE

The air in the cream walled corridor smelled faintly of carbolic and stale cabbage. Matt made his way past the green painted door of Inspector Lewis's office and further along to the chief inspector's room. He knocked on the closed door and waited until the chief inspector bade him enter.

Promotion had not made Chief Inspector Greville any more tidy and organised than when Matt and Kitty had first encountered him as an inspector. The office was filled with stacks of manila files and folders. Some were balanced precariously on chairs, others in heaps on the floor. An overflowing ashtray was set amongst the papers strewn on the top of the large desk along with what looked suspiciously like cake crumbs.

Joshua Payne sat opposite the chief inspector nervously twisting his cloth cap between his hands on his lap. He looked up as Matt entered, appearing surprised to see someone not wearing a police constable's uniform. A constable stood discreetly at the back of the room behind Joshua Payne.

'Ha, Captain Bryant, most fortuitous that you could join us. I don't believe you've actually met Mr Joshua Payne before.' The chief inspector made the introductions and Matt shook Mr

Payne's hand, before taking the other vacant seat. The constable received a nod from the chief inspector and went to wait outside the office door.

'Captain Bryant did a great deal of work to assist us in locating you, Mr Payne. He and his wife frequently work in collaboration with us here since our manpower is often insufficient when a major case is underway,' Chief Inspector Greville explained. 'Inspector Lewis would normally be here, but he is busy on Dartmoor looking for a gentleman you might recall, Mr Payne, a Mr Arthur Maldon, a former publican previously from Kingswear.'

'I used to know somebody of that name years ago,' Joshua Payne admitted. 'What's all this about? Your police constable fetched me from my lodgings in Plymouth and brought me here without really saying what it was you wanted. Then you say this gentleman was engaged looking for me.' He inclined his head towards Matt. 'I've been away at sea for three months so I don't know what I can tell you about anything.'

'Do you also recall a Mr Thomas Crabtree?' Chief Inspector Greville asked.

A dull, ugly, red flush crept up Joshua Payne's neck and into his cheeks. 'That cheating old scoundrel. I'm hardly likely to forget him even after all this time. He cheated me out of the best part of fifty pounds and refused to pay it back when I confronted him with proof. Last I heard he went missing. Probably with my money and the money he'd took off his own son as well. Ten years ago, that was. I went back to sea just as they found his farmhouse empty. Never heard no more of him.'

'You lost the money gambling in an illicit game at Mr Maldon's public house,' the chief inspector said. It was a statement not a question.

Joshua fidgeted on the hard bentwood seat. 'Listen, that game was private in Maldon's own quarters. It weren't in the public saloon and it was amongst friends. I didn't know then as I'd fell into a den of thieves.'

'You fought with Crabtree and made various threats before Mr Maldon barred you from the premises, throwing you out into the street. A constable attended and escorted you onto the river ferry.' Chief Inspector Greville appeared to be consulting from a folder that lay open in front of him.

'That was years ago. What of it? He robbed me, I was angry. It was almost Christmas and I had plans for that money. Maldon threw me out and I left and went back to Plymouth a few days later to get my ship. Why are you asking me questions now?' Joshua Payne scowled at the chief inspector.

'The remains of Thomas Crabtree have recently been discovered, buried in the piggery of Midwinter Farm. It seems that he didn't simply disappear, he was murdered. I don't know if you may have seen it reported in the newspapers?' the policeman replied mildly.

Matt watched Payne closely to see how he reacted to this information.

The man rubbed his face wearily with his hand. 'I haven't taken much notice of the news. I came home from my tour and found out my mother had passed away while I was at sea. I had a notice from the landlord to clear the place and to be gone by Christmas Eve as he had new tenants ready to rent it. He didn't even offer for me to keep it on. I haven't exactly been in the best frame of mind to read the papers.'

The chief inspector nodded.

'I'm sorry for the loss of your mother. I can imagine it must have been the most terrible shock,' Matt said.

'She'd been ill for a bit but nothing serious. I hadn't had a letter but that was nothing unusual. She weren't a good hand with a pen. The neighbour broke it to me what had happened. The funeral had been held and everything. All I got was the bill and an eviction notice.' Payne's tone was bitter, and Matt didn't blame him.

'I am most sorry to hear what has happened.' Chief Inspector Greville looked at Joshua Payne. 'However, you must understand that the discovery of Mr Crabtree's remains means that we have reopened the case. This means talking to everyone who had a dispute or dealings with the man in the days before he disappeared. Did you see him or contact him again after the fight you had with him over the card game?'

'No. I went back to my mother's house. I spent a day or so there and then took the train to Plymouth as I was due to sail.' The man met the chief inspector's eyes with a level gaze.

'Hmm, I see. Also, around that time there was a series of robberies in the area. The last one being a couple of weeks before Thomas Crabtree disappeared. That robbery was at Seacliffe House, home of Lord and Lady Massey. A valuable tiara, some other diamond jewellery and some silverware was stolen,' the chief inspector said.

Joshua Payne gave a careless shrug of his shoulders. 'I was probably at sea, Chief Inspector. Why would I know anything about robberies?'

Matt watched as the policeman made careful notes in his book.

'Do you recall Mr Maldon's daughter at all, Tilly? She would have been about seventeen when Mr Crabtree disappeared. She resided with her father at the pub,' the chief inspector asked.

'Tilly?' Joshua Payne appeared to pause to think but Matt was not entirely convinced the man's actions were genuine. He thought that Joshua Payne did remember Tilly but for some reason was playing for time.

'Yes, I think so, a pretty girl, she was walking out with a bloke who worked on the ferry. Old Crabtree kept trying to flirt with her, but she was having none of it.'

Chief Inspector Greville raised an eyebrow as he jotted the comment down. 'This man who worked on the ferry, did you know him at all?'

Again, Matt thought Joshua Payne looked a little uncomfortable. 'Not especially. I know he had a big fight with Maldon and with Crabtree. I heard about it when I was heading back to port and called for a drink at the pub near Mother's house before I left. I ran across a bloke who knew both of them and he told me. He'd heard as I'd already fell out with both of them.'

'Did you ever speak to this man at all? Fred Smith? Find out what the fight was about?' Chief Inspector Greville asked.

Payne shook his head. 'No, I only used to see him in passing when he called for the girl. Like I said, I only found out about his fight with Crabtree by chance as I was getting ready to leave.'

'It is quite a way from Paignton to Kingswear. How did you get to meet Mr Crabtree and discover his penchant for cards?'

Matt thought this was an interesting question from the chief inspector. Payne clearly didn't have a car, and the buses only ran at certain times. He could have gone by train but how had he met them in the first place?

'I was looking for some action. Life ashore is boring when you're used to being with company. I was drinking in one of the local pubs and I heard that if I wanted a game then Maldon in Kingswear was the man to go and see,' Payne explained.

'So it was Arthur Maldon who introduced you to Crabtree originally?' Chief Inspector Greville's pen raced across the page.

'Yes, there were four of us playing to start with but the other two dropped out when the stakes went up. Then it were just me and Crabtree left. We'd played before and it had all seemed above board but that night were different. It took me a couple of hands, but I spotted he was cheating.' Payne scowled at the table as if reliving the moment. 'By then he'd took best part of fifty pounds and I wanted it back.'

'Thank you. Did you know Thomas Crabtree's son William at all, or his wife, Lavinia?' the chief inspector asked.

'I never met the son. I heard he was seriously ill at the time. It was the talk of the village about how his father wouldn't help him and had borrowed money from them that they desperately needed. His wife was ill too and they had a baby,' Payne said.

'Did you meet him at all either then or since?' the chief inspector persisted.

'No, not that I recall. Listen, is there much more, Chief Inspector, only I don't see how I'm really able to be much help to you.' Joshua Payne fidgeted in his seat and glanced towards the door of the office where Matt was certain a constable was standing outside.

'Captain Bryant, do you have any questions for Mr Payne before he returns to Plymouth?' Chief Inspector Greville looked at Matt.

'You have spent many years now at sea, Mr Payne. Do you have regular routes?' Matt asked.

He had an idea percolating at the back of his mind and wanted to see if he was correct.

The man appeared surprised by the question. 'I have regular port stops. New York, South America, that kind of thing.'

'And that has been the case over the last ten years?' Matt smiled genially as if just making casual conversation.

'Yes, but what's that got to do with anything?' Payne lifted his chin belligerently as he spoke.

'I was just curious,' Matt said as Payne eyed him with suspicion.

'Thank you for your cooperation, Mr Payne, it's much appreciated. By the way, may I ask where you were on Sunday morning?' the chief inspector asked as Payne was about to get up from his seat.

Payne dropped back down on his chair, his cap still in his hand. 'Sunday?'

'Yes, this Sunday morning.' Chief Inspector Greville looked at him expectantly.

'I don't... I mean, I'm not sure. I think I went back to Mother's to collect some papers and a few small sentimental pieces for the last time, then, I don't know. I may have wandered about a bit down by the pier on Paignton seafront.'

Matt thought the man looked decidedly shifty.

'Did you see anyone you knew, or meet anyone?' Chief Inspector Greville asked.

'I don't think so. I mean there were people out walking their dogs. It was cold down there, a wind blowing in off the sea with some decent waves,' Payne said.

'You didn't take the bus or the train to Totnes at all?' Chief Inspector Greville asked.

'Why would I go to Totnes?' Payne demanded. 'What's this about?'

'Tilly Maldon was murdered there on Sunday and her body thrown into the river.' Chief Inspector Greville's eyes were flinty.

'I haven't seen Tilly Maldon for years. How would I know where to find her even if I wanted to? Which I didn't. I certainly wouldn't be there to kill somebody I barely knew ten years ago,' Payne said.

'We do have to ask everyone who may have been connected to Thomas Crabtree and now Tilly Maldon.' Chief Inspector Greville's tone was mild.

'Well, you can scratch me off your list.' Payne glared at him. 'If we're done, I need to get back to Plymouth. I've things to do, like finding a permanent place to stop over Christmas before I'm due to get my next ship.'

Chief Inspector Greville called out to the constable and Joshua Payne was escorted out of the room, still looking angry about the policeman's question.

'Well, Captain Bryant, what did you make of our friend, Mr Payne?'

Matt looked at the chief inspector. 'I don't think he was being entirely honest with us.' In fact, Matt got the distinct impression that Joshua Payne had known exactly where Tilly Maldon lived.

Chief Inspector Greville's moustache lifted upwards as he smiled. 'I agree. We shall be keeping a close watch on him until he sails.'

* * *

Kitty's decision to telephone Alice so they could meet up the next day was spurred on by what Matt told her on his return home. She set aside her writing paper and the last few Christmas cards she had to post to one side. He told her all about the interview with Joshua Payne and what his impressions had been of the man.

'Both you and the chief inspector thought he was less than honest?' Kitty said. 'Oh dear. Do you think he may have gone to see Tilly?'

'I don't know. I can't see how he would know where she was unless someone told him. If they did tell him, then why?' Matt patted the top of Bertie's head as the dog rested his nose on Matt's knee.

'Maybe Tilly herself contacted him somehow?' Kitty suggested.

'If he wasn't at his mother's then how would she find him?' Matt countered.

'Hmm, I suppose she couldn't then. And you asked him about his routes and the ports?' Kitty looked at her husband.

It was a question she would have asked given the timing of the robberies and how often Joshua Payne might return home.

'Regular routes for much of the time. The Americas mostly are his main ports of call,' Matt said. 'That means he is often away for three or six months at a time before returning back to Plymouth depending on the trade route.'

Kitty nodded, an idea of her own niggling at the back of her mind. 'He said he met Mr Maldon because he was looking for a card school?' She knew gambling in such a way was illegal but a sailor with money in his pocket to burn would have been tempting prey to Thomas Crabtree and his friends.

'That was his story. He claims he only knew Fred Smith in passing and the same for Lavinia Crabtree. He never met William as he was ill. Inspector Lewis and his men are still on Dartmoor searching for Arthur Maldon,' Matt said.

'It's strange how the man has managed to disappear so completely. It's like one of those conjuring tricks with smoke and mirrors. You know, look over here instead of over there and poof, gone in a puff of smoke.' Kitty was deeply suspicious of why there had been no trace of Mr Maldon.

By all accounts he had seemed a larger-than-life character with a lot of connections and influence in the crooked world in which he lived. Surely by now some trace of him would have emerged. She had no doubt that if the man was alive, he must have heard that the police wished to speak to him.

'Let us hope he is still alive. The longer time goes on without him being found, it does raise the question that he may be another victim,' Matt said.

Kitty knew her husband was right. She had been thinking the same thing. She had a feeling however that Maldon was in hiding, not dead. 'He may be frightened for his life,' she said. 'That could well be another reason he has not come forward. If he has heard somehow about poor Tilly.'

'You have a point. There seems so much that was going on

back then that was not above board. Even if any or all of them are lying, it's hard to know what they may be lying about. It could just be over the gambling or that Arthur Maldon and Thomas Crabtree seem to have been hiding and fencing stolen goods. Then we don't know if any of them were involved in the robberies and if Tilly knew something about that which could have got her killed,' Matt said.

'If we assume that all of them have lied to us at some point then who do we think has been the most truthful?' Kitty asked.

Matt considered her question carefully. 'Probably William and Lavinia Crabtree,' he suggested.

'Then let's go from there and see if we can untangle all of this,' Kitty said. 'I'll make some tea and get us a slice of Christmas cake.'

CHAPTER TWENTY-TWO

Armed with tea and a slice of rich iced fruit cake they went back over everything that Lavinia and William had both told them about Thomas Crabtree.

'Lavinia was clearly furious that William's father had tricked or pressured him into giving him what little savings they had while he was so ill,' Matt said as he picked the last of the cake crumbs from his plate.

'I can understand how she felt. She wasn't well herself and she said their eldest daughter was only a few months old at the time. Lavinia said the church had come to their rescue and saved them from eviction. It was why she does so much for the church even now,' Kitty said thoughtfully. 'I wonder.' She jumped up from her chair, startling Rascal who meowed a protest as Kitty went out to the telephone in the hall.

'Hello, Mrs Craven, I hope I'm not disturbing you?' Kitty never enjoyed calling Mrs Craven and she knew she ran the risk of being volunteered into another unwanted job by doing so.

'Not at all, Kitty, dear, my committee ladies have just gone home. How can I help? Is it another case? The Crabtree one? Thank you for returning my china by the way. Dora inspected it thoroughly and it was such a relief to see it unscathed,' Mrs Craven asked.

Kitty suppressed a sigh and tried to sound cheerful. 'It was just something Lavinia Crabtree mentioned on Sunday about the time when her father-in-law disappeared. He had borrowed a sum of money from them, this was when her husband was seriously ill. She mentioned that the church had assisted them. She seemed very grateful for the help, and I assumed it must have been something substantial. I wondered if you knew anything about that?'

'Well, my dear, I'm sure as good Christians the church hardship fund would have certainly helped but it would only have been in a small way. Food for the children and perhaps some knitted garments from the mothers' group. Let me think, I would have been on the parish and church councils when the decisions were made for funding, I'd certainly remember if we had done something out of the ordinary.'

Kitty waited for Mrs Craven to think back. She knew the older woman to have an excellent memory when it came to her committees and their funds.

'Yes, now I remember. She did have some relief from the parish fund but only a small amount. We had quite a debate at the committee meeting about what we could offer. If I recall correctly a distant relative of Lavinia's stepped in with a loan to cover their rent. Most generous and just in time to save them from eviction. It also meant she could cover the doctor's fees and the medication for her husband. A true Christmas miracle I thought at the time.'

'Lavinia was certainly most fortunate. Thank you so much, Mrs Craven. I'm afraid I must dash, Matt is calling me.' Kitty put down the receiver quickly before she could be engaged in further conversation.

'That was an interesting piece of information,' Kitty said as she relayed the content of the conversation to Matt.

'Hmm, it sounds to me as if Lavinia may have recovered the money from her father-in-law. I'm inclined to suspect this other mystery donor doesn't exist especially as she always gives the church credit for their help at that time.' Matt looked thoughtful.

'Do you think she recovered the money before or after his murder?' Kitty asked.

Could Lavinia have killed him during another argument? One that had taken place at the farm? If she was the murderer then who had killed Tilly and why? Were the murders not linked after all? It seemed unlikely that William Crabtree could have killed the girl. His hand had been heavily bandaged after Kitty had hit him with the poker and he had been with his children.

'She may have gone to the farm before it was found he had vanished. She could have gone to confront him, found the place empty and spied her chance to go inside and take what was theirs,' Matt suggested.

'If that was the case then I could see why she wouldn't say anything about it in case anyone thought she was a thief or had something to do with his disappearance,' Kitty agreed.

'Then when we found his body that made her position worse if that is what happened. She would become the main suspect,' Matt said.

'I suppose if she did take the money then that accounts for why that wasn't found after her father-in-law disappeared. I wonder if her husband realises that's what she did? I mean if he was looking around the farm, then maybe he believes her story that the church helped them,' Kitty said.

'He was seriously ill at the time so he may well not have realised. The money that was missing now seems to be accounted for if we accept that Lavinia took it but that still leaves the mystery of the stolen jewels.' Matt scratched his chin as he stared into the glowing wood in the fireplace.

A log shifted sending a shower of sparks up the chimney and Bertie raised his head to glare at the offending piece of firewood.

'Perhaps someone else collected those. That could well be the person who killed him and who may have also killed Tilly.' Kitty gave an involuntary shiver.

'One of the members of the gang of thieves perhaps?' Matt suggested. He reached into the log basket for another piece of firewood to drop onto the fire.

'Who were those thieves? We know that Maldon was the man who moved the goods on. Crabtree was the bagman, keeping the goods hidden until Maldon had a buyer, but then who stole them?' Kitty asked as she watched Matt rearrange the fire so that the wood would catch light safely.

'I think Joshua Payne knows far more than he was letting on. His trips could have provided Maldon with a way to move anything that was too hot to sell in this country overseas.' Matt looked at Kitty.

'I agree. That was what I was thinking. I don't know if he also may have taken part in the robberies when he was ashore. It would account for the pattern of several happening together and then a gap of several weeks or months before the next ones. That would have given them time to stash the goods and for Maldon to find a buyer here. Anything that was considered too risky Payne could have taken with him for disposal abroad.' Kitty had been giving the matter some considerable thought.

'That does seem to fit. Is Fred Smith involved in the thefts at all, do you think? Or even William Crabtree before he was ill? He could possibly have been in on it.' Matt replaced the fire irons in the brass stand.

'It's possible. Maldon may also have participated. Having one role in a gang like that doesn't stop them from having other jobs. He could have been actively involved in the robberies. That would make Thomas Crabtree's murder possibly the result of a falling out amongst thieves. Did he try to double-cross them do you think? Or was he going to try and get the reward for information about the robbery? That tiara with such a distinctive stone would have been virtually impossible to get rid of at least in this country,' Kitty said.

'True, but none of our suspects appear to have gained materially since the robbery at Seacliffe House and Crabtree's death, so what has become of the jewels in the meantime? Did Crabtree hide them somewhere in his role as bagman and they haven't ever found them?' Matt asked.

'You mean Betty could be right about the jewels still being hidden somewhere at Midwinter Farm? Unless, of course, Arthur Maldon is secretly very wealthy and has lain low about it all this time. I wonder if the inspector has finally found him. I really want to know what he has to say about all of this,' Kitty said.

'Unfortunately, we shall have to wait and see. I think until they do discover what has become of the man, we should keep our thoughts on this to ourselves for now. We have no real proof, only our suspicion of where Lavinia obtained the money to save her family. Perhaps by tomorrow we may know much more, and we can approach the police with our thoughts then,' Matt suggested.

Much as it irked Kitty to agree, she knew he was right. She longed to jump in her car and head for the moors to search for Maldon herself. Not that it would do any good unless they could narrow the search area. If the police were struggling to locate him with all their resources, then she and Matt stood little or no chance.

Even so it was all very frustrating. She was sure they were on the right track about the robberies at least. The big question was how did it tie in with the murders? Or was it even anything to do with the murders? Thomas Crabtree had made plenty of enemies without his death being related to the goods he had probably been minding.

He had swindled Joshua Payne at cards, something that even now the sailor clearly deeply resented. Fifty pounds was a very large sum of money. Lavinia had hated him for taking money from his son while he had been seriously ill. Fred Smith had resented the way he had ogled Tilly Maldon, pestering and leching after a girl young enough to be his daughter. Tilly had disliked him and who knows what her father, Arthur Maldon, had thought.

He had barred him from his pub, and they had clearly fallen out despite any connection they may have had over the robberies. Or over any other goods that Crabtree may have stored for Maldon previously. Which then took her thoughts to Tilly's murder. Why had the girl been killed? There had to be a connection. It surely wasn't just a coincidence.

Matt glanced her way and smiled. She knew he could tell what she was thinking.

'I'm going to telephone Alice this evening. It's her day off tomorrow from the shop and I want to see if she might be free for an hour for lunch,' Kitty said.

'You want to go back to Midwinter Farm, don't you?' Matt looked at her. 'Are you going to tell Alice everything else that you've discovered?'

'I think she should know, don't you? I mean we've pieced together so much more since you last spoke to Robert,' Kitty said. It had been playing on her conscience that perhaps her friend might be in the dark about some of the developments in the case which might affect her.

'That's true. I do think perhaps we should let Alice know everything, about Tilly and about what we think Thomas Crabtree was doing at the farm.' The smile faded from Matt's face to be replaced by a grave expression. 'I just hope it doesn't upset her or make her feel more negatively about living there.'

'I know, but in a way I think it may make her feel better knowing there was a reason or reasons why Thomas may have been murdered. It means that it's not a bad place or an unlucky one. It just had one bad former tenant,' Kitty said. At least, she hoped that was how her friend would feel.

'I hope you can help her to see that. I suppose too that you'd like to go and poke around the farm and the outbuildings in case you can stumble upon Thomas Crabtree's hiding places?' Matt's smile returned.

Kitty looked slightly abashed. Her husband knew her all too well. 'It wouldn't hurt just to double-check everything. Put Betty's theory to the test. I know Robert has done a lot of work to the place so the potential for finding a hiding place must be small. Even so it has to be worth a shot and Alice may feel better knowing it's all been checked.'

'I suppose you have a point,' Matt agreed.

'Besides,' Kitty said impishly. 'You know that you would like to have a look around the place yourself, admit it.'

Matt chuckled and was forced to agree.

After supper Kitty telephoned her friend. She had waited until Alice had a chance to have closed up her shop and rested for a while before her own supper. Kitty knew how exhausting running the shop was for her friend, especially with Christmas so close and so many people needing her services as well as purchasing gifts.

'Kitty, how is everything? Have the police found who killed Mr Crabtree yet?' Alice asked as soon as Kitty had greeted her.

'I think they are getting closer to working things out. I have lots to tell you. Are you free tomorrow at all? We could finish off hanging the curtains at the farm and Matt and I can tell you everything we've discovered. We could even get a fish supper afterwards,' Kitty wheedled.

'I suspect that I'm not going to like everything you're going to tell me. Robert has told me as much as he knows but it sounds from the way you're talking that even more things have come to light,' Alice said, a hint of suspicion in her tone.

'You did want to get the house looking more lived in this side of Christmas,' Kitty said.

'Why are you so keen to go back to the farm? You aren't planning on whacking no one else with a poker, are you?' Alice teased.

'I do hope not.' Kitty shuddered at the thought. 'There's just a few things we want to look at and it might help if we all go back and see that everything really is perfectly lovely there.'

'Throw off any badness?' Alice asked in a slightly worried tone.

'Yes, give the house good, positive feelings again with your lovely curtains,' Kitty said.

'All right, I can spare a few hours. I need a break and I'm holding you to a fish supper. Robert is too busy with work at the moment, so he won't be able to come,' Alice said.

'That's a shame but I'm sure he'll be pleased that you're going back there and preparing the house for after the wedding.' Kitty arranged a time to collect her friend the next day and ended the call.

She might not be able to track down Arthur Maldon but at least she could help her friend and check the farm over in case something was still hidden somewhere on the premises.

There was a sharp frost the following morning and Kitty's breath hung in a white cloud in front of her face as she, Matt and Bertie bundled into her car to go and collect Alice. Kitty drove with care on the icy road into Paignton to Alice's shop.

Matt jumped out and assisted Alice with her brown paper parcel of curtains while Kitty persuaded Bertie to make room on the back seat for her.

'Go on then, tell me the worst and get it over with on the

way to the farm. If it's too bad then you'll have time to turn around and take me back home again,' Alice said as she adjusted her warm emerald-green knitted scarf around her neck.

Matt glanced at Kitty, who was still concentrating on the slippery road, and he launched into a precise report of everything they knew.

'Another murder?' Alice asked in a horrified voice. 'And this Tilly was the landlord's daughter, the one who was seeing Fred Smith?'

'That's right,' Kitty said. They were back up at Hillhead now and almost at the turn down the hill towards the old toll house. The frost was thawing quickly from the fields leaving behind bare, wet branches in the hedgerows.

'Dear me, and is it all connected do you think with this Thomas Crabtree and whatever he was up to?' Alice asked.

'We think so but there is no proof right now. The chief inspector and Inspector Lewis are using all their manpower on the case,' Matt assured her.

'Oh, don't I know the sacrifices Inspector Lewis is making. Our Betty never fails to remind me of how busy and important he is. James this and James that. She said he had been working on the moor yesterday near Ashburton.' Kitty glanced in the driver's mirror and saw Alice roll her eyes as she spoke.

She could imagine Betty dropping her boyfriend's name into every conversation, especially now he was involved in trying to solve the Crabtree murder. She turned the car down the narrow lanes that led to Alice's house. Everywhere looked bleak and deserted. The red earth in the arable fields lay bare of crops with the black crows pecking over the exposed soil.

The lone pine tree that stood beside the gate loomed up out of the mist that had started to descend the closer they had drawn to the farm. Alice hopped out of the car to unlock the gate's padlock and opened it ready for Kitty to drive into the yard and park near the large stone barn where Robert stored his vehicles.

Kitty parked her car and Matt lifted Bertie from the back seat, while Alice gathered up her curtains. A pair of crows cawed mournfully to one another from the top of the tree and the chimney pot on the farmhouse roof. The sound seeming to echo in the gloom.

'Brr, let's get inside and get the fires going,' Alice suggested as Matt came to help her with the curtains. 'A cup of tea wouldn't go amiss either, afore we start.'

She led the way to the front door and unlocked it so they could all go in. Bertie followed them, happily sniffing at all the different scents, clearly delighted at having a new place to explore. Matt draped the parcel of curtains over the back of one of the kitchen chairs and set to, lighting the fire. Alice filled the kettle and put it on the hob to make tea.

Kitty switched on the kitchen light since the mist and accompanying drizzle was making the room feel dark and dreary. With the light on and a minute or two later orange flames licking at the kindling in the grate, the atmosphere soon changed to one of cosy warmth.

'Right ho then, now what are we doing first? Hanging these curtains upstairs or poking about the house and barns looking for whatever might be hidden here?' Alice asked as she placed a tray of tea on the kitchen table.

CHAPTER TWENTY-THREE

Matt proposed they make a plan while having their tea. They agreed to spend an hour looking around the farmhouse and the outbuildings for possible hiding places. Then they would stop and hang the curtains before having some lunch.

'I will feel easier once I know as there's no possibility of anything having been left here by that Mr Crabtree,' Alice said.

'We can help you spread the word afterwards too that the place has been searched. That should stop anyone from getting fanciful ideas about looking for treasure up here.' Kitty thought this should make Alice feel safer.

'Like our Betty you mean?' Alice smiled as she spoke.

'We should split up to search and do each area in order,' Matt suggested.

Kitty and Alice agreed.

'There isn't a cellar in the farmhouse. The floors are tiled all in here and the hall and scullery space and there's no loose boards in any of the ground floor rooms. Robert had them all fixed by the carpenter as a few of the planks were rotten,' Alice said as she sipped her tea.

'William said he had checked the floorboards downstairs years ago, before his father even disappeared and there were no hiding places there then,' Matt said.

'What about the attic?' Kitty asked as she slipped Bertie half a broken biscuit from the tin Alice had produced from her pantry.

'You can look if you want but again, Robert had the carpenter go up there to fix one of the joists as it was wet from where some of the tiles had to be replaced. The hatch had been nailed shut and he had to prise them out to get inside. I remember him saying it was completely bare.' Alice looked sternly at Bertie when he sidled up to her in case she too might have a biscuit.

'Well, that saves us from going up there.' Kitty couldn't help feeling relieved. She hadn't fancied looking up in an attic or down a dank cellar. She knew Matt, with his fear of enclosed spaces caused by his experiences in the Great War, would feel the same way.

'The bathroom is all new and the boards came up to lay the pipes for the plumbing so that won't have anything.' Alice frowned as she spoke.

'This is really helpful, Alice, thank you. It'll save us a lot of time while we're searching the house by ruling some of the rooms out,' Kitty said in an encouraging tone.

'What about the barn where Robert keeps Daisybelle the old charabanc, and the tool shed?' Matt asked as he finished his tea and replaced his cup on the tray.

'I suppose they might be a possibility. He did clear the old hayloft though so I don't think there will be anything up on that level. I don't know about the one part of the barn as there was some old machinery there.' Alice too finished her drink and prepared to carry the tray to the sink.

'I'll go outside and start with the outbuildings. Kitty, is the torch still in the glove box of your car?' Matt asked.

'Yes, I think so.' Kitty finished her tea and went to help Alice wash the tea things before embarking on her own search of the farmhouse.

Matt wrapped his scarf around his neck and tugged his cap down low before venturing back out into the cold. Bertie happily accompanied him, eager to explore the many enticing scents in the old farmyard. Kitty and Alice washed the tea things and then headed upstairs.

'We might as well take these curtains up with us. There's no point in wasting a journey,' Alice pointed out.

Kitty assisted her friend in taking everything up. The set of steps was already in the front bedroom.

'Where shall we start looking then?' Alice asked as she cast a dubious eye around the bare room. The walls had been freshly painted in primrose yellow, and the floorboards were bare. Alice was saving for a set of bedroom furniture from the second-hand shop in Paignton which she hoped to buy to furnish the room.

'Tap the walls and the skirting boards and look for any loose floorboards,' Kitty suggested. 'Is it worth looking up the chimneys?'

'Robert had them swept and inspected. They was all clean, nothing on any ledges, not even those witch things that people used to put in olden times. Although, I have to say, I were glad about that. I didn't fancy them finding a dead cat or no old shoes or something.' Alice shivered in distaste.

'I know what you mean. I don't think I would have liked that either,' Kitty agreed. She knew that many old houses had things placed in their chimneys to ward off witches or evil spirits. Midwinter Farm was certainly old enough to have been one of those places.

The two women went around the room systematically tapping and probing all the surfaces including the broad wooden windowsill.

'There's nothing in here. Let's try next door,' Alice said.

The second bedroom was another good-sized room and overlooked the orchard at the back of the farm. The walls again had been freshly painted. This time in white, and the only furniture was a pine chest of drawers that Robert had procured from a customer who was throwing it out. He had mended a broken drawer, and they had placed it in the room to use as a linen store.

Once more they went around the room tapping and probing every surface, sill and baseboard.

'There's just the box room left to try now,' Alice said. The box room was a small, single room which housed the slope for the head of the stairs. Kitty refrained from saying it was a perfect size for a nursery.

Again, the floorboards were bare and there was no furniture in the white painted room. 'Not a sausage.' Alice brushed her hands together to knock off the dust she had acquired from probing a loose floorboard.

'Did you hear Bertie?' Kitty frowned and strained to listen. 'I thought I heard him barking. I do hope he hasn't found a mouse or something stinky to roll in.'

She went back into the front bedroom to look out of the window towards the barns. Any barking had ceased so she guessed Matt must have found whatever her dog had discovered.

'I can't hear him now, or see them. They must be inside the barn.' Alice had joined her. 'Landing next and the cupboard?'

Alice once more checked the floorboards and skirting while Kitty probed inside the spacious cupboard on the landing.

'Nothing again.' Kitty couldn't help feeling a little crestfallen. She had been certain they would discover something of interest during their treasure hunt.

Alice, however, had grown ever more chirpy with every room that contained nothing more than a hint of dust and a splash of paint.

'That's it for up here then. Well, we'd best go and check downstairs I suppose. Best not to rely completely on William Crabtree. He might not have been telling the truth,' Alice said. 'Then we can hang these blessed curtains.'

Kitty reluctantly followed her friend down the staircase.

'I must get Robert to look at this step again. I thought as he'd fixed this creak,' Alice said as the third step from the bottom groaned as she stood on it.

'The stairs, we need to check the stairs. Alice, look at the one you're standing on,' Kitty urged, her pulse quickening.

'It's just a loose board. I was sure he had nailed it down. I've asked him enough times,' Alice grumbled as she stepped down into the hall and turned to examine the faulty step.

Kitty came to stand on the step above the one Alice was probing. 'There, Alice, press down on that little notch.'

Alice obeyed, leaning her thumb on a barely discernible notch at the side of the step where it was set into the wall. As she did so the tread of the step lifted like a lid. Kitty's heart raced as her friend moved the piece of wood aside and peered into the gap below. Concealed under the step was a dusty brown canvas drawstring bag.

'Oh my days, I think we may have found it,' Alice said as she lifted the bag from its hiding place. 'There was something here after all. Our Betty will never let me hear the end of it if she's right. Gosh, it's heavy.'

She heaved the bag out of its hiding place. As she passed it up to Kitty something clanked inside the bag. Alice replaced the tread of the stair, so Kitty would be able to come down to join her. 'Bring it into the kitchen and put it on the table. Let's see what we've got,' Alice urged as Kitty hurried down to the hall.

Together they went through to the kitchen and placed the mysterious bag on the table. Kitty's pulse raced with excitement at their discovery. Alice opened up the drawstring and pulled the canvas open. They gasped in unison as the contents were revealed.

Tarnished silver candlesticks, rose bowls and a couple of vases, a snuff box and a set of spoons. Red velvet-covered jewellery boxes and a larger cream coloured leatherette box. Kitty's hand shook as she raised the hinged lid on the larger box to discover a magnificent tiara. The stones twinkled and blazed with an iridescent colour under the brightness of the overhead electric light. The centre stone shone a soft yellowy-orange colour sending fragments of light dancing around the room.

'Oh my goodness, we must go and get Matt,' Kitty said.

'I don't think it'll be necessary to get anyone.' A male voice from behind them in the kitchen doorway made them both whirl around in shock.

An older man dressed in a dark coat and cap blocked their exit into the hall. Behind him the front door stood slightly ajar allowing a cold draught to blow along the hall.

'Who are you? Where did you come from?' Alice demanded as she grabbed at Kitty's arm for support.

'I should thank you, ladies. I've been looking for my property for a good long time now.' The man was in his mid-sixties, Kitty guessed. He was heavyset with cold eyes and a swarthy complexion. A handgun was cocked and primed ready in his hand and he had the barrel pointed right at them.

'Arthur Maldon, I presume,' Kitty said.

The man smiled a thin, humourless grin that revealed brown, broken teeth. 'Correct. I wouldn't bother shouting for help if that was what you was planning. The gentleman and his dog are busy right now in the barn.'

'If you've hurt Matt or Bertie.' Panic filled Kitty's chest, and she glared at the man they had all been searching for. The barking she thought she had heard must have been Bertie trying to warn them.

'Not at all. He's just cooling his heels for a bit in there. Got a good lock fitted on that door,' Arthur Maldon remarked.

Kitty's immediate panic quelled a little at his words and she hoped he was telling the truth about having merely locked Matt inside the outbuilding.

'The police have been looking everywhere for you,' Kitty said.

'So I gather. I don't know what I'm supposed to tell them though,' Arthur observed.

'Perhaps you could begin with how you killed Thomas Crabtree?' Kitty suggested. 'Although you miscalculated there didn't you, because you couldn't find where he'd hidden this lot. I can see these are the things stolen from the Massey house.'

'Thomas's death were an accident. The plan was to have a chat with him and collect the goods. A tap on the head to make him see reason but he fell awkward and hit a big stone. It had seemed a good plan that we had. I'm not a violent man by nature.' Arthur looked at Kitty.

'Why did you come here that night? We know that you and Mr Crabtree had argued, and you had barred him from your pub. Was it just to retrieve the jewels?' Kitty asked. Alice's fingers dug into the flesh of her arm, and she knew her friend was scared.

'Thomas had become a liability. The fight with Fred Smith was one thing but then when Joshua caught him cheating with the cards, then I knew we needed to cut him out of the loop.' Arthur's eyes narrowed as he studied Kitty. 'You seem to know a lot about it all.'

'I'm a private investigator, as is my husband, the man you have locked in the barn. I think we have quite a lot of it worked out. I expect Chief Inspector Greville and Inspector Lewis have too. You were angry over him upsetting Joshua Payne because he used to dispose of items too hot to sell in this country on his trips overseas.' Kitty lifted her chin and met Arthur's gaze. Alice drew a little closer to her.

'Crabtree was reckless. The police had been sniffing round, and we needed to get the stuff out of the country. We came here to reason with him. I was going to pay him his cut early. He was desperate for money. Lord Massey's land agent was going to evict him as he was behind on the rent.' Arthur kept his gun levelled at Kitty almost as if daring her to question what he had told her.

'How did you lure him outside and why?' Kitty asked.

A crafty smile tugged at the corner of Arthur's lips. 'I knew Thomas would be wary if I cornered him in here. I thought that outside I stood a better chance of talking to him. I had a couple of people to assist me in case he didn't want to give up the goods.'

'You made a noise out by the hen coop in the old piggery so he would think it was a fox,' Alice chipped in, drawing Maldon's attention in her direction.

'That's right. I knew he hadn't got his shotgun no more since the constable had confiscated it. He had to go out himself to scare a fox away. That's when he had the bump to his head,' Arthur confirmed.

Kitty could see what had happened, Thomas being lured outside by the hens squawking. The hit on his head to knock him out. Then the man falling and hitting his head for the second time, on that occasion fatally on the broken-down stone wall.

'Where does your daughter, Tilly, fit into all this?' Kitty asked.

Arthur frowned. 'Only that she was the one who set the hens off while I lay in wait for Thomas. I'd promised her some money. She wanted to go on the stage.'

Kitty had the uneasy feeling that they were not getting all of the answers from Arthur but before she could ask anything else he motioned the gun at them. 'Enough talking. Outside, both of you. I reckon as you can join the bloke in the barn while I reclaim my property.'

Alice kept hold of Kitty's arm as Arthur forced them both out of the kitchen and along the hallway and out of the front door. The cold air made her gasp as the mist moved blurring their surroundings.

The gravel crunched under their feet as Arthur marched them across the yard past Kitty's car towards the barn door. Alice stumbled as she walked, earning her a gruff rebuke from the man with the gun.

'Why did you kill Tilly? Was it because she was going to go to the police about what happened that night?' Kitty asked as Arthur took out the key to the padlock with his free hand. She couldn't see why Tilly would have waited all those years and not said anything. Her father had abandoned her at her time of need and treated her cruelly. She could have had no loyalty to him.

She saw a range of emotions flick across Arthur's face. 'I've never hurt Tilly and never would, not even after all she's done. What do you mean, she's dead?'

'That was why the police were so desperate to talk to you. They left messages all over the place. Someone murdered her on Sunday in Totnes. They throttled her and pushed her into the river,' Kitty said. She could see that what she was saying was a complete surprise to Arthur. 'Who else was with you that night when you came to get the jewels from Thomas Crabtree?'

He had mentioned a couple of people. Tilly had been one so who had been the third?

'I don't believe you. There wouldn't be no cause to hurt Tilly,' Arthur said.

'I'm afraid it's true, Mr Maldon,' Alice said. 'The police were searching for you to tell you, as well as investigating Mr Crabtree's death and the jewel thefts.'

Kitty saw the effects of Alice's confirmation of his daughter's murder on Arthur's face.

'That double-crossing...' Arthur snarled the words out before breaking off mid-sentence. 'Never mind that now. I'll get you two in here and then I'm away. It'll take them a while to find you I expect. The man with the touring bus will be back this evening.'

'That's my fiancé. He owns this property. Have you been watching us?' Alice asked.

'Only to see when the coast was clear so I could come and do a bit more searching. I saw William Crabtree poking around, and you.' He inclined his head towards Kitty. 'Then the police and the telephone people.'

Kitty had been listening for any sounds from within the barn. The building was a sturdy one, built of local stone with a heavy pair of tall, wooden sliding doors which gave an opening big enough for Robert to park his buses inside. The door Maldon was about to open was a pedestrian door cut into the larger doors to save having to open the whole thing when just one person needed to enter the building.

She thought she could hear the muffled sound of Bertie barking and Matt's voice calling her name from inside the barn.

'Matt!' she shouted his name, hoping he could hear her and know she was by the door.

Arthur scowled and inserted the key in the padlock, stepping around behind Alice and Kitty ready to pop open the lock to usher them inside.

Much to Kitty's relief she heard Matt's voice again calling her name. He sounded much closer, and she guessed he was standing on the other side of the door.

'He's got a gun, Matt, stand clear!' She hoped he could hear what she was saying. If Maldon undid the lock and Matt came to charge out she was under no illusion that he would probably shoot.

'Once you two are safely out of the way then I'm off,' Maldon said as he prepared to remove the lock, his attention temporarily on the door.

'Oh no you don't. You don't get to swindle me twice, Maldon.' Another male voice sounded through the mist behind them. Kitty, Alice and their captor turned to see who had joined them.

CHAPTER TWENTY-FOUR

Kitty didn't recognise the voice or the man emerging from the dense, freezing fog. He was of average height and build, his face shaded by the brim of his dark-brown hat. She could, however, see that he too carried a gun, and his weapon was pointed at Arthur Maldon.

'Joshua, long time no see,' Arthur greeted the stranger in a level tone. He seemed unsurprised by the stranger's sudden arrival.

Alice looked at Kitty and mouthed, 'Joshua Payne?'

Kitty gave a quick affirmative nod of her head. She couldn't see who else it could be.

Tension seemed to mount as thick as the dense winter mist that surrounded them as the two former friends faced one another at the door of the barn.

'It's been a while. I take it you finally found the goods then? Planning on keeping it all for yourself, I suppose?' Payne asked, an edge of menace in his tone.

Kitty's heart banged against her ribcage, and she could hear Matt echoing the sound with his fist against the thick wood of the barn door. Her husband was no doubt wondering what was happening outside in the yard.

'I didn't think you'd be back. My condolences, I hear your mother has passed away.' Maldon's own tone was even but Kitty could see his grip had tightened around the handle of his gun.

'She has. It's lucky for me then that I decided to call here when I did. I had intended to return to Plymouth to wait for my ship,' Payne replied.

Kitty gave Alice a gentle, discreet nudge to try and move slowly backwards out of the direct line of fire from the two men while their attention was on each other.

Alice bit her upper lip and slackened her hold on Kitty's arm moving a fraction of an inch away from the door and closer to where Kitty's car was parked.

'I take it you heard that the police found Crabtree's body?' Arthur asked.

'It took them long enough.' Payne's attention was still on Arthur, and Kitty joined Alice in making a slight move away from the men. 'Ten years, and now you have the jewels and the silver he had hidden away all this time.'

'There is plenty there for both of us,' Arthur said.

'Now you want to share, how very gentlemanly of you,' Payne sneered.

Arthur didn't reply. Instead, he fired his gun at Payne. Kitty and Alice screamed at the unexpected sound of the shot. Kitty automatically shoved her friend to the floor and dived down with her as the younger man dropped like a stone, a surprised expression on his face.

Alice huddled closer to Kitty, her face white with fear, as Maldon stepped forward a few paces to kick Payne's gun from his hand.

'You murdered my girl,' Maldon spat at the injured man.

Bertie barked inside the barn and Matt's banging on the door grew more frantic after the gunshot.

'She was going to the police. Had to stop her. We didn't

mean to kill Crabtree.' Payne was curled over, his hands pressed against his abdomen in a vain attempt to staunch the flow of blood. His gasps for breath grew shorter and Alice buried her face against Kitty's shoulder. Kitty could feel Alice trembling.

'You two, up and into the barn.' Maldon turned back to Kitty and Alice.

Kitty helped Alice to her feet. Her friend had begun to sob quietly, and Kitty couldn't bring herself to look at Payne's prone form where he was now lying still on the floor. She couldn't tell if he was alive or dead. Maldon steered them back to the barn door and removed the padlock.

'Stand aside in there or I'll shoot,' he shouted as he cracked open the door.

Before he had time to open it fully and push Kitty and Alice through the gap, Bertie charged out. He had wriggled his way through the opening space and made a dash for freedom.

The dog cannoned into Maldon's legs throwing him slightly off balance and Kitty dived forward hurling herself with all her weight onto the man to bring them both to the floor. The impact knocked the breath from her body and she fought to try and keep Maldon from breaking free.

Alice sprang after her, scrambling across the gravel to get to the gun which had been knocked clear of Maldon's grasp.

'I've got the gun, and I'm not frightened of using it.' Alice stood over Maldon, her words coming in little gasps as Matt burst out from the barn to see what was happening. Bertie continued to cavort around Kitty as she struggled to her feet while her dog attempted to lick her face.

'Give me the gun, Alice. Kitty, go and telephone the police and an ambulance for Mr Payne.' Matt took the weapon from Alice's trembling fingers and kept it trained on Maldon who remained still and winded on the floor near his former friend.

Kitty and Alice ran back inside the house leaving Matt to stand guard. Kitty dialled the number of the police station with trembling fingers to summon help. Alice, practical as ever now the shock was leaving her system, found some old towels from the kitchen. She hurried back outside to see if there was anything that could be done for the wounded man.

Once Kitty knew the police and an ambulance were on their way she went out to Alice and Matt, with Bertie sticking close to her heels. Matt had taken a leaf out of Maldon's book and had secured him inside the barn. Her husband was now kneeling beside Joshua Payne's motionless form and was administering what aid he could.

Matt was clearly using his experiences during the Great War to try to assist the wounded man. Kitty could only hope the ambulance or a doctor could reach him in time.

'Maldon, mastermind behind robberies,' Payne gasped between gritted teeth. His voice was barely audible, his face contorted in pain.

'Try not to talk,' Matt ordered as Alice, pale but determined, tore up her thin cotton towels into strips to make packing for the man's wound.

'Tilly was lookout, going to police.' Payne's voice grew fainter, and Kitty and Alice exchanged anxious glances.

'It sounds as if she was part of the gang.' Kitty helped Alice with her task, crouching down on the cold gravel to hand Matt the makeshift bandages.

'Yes, she took the money to Lavinia.' Joshua barely managed the last few words before losing consciousness.

'Oh thank heavens, someone's coming,' Alice said as they heard the distant sound of a fast car growing ever closer.

'It's Doctor Carter, he must have come up from Dartmouth.' Kitty breathed a sigh of relief as the doctor's familiar sporty car shot into the yard and pulled up beside hers in a small shower of gravel.

The doctor jumped out of his car with surprising speed for his shape and hurried to join them, his medical bag ready in his hand. Kitty and Alice stepped back to allow him to take over with Matt.

'My word, Mrs Bryant, Captain Bryant, this is a pretty pickle.' The doctor popped open his bag and started work.

'We can't do anything else out here. Let's go back inside the house and make some tea ready,' Kitty suggested. 'I think I hear more cars coming so the police and ambulance cannot be far away.' She could see that Alice had begun to shake again now the shock of what had happened took hold.

She led her friend back inside the house and prepared a fresh tray of tea while Alice washed her hands. Kitty wished there was some brandy or spirits in the house. Bertie was rewarded with a biscuit for his bravery at helping in the capture of Arthur Maldon.

'Oh, I've come over all of a wobble.' Alice collapsed down suddenly onto a kitchen chair as if her legs had given out from under her.

Kitty rushed to her side to hold her friend's hands and to check on her. 'I'm not surprised. That was all pretty awful out there. You were so brave.'

'I didn't feel very brave.' Alice managed a weak smile as Kitty fetched her a glass of cold water to sip.

'There's no brandy, I'm afraid, unless Doctor Carter has some in his medical bag. The tea will be ready in a minute, some sugar will help with the shock.' Kitty was relieved to see a trace of pink returning to Alice's cheeks.

'Do you think he'll live?' Alice asked, glancing through the kitchen doorway to where they could just make out the huddle of figures in the fog beside the barn.

'I don't know. Doctor Carter will do his best. Maybe, but then he has committed murder.' She bit her lip, leaving the conclusion unspoken. Even if Payne was saved now it could not be for long. He had been responsible for murdering Tilly Maldon.

There were more vehicles and male voices. Kitty saw them preparing to get Payne onto a stretcher so guessed the ambulance was ready to take him to Kingswear and across the river to the cottage hospital in Dartmouth. She knew he would need to be seen quickly and could not survive the journey to the larger hospital at Totnes.

The jewels they had discovered earlier sparkled on the table before them under the electric light which was still on from earlier. Kitty retrieved the kettle from the hob where it had boiled. It was lucky it hadn't filled the kitchen with steam or burned a hole in the base while they had been busy with Joshua Payne and waiting for the police.

She judged that Matt would soon be coming inside and no doubt whoever had arrived from the police would be accompanying him.

'I'll make the tea now.' She busied herself warming the pot while the ambulance departed, its bell clanging. Doctor Carter also roared away, following behind it down the track. His skills would be needed once his patient reached the cottage hospital.

Matt emerged from the mist and entered the hall, his face sombre and gaunt. 'Payne has gone to the hospital. Inspector Lewis is taking Arthur Maldon to the police station in Torquay.'

Kitty rushed to embrace her husband. 'Oh, Matt, are you all right? I was so scared when Maldon said he had locked you and Bertie in the barn.'

Matt nodded. 'I could kick myself. Bertie and I were at the far side of the barn with the torch. We were examining some boxes behind Daisybelle when the door suddenly closed. I knew it couldn't be the wind because everything was so still with the fog. I went over straight away and realised we had been locked in. There was no way to warn you or to escape. I had no idea who it was or what they wanted.'

Alice rose from her chair. 'Come and sit down. Kitty has made tea. Is Chief Inspector Greville here?'

'Yes, he's just coming now. He must have driven at a hell of a speed to get here from Torquay so quickly.' Matt sank down on one of the other chairs. Kitty could see his hands were shaking and stained with dried blood from where he had been tending to Joshua Payne.

'Come and wash your hands, darling.' Kitty gently assisted Matt to stand and walked with him to the sink where he scrubbed at his hands until they were clean. Once completed, he retook his seat.

Alice added more kindling to the fire which was burning low. The fog which had seeped inside the house through the open doors had removed what little heat it was still throwing out. Kitty shivered and poured a cup of tea for her husband. She could see that he was not himself.

There was a knock on the still open front door and Chief Inspector Greville entered the hall, wiping his boots on the mat. He closed the door behind him and Kitty surmised that the rest of the police must have now departed with the prisoner.

'Come in, Chief Inspector.' Alice pulled out a chair.

The policeman's eyes widened when he saw what was on the kitchen table. 'I take it this is the Massey family property?'

Kitty and Alice nodded. Matt looked at the jewels as if just noticing them for the first time. Kitty set out cups and saucers to pour the tea for the rest of the group. She was worried about Matt, knowing that being confronted with Joshua Payne's wounds may well have brought back his wartime experiences.

'Thank you, Mrs Bryant,' the chief inspector said as Kitty placed a cup before him. Kitty added sugar to Matt's cup, gently urging him to drink.

Alice put out the last of the biscuits on a plate and Kitty rewarded Bertie with an extra one before they all disappeared.

'Mr Maldon has gone to Torquay Police Station with Inspector Lewis. Captain Bryant has given me the gist of what you learned outside, but perhaps you can tell me the rest?'

Chief Inspector Greville asked as he helped himself to the biscuits.

Kitty went through what they knew about the robberies including that Joshua Payne had implied that Tilly had been the lookout for the gang.

'She was here at the farm then when Crabtree was killed?' the chief inspector asked.

Alice nodded. 'That was what Mr Maldon said. She had lured Crabtree outside to the old piggery. His death sounded like a combination of an accident when he hit his head on a rock after Mr Maldon struck him. They hadn't wanted to kill him because he had these.' She waved her hand towards the bag on the table. 'Then after, once he was dead, they couldn't find the hiding place. They must have just hid his body and left.'

Kitty explained that it had sounded from what Joshua Payne had said that Tilly had found the money Crabtree had taken from his son and she had given it back to Lavinia.

'I assume that Tilly swore Lavinia to secrecy about where the money had come from. Lavinia obviously didn't care to ask too many questions about what had happened to her father-in-law,' Chief Inspector Greville said.

'Payne said that Maldon had organised the gang and the robberies.' Kitty looked at her husband. He was unusually silent, and she could see that he was struggling with the conversation.

'And he silenced Tilly, afraid that after all this time she was going to go to the police now she had fallen out with her father and had nothing to lose. Now Crabtree had been discovered she was probably afraid that she would be implicated in the crime somehow,' the chief inspector said.

'That was when Mr Maldon shot him. He didn't know until we said, you see, that Tilly was dead, and he knew it had to be Joshua Payne who had killed her.' Alice gave a shudder. 'Will

Mr Payne survive, do you think?' She looked at the chief inspector.

'Doctor Carter was not hopeful, despite the sterling work you and Captain Bryant did trying to save him. He was going straight to the operating theatre.' The chief inspector finished his tea and biscuits. 'I must get off to assist Inspector Lewis. Will you be all right, Miss Miller?'

Alice nodded. 'Yes, thank you. I have Kitty and Matt with me and Robert should be returning soon from his day trip. It was more local today.'

'There will be a lot to tell him.' The policeman rose and gathered up the canvas bag and its contents. 'I shall inform the Massey family that their things have finally been recovered. I shall also ask if the reward still stands for return of the jewels. I rather think you deserve it.' He smiled genially at Alice who blushed fiery red.

'I'll see you out, sir.' Alice walked the policeman to the front door leaving Kitty and Matt alone for a moment.

'Are you all right, Matt? Do you wish to go home?' Kitty asked in a low voice. She tried not to let her anxiety for her husband show in her voice or her expression.

'I shall recover in a while, I promise. Don't fret, old thing.' He smiled briefly, and she kissed his still cold cheek hoping he was right.

CHAPTER TWENTY-FIVE

The next time Kitty and Matt saw Lavinia Crabtree and her family was two days later. It was Midnight Mass on Christmas Eve at St Saviour's in Dartmouth. They had gone to the service at the ancient church where they had married a few years before and where Kitty's mother lay at rest in the graveyard.

The stone-built church was full, as always, for the service. The air filled with the scent of pine from the tree near the advent scene beside the altar mingling with beeswax from the freshly polished oak pews. There was a hum of chatter and good humour as people wished one another a merry Christmas.

Matt had not been well since the incident at Alice and Robert's house. His nightmares about his time in the trenches had returned with a vengeance despite Kitty's tender care. She had been forced to clear his bedroom and lock his door at night to prevent him from sleepwalking and destroying the house.

Kitty hoped that the combination of it being their wedding anniversary and Christmas might help to soothe his mind and replace the bad memories with happier ones. They had received word from the chief inspector that Arthur Maldon had been charged with robbery and murder. Joshua Payne had not survived his injuries despite Doctor Carter's best efforts. Kitty couldn't help but feel that perhaps this was for the best under the circumstances.

The Massey family had agreed to honour the old offer of a reward and Chief Inspector Greville had informed Alice and Robert that it would make a handsome wedding present. Alice had tried to persuade Kitty and Matt to share the money, but they had declined. Kitty thought that perhaps being able to furnish and equip her house would help Alice to come to terms with its history.

The service began and Kitty forced herself to focus on the music, readings and prayers that she had known since her childhood. The familiarity providing her with comfort and peace after the last few days. She glanced across at Matt and was relieved to see that the lines of strain around his mouth and eyes seemed softened. She spotted Mrs Craven on the front row of the pews, the feather in her hat waving as she sang.

Once the service was ended and the congregation started to file out, Kitty became temporarily separated from Matt in the crowd. Lavinia Crabtree brushed up against her in the queue for the door.

'Mrs Bryant, I just wanted to thank you on behalf of William and me. The policeman, that chief inspector, he told me in private that he knew what Tilly had done. He said you worked it out from what that Joshua Payne said.' Lavinia bit her lip. 'William don't know anything. I always told him the money was from the church.'

'Then he won't hear anything from me. You only had back what was yours,' Kitty said.

Lavinia inclined her head. 'It's been a burden all this time. I never asked Tilly what had happened. She gave it me before Thomas was reported missing. I thought it best not to know if he give it her or if she took it.'

'Well, it is all over now at last. Happy Christmas to you and your family,' Kitty said as Lavinia's daughters squeezed through the crowd to seize their mother's gloved hands, their father following behind them with their young son.

Kitty spotted Matt just ahead of her and worked her way back to his side.

'I wondered where you had gone.' He smiled down at her as they stepped through the doorway out into the crisp, winter night. They shook hands with the vicar and started back towards Kitty's car.

'I was just wishing a few people a merry Christmas,' Kitty said.

'Ah, Kitty, Matthew, just the people I hoped to see.' Mrs Craven's clarion voice carried in the clear night air and she waved imperiously at them.

Matt's gaze tangled with Kitty's and she saw the spark of mischief ignite in his bright blue eyes. 'Happy Christmas, Mrs C. Can't stop, I'm afraid. It's still our anniversary,' Matt called as he and Kitty escaped down the hill to her car giggling like children.

A LETTER FROM HELENA

Dear reader,

I want to say a huge thank you for choosing to read *Murder at Midwinter Farm*. If you enjoyed it and would like to keep up-to-date with all my latest releases, just sign up at the following link. Your email address will never be shared, and you can unsubscribe at any time. There is also a free story – *The Mysterious Guest*, starring Kitty's friend, Alice.

www.bookouture.com/helena-dixon

This book was a joy to write as it's set so close to my home. It also mentions one of my favourite places in the world, the gorgeous Coleton Fishacre. This now belongs to the National Trust so you can visit and enjoy a wonderful jazz age house and glorious gardens. If I could own any house, it would be this one. I do hope you loved *Murder at Midwinter Farm* and if you did, I would be very grateful if you could write a review. I'd love to hear what you think, and it makes such a difference helping new readers to discover one of my books for the first time.

I love hearing from my readers – you can get in touch through social media or my website.

Thanks,

Helena Dixon

KEEP IN TOUCH WITH HELENA

www.nelldixon.com

ACKNOWLEDGEMENTS

Thank you to the brilliant staff at Coleton Fishacre for their assistance in writing this book. My wonderful readers and friends in Torbay who provide me with so much information. Torquay museum for their help and support. My fabulous team Kitty at Bookouture and my incredible agent, Kate Nash. Writing and publishing a book is a team effort and I couldn't do it without all of you.

PUBLISHING TEAM

Turning a manuscript into a book requires the efforts of many people. The publishing team at Bookouture would like to acknowledge everyone who contributed to this publication.

Audio
Alba Proko
Melissa Tran

Commercial
Lauren Morrissette
Hannah Richmond
Imogen Allport

Cover design
Debbie Clement

Data and analysis
Mark Alder
Mohamed Bussuri

Editorial
Cerys Hadwin-Owen
Charlotte Hegley

Copyeditor
Jane Eastgate

Proofreader
Shirley Khan

Marketing
Alex Crow
Melanie Price
Occy Carr
Cíara Rosney
Martyna Młynarska

Operations and distribution
Marina Valles
Joe Morris

Production
Hannah Snetsinger
Mandy Kullar
Nadia Michael
Charlotte Hegley

Publicity
Kim Nash
Noelle Holten
Jess Readett
Sarah Hardy

Rights and contracts
Peta Nightingale
Richard King
Saidah Graham

Dear Reader,

We'd love your attention for one more page to tell you about the crisis in children's reading, and what we can all do.

Studies have shown that reading for fun is the **single biggest predictor of a child's future life chances** – more than family circumstance, parents' educational background or income. It improves academic results, mental health, wealth, communication skills, ambition and happiness.

The number of children reading for fun is in rapid decline. Young people have a lot of competition for their time, and a worryingly high number do not have a single book at home.

Hachette works extensively with schools, libraries and literacy charities, but here are some ways we can all raise more readers:

- Reading to children for just 10 minutes a day makes a difference
- Don't give up if children aren't regular readers – there will be books for them!

- Visit bookshops and libraries to get recommendations
- Encourage them to listen to audiobooks
- Support school libraries
- Give books as gifts

There's a lot more information about how to encourage children to read on our websites: **www.RaisingReaders.co.uk** and **www.JoinRaisingReaders.com**.

Thank you for reading.